THE CHRYSANTHEMUM TIGER

Also by Alys Clare from Severn House

The Gabriel Taverner series

A RUSTLE OF SILK
THE ANGEL IN THE GLASS
THE INDIGO GHOSTS
MAGIC IN THE WEAVE
THE CARGO FROM NEIRA

The World's End Bureau mysteries

THE WOMAN WHO SPOKE TO SPIRITS
THE OUTCAST GIRLS
THE MAN IN THE SHADOWS
THE STRANGER IN THE ASYLUM

The Aelf Fen series

OUT OF THE DAWN LIGHT
MIST OVER THE WATER
MUSIC OF THE DISTANT STARS
THE WAY BETWEEN THE WORLDS
LAND OF THE SILVER DRAGON
BLOOD OF THE SOUTH
THE NIGHT WANDERER
THE RUFUS SPY
CITY OF PEARL
THE LAMMAS WILD

The Hawkenlye series

THE PATHS OF THE AIR
THE JOYS OF MY LIFE
THE ROSE OF THE WORLD
THE SONG OF THE NIGHTINGALE
THE WINTER KING
A SHADOWED EVIL
THE DEVIL'S CUP

THE CHRYSANTHEMUM TIGER

Alys Clare

SEVERN
HOUSE

First world edition published in Great Britain and the USA in 2024
by Severn House, an imprint of Canongate Books Ltd,
14 High Street, Edinburgh EH1 1TE.

Trade paperback edition first published in Great Britain and the USA in 2025
by Severn House, an imprint of Canongate Books Ltd.

severnhouse.com

British Library Cataloguing-in-Publication Data
A CIP catalogue record for this title is available from the British Library.

ISBN-13: 978-1-4483-1300-6 (cased)
ISBN-13: 978-1-4483-1714-1 (trade paper)
ISBN-13: 978-1-4483-1301-3 (e-book)

All Severn House titles are printed on acid-free paper.

Typeset by Palimpsest Book Production Ltd.,
Falkirk, Stirlingshire, Scotland.
Printed and bound in Great Britain by CPI Group (UK) Ltd,
Croydon CR0 4YY.

The manufacturer's authorised representative in the EU for product safety is
Authorised Rep Compliance Ltd, 71 Lower Baggot Street, Dublin D02 P593
Ireland (arccompliance.com)

Praise for the Gabriel Taverner mysteries

"A must for historical mystery readers"
Booklist on *The Cargo from Neira*

"A historically detailed mystery full of action and philosophizing"
Kirkus Reviews on *The Cargo from Neira*

"A haunting, eerie tale with otherworldly twists, a multilayered plot, and Clare's excellent period details make this a fine choice for historical-mystery fans"
Booklist on *Magic in the Weave*

"A complex, exciting mystery whose rich historical background is disturbed by some truly chilling events"
Kirkus Reviews on *Magic in the Weave*

"Excellent . . . Clare matches well-drawn characters, in particular the charismatic lead, with a head-scratching puzzle and creepy atmospherics. Imogen Robertson fans will be pleased"
Publishers Weekly Starred Review of *The Indigo Ghosts*

"Impressive . . . The mystery satisfies with a tragic, far-reaching conclusion. Clare reinforces her place among the top rank of historical writers"
Publishers Weekly on *The Angel in the Glass*

"A superb storyteller whose clever, twisty plots; believable characters, and skilful writing will engross the reader from first page to last"
Booklist Starred Review of *A Rustle of Silk*

About the author

Alys Clare lives in the English countryside where her novels are set. She went to school in Tonbridge and later studied English and psychology at the University of Keele and archaeology at the University of Kent. She is the author of the Aelf Fen, Hawkenlye, World's End Bureau and Gabriel Taverner historical mystery series.

Dedicated to the memory of travels and encounters
on the other side of the world.

PROLOGUE

The sun was setting in the west. After almost two weeks of tempests, howling winds and roaring seas that had strained the crew to the limit and savaged the ship as if they hated her, now it was blessedly calm. I stood by the port rail and watched the sparkling gold coins dancing on the gently ruffled surface of the ocean.

For the first time in what felt like months, I had nothing demanding my attention. Not immediately, anyway, although there was a man below in considerable pain from a badly broken humerus who would soon be needing another draught if he was going to get any sleep tonight, and the strange case of the lad with the inexplicable fever still troubled me. Presently, I told myself. For now, I was going to take the time to stand and reflect.

What a time it had been.

I had seen sights I thought only belonged in dreams, in nightmares. I had encountered men who looked so strange that they might have come from a different species. I had learned three new languages; I would not have called myself fluent in any of them, but I had picked up what a native speaker of one of them referred to as an adequate working knowledge. One of these tongues was written in different letters; only they weren't letters, they were more like little pictures, drawn on heavy, thick paper with brushes loaded with black ink. I had eaten the most unlikely foods: fish that was still moving as I poked it out of its shell; the young green shoots of a plant that, if left to grow, turned into thick poles strong enough to support the weight of houses; immeasurable quantities of rice and, unforgettably, fat grasshoppers deep-fried in savoury batter. The memory of the grasshoppers made me smile. I'd been at a day-long feast, I'd drunk a deal more than was good for me, and when my companion slapped coins on the low table and said *I bet you can't eat THAT*, of course I had to. It wasn't too bad, in fact; as long as I told myself it wasn't really a faintly repulsive-looking insect, it tasted much like any other fried morsel.

I had seen extreme ugliness; the worst that human beings can do to each other. I had patched up wounds that, even after my many years as a physician, had forced me to swallow down the nausea and fight the threatening faintness. I had encountered greed of the most ruthless, self-serving kind – the sort that puts money and position above loved ones; above, indeed, pretty much everything. I had seen perfection in the form of exquisite artefacts made long ago by human hands.

We speak of one short life, a man had once said. *What is that against a treasure from the ancient past that will last for all eternity?*

What indeed.

I had seen beauty; such beauty that at times I had stood in silent awe with the tears on my face. I had felt the utter stillness of a winter morning when there was snow on the ground that blanketed all sound, and the long rays of an early sun made shadows as tall as giants. I had seen ecstasy on the face of an old man as he bowed before the shrine he had tended since he was a boy, and for an unforgettable instant I had felt the over-powering universal spirit overwhelm me as I stood beside him. I had lain on a straw mattress in the attic of an inn and smelt the smoke of a fire that had burned in the hearth for decades – centuries, according to the innkeeper – and sensed the endless past of the ancient wooden building crowding around me in the profound darkness. I had stood alone in the night staring up at the sky, making out patterns in constellations made unfamiliar by the different angle. I had seen a mountain on fire, and felt the earth tremble and jerk beneath my feet as if the gods were angrily shaking a rug.

I had encountered anger, hatred, envy and violence, each savage emotion aimed squarely at me. Not that I didn't deserve it: my actions had been far from blameless, and I understood why men wanted to kill me, preferably slowly and as painfully as they could.

I had encountered love. I had been loved; I had loved. I still did, more deeply with every day; there was a sort of love finding its way into my heart that had hitherto been quite unknown to me.

And it was the consequences of this new emotion – as fierce and furious as all those negative ones – that I feared the most.

'Gabe! *Gabriel!*'

Someone was calling me; it was Piet, the young man I had been training as my apprentice. My patient with the broken arm must have been complaining; it was time I went below to attend him.

ONE

I set sail on the *Luipaard* in March 1605. We embarked from Plymouth, and, for all it was only a handful of miles to my house and the homes of the people I cared about, there was nobody to see me on my way. I'd wanted it that way; I'd told them all not to come. But nevertheless, I was sad as we left the port behind.

The ship was beautiful. Long and lean, she looked fast, and very soon I discovered that she was. She had already proved her worth as a trading vessel, and belonged to a man called Walter Haverleigh. He was a highly successful and adventurous merchant who lived in a grand house with well-hidden, carefully guarded and securely stocked storage barns that held goods worth more than I could imagine; I and almost everyone else, for surely only the King could have that sort of wealth. Walter Haverleigh had allowed me to see inside his barns.[1] Back then, I had not understood what a very rare privilege that was, nor what his purpose was in showing me. It was not long before I found out. He had put a proposition to me, that I join the company of the *Luipaard* on her next voyage to the Eastern Seas as ship's physician.

'I lost men on the last trip and I'm not prepared to risk the needless expense of losing more,' Walter had said bluntly. 'They fell to accidents and to sickness. Now I choose my crew with care, Doctor, and I invest time and money in having them trained to a very high standard of efficiency. I do not like it when they die, for it takes time and money to replace them. Several of the casualties would not have succumbed had a physician been at hand. I am told you are good; that you have long experience of the hazards of the sea and how to counter them. I will equip your surgeon's cabin with the finest equipment that money can buy. You can have whatever you need,

---

1 See *The Cargo from Neira*.

you can write your own list. And,' he had concluded almost as a throwaway remark, 'you will, of course, earn yourself a small fortune.'

It wasn't the vision of a surgeon's cabin full of the best physician's tools money could buy that persuaded me, nor the promise of vast wealth. It was something inside myself.

I had served on the late Queen's ships for nearly fifteen years, and I had loved the life. Then on a hot, humid day in a hectic Caribbean port, the world came crashing down. A careless sailor loading supplies let a rope slip, and a heavy crate swung violently and hit me just behind my right ear. I wasn't dead, as they'd all assumed, but when I returned to consciousness two days later on the voyage home, I wished I was. I was seasick. I'd never known anything like it. It was violent, relentless and continuous, my head swimming with vertigo and my stomach heaving up yellow bile that burned as it came out. I wanted to die but I didn't, because, despite my feeble efforts to fight him off, my captain wouldn't let me. '*Drink*, you fucking idiot!' Captain Zeke yelled at me, forcing the cup to my lips, 'even if it comes straight back up again, for it's your only hope!'

When we finally arrived in Plymouth, I knew already that my days as a ship's surgeon were over. I made a new life ashore. I'd have said I was contented, for it was a fine life; I did a worthwhile job, I had family and very good friends. And, besides, I told myself there was no alternative.

I was wrong.

I had found myself at sea again, taken unconscious on board a small craft whose lively motion on the temperamental waters of the Channel provided a stern test of my enduring susceptibility to seasickness.

And I discovered that it had gone. I wasn't sick; I didn't feel so much as a twinge of nausea or vertigo. I had no idea what injury had been done to me by that heavy wooden crate, but it seemed that, after eight years, it had healed.

I had tried to deny the fact that I was longing to go to sea again. I had responsibilities and commitments in my life on land; people who cared about me, loved me, and whose affections I fully returned. But when Walter Haverleigh asked me to be his surgeon on the *Luipaard*'s next voyage, I said yes even before he'd finished the question.

The voyage on Walter Haverleigh's beautiful ship began presenting surprises right from the start. I knew money had been no object in fitting her out, and, as I'd anticipated, my surgeon's cabin was crammed with crates of medical supplies. If I had expected luxurious accommodation, however, I was to be disappointed. My personal quarters amounted to a tiny cabin and a hard shelf of a bed, and there would have been no point in complaining because nobody else fared any better. Even the captain – a stocky, broad-shouldered Dutchman called Ambroos Leyn who walked with his hands held away from his body as if constantly expecting the sort of threat that would make him draw his knife – had only a few feet more space than I did.

There was a good reason why the ship's company had to make do with such spartan conditions. The *Luipaard* had been built to carry cargo, but the most important factor in her design was speed. Like the fast ships of the privateers, she was similar in design to the navy's race-built galleons, and the upperworks at the prow had been sliced away to leave the long, aggressive 'beak'. She was narrow, sleek, she rode the seas with the swift, effortless grace of the leopard she was named for, and her crew loved her because she responded to the merest twitch on the helm or adjustment in the canvas as fast as a dancer.

The first surprise, then, was that she was even swifter and nimbler than I'd dreamt.

The second surprise was her company. My first introduction to Walter Haverleigh's world had been a Dutchman called Hieronymus Petrarcus, who, despite behaviour that was more than a little questionable when we first met, in the close confines of shipboard life was fast becoming my friend. Given his nationality and that of the captain, I took it for granted that the crew would all be Dutch. They weren't; I was the only Englishman, but four of the men were Portuguese. And these men weren't just run-of-the mill seamen. They might have worked as hard as everyone else – the company was not over-generous in number – but, no matter how he tried to disguise it, each had his own sophistication. One drew maps, one had a head for figures, one was learned in the history of the East. One was firmly believed by his Dutch companions to have magic powers: for three and a half unforgettable days, the *Luipaard* had lain becalmed in the vicinity of the equator, the water ran low, half a dozen men were running a high fever and fear was growing like a fungus. The Portuguese – his name was Flávio, and they called him Flavinho – was a man of middle age, with close-cropped iron-grey hair, intensely dark eyes and a way of watching you without moving or even, apparently, breathing. In their despair, a couple of his countrymen asked him to whistle up a wind. I thought they were joking, although, God knew, there was nothing to joke about. But then, softly to start with and building rapidly to a pitch that was so high that it first hurt the ears and then became inaudible, Flavinho began to whistle.

Within the hour – and long before that, if I must be honest – the wind began to rise.

I told myself it was nothing but coincidence.

Apart from anything else, why would a man suffer nearly four days becalmed in scorching, broiling heat where there was no shade and going below decks felt like descending into an oven when the remedy was in his own hands?

Yes, I tried hard not to be convinced by Flavinho and his powers.

But I wasn't sure I succeeded.

Other than that distressing, troubling incident, our voyage south past Brittany, Portugal and all the way down the west coast of Africa passed with no more than the usual minor calamities of life at sea. After an initial and difficult period of adaptation – for I had become used to the comforts and security of life ashore – I soon began to feel like a sailor again. Much of the daily round was very familiar, and I noted quickly that Master Leyn ran his ship with as ruthlessly firm a hand as any of the captains I had served under in the late Queen's navy. I was seeing my friend Hieronymus Petrarcus in a new light; I think I had thought that he was a diplomat, concerned always to be courteous and mannerly, and I had allowed this impression to override what else I knew about his character. Now, seeing him on the *Luipaard*, answerable to an exacting captain who brooked no indiscipline or inefficiency, I recognized that his steelier elements had come to the fore.

There were two main differences from life at sea as I had experienced it before. The first was that the food was a great deal tastier; the *Luipaard*'s company was smaller than that of the *Falco* or the *Nightbird*, the largest of the Queen's ships I'd served on, and it appears to be a rule at sea that the bigger the number of men to be fed, the more bland and uninteresting the food. Ambroos Leyn's cook and his apprentice were Portuguese, and they knew their craft. The second major difference was that the *Luipaard* flew over the seas far more swiftly than any vessel I'd served on. By the beginning of August, we were undertaking a major reprovisioning in the bay under the mountain in Saldania, at the Cape.

I had planned to ask Captain Leyn to allow the company at least a couple of weeks of rest and recuperation, but although I insisted on giving every man a health check, I could find little wrong with any of them. Among my preliminary requests I'd included a generous supply of lemon juice, to be replenished at every opportunity, but my request hadn't been necessary because the company had already been in the excellent habit of taking three spoonfuls per man per day, and this wise precaution had entirely kept at bay that scourge of the South Atlantic, scurvy.

The long voyage resumed, and we headed into the southern spring. The Cape was our southerly limit, and now we made for Madagascar and out into the ocean beyond. I had sailed these waters before, although my experience when in the service of the Queen had taken me further north, into the Arabian Sea, and to the Gujarat and Malabar coasts that border the Indian Ocean on the west side of the Indian subcontinent. This time our course lay north-east, as far as a mere ship's surgeon could determine it, and we sailed straight out across the ocean and ended up in Sumatra.

The company were awarded a decent rest here. Ambroos Leyn was not a man to show much emotion; the pale blue eyes watched, assessed, but gave little away, but even he could not resist expressing pleasure at the speed of our voyage. He sought me

out and poured me a very generous measure of rum, in recogni-
tion of the fact that, as he phrased it, I had managed to preserve
the lives of all but two of his men in the course of the voyage.
Of the dead men, one had been lost to an infected insect bite
that had swollen him up with some fearful poison I could neither
identify nor counteract, the other perished through his own folly:
he returned to the ship very drunk when we were in port in
Madagascar, slipped and knocked himself unconscious, and was
found drowned by his shipmates the next morning.

We set out from Banda Aceh at the beginning of October. This
time I had made sure to consult the charts, and I was confidently
expecting that the *Luipaard* would sail south-east, along the south
coast of Sumatra, through the Sunda Strait and past the Dutch
port of Batavia, then on eastwards for the hundreds of miles to
the Banda Islands and the port of Neira, where we would take
on the unbelievably profitable cargo of nutmegs that was the sole
purpose of our voyage.

But the *Luipaard* did not take that route.

From Banda Aceh we sailed down Sumatra's north coast, along
the Strait of Malacca. It wasn't for me to protest; Master Leyn
would have given me short shrift if I had, and in any case I was
fully occupied with tending several sailors who were in the
agonizing, tormenting throes of acute malaria, two more who
had severe dysentery and one whom I had isolated because I
suspected he had typhoid.

Emerging from the Malacca Strait, we turned abruptly to the
north. Too busy to take much notice, I did understand that,
wherever we were bound, it wasn't Neira. From listening carefully, I deduced we were in the South China Sea. It was
apparently endless; I wondered if this journey would ever reach
its destination.

After almost a month, I woke one morning in my cramped
quarters full of anger. All my patients were either back at their
posts or well on the way to recovery, and their improved health
was entirely down to my ceaseless efforts to heal them. Stoking
my fury by telling myself I'd like to see Ambroos Leyn emptying
his tenth bucket of stinking brown diarrhoea over the side, or
holding a sweaty, howling man still while I extracted a huge, fat,

glistening, wriggling white parasitical larva from the flesh of his buttock, abruptly I came to the decision that I'd had enough of being hoodwinked and taken for a fool and that I was going to seek out the captain right now and demand an explanation.

He was taking his breakfast when I burst into his tiny cabin. He ate frugally: a small bowl of rice, a few pieces of cooked vegetables, a slice of mango. 'Gabriel,' he greeted me, 'will you join me?'

'No,' I said rudely. 'I don't want food, I want the answers to some questions, and I'm staying here until you tell me what I want to know.'

He inclined his head courteously. There was a smile playing around his thin-lipped mouth. 'Please, ask,' he said.

'I was taken on as ship's surgeon for a voyage to Neira, in the Banda Sea, and Walter Haverleigh promised I would earn a great deal of money from the profits,' I said forcefully. I had refused his offer of a seat and was looming over him; even when we were both on our feet, I was a head taller than him and considerably broader. 'But we're going the wrong way, and if you thought you were getting away with it and that I hadn't noticed the deception, then you're wrong because I have!' I paused, feeling the sweat break out on my chest. He was still smiling, and I had to fight the desire to punch him. 'Well? What have you to say?'

'I must assure you, my friend, there is no intention to deceive,' the captain said mildly, having waited a moment or two to see if I'd finished. 'It is true that there might once have been a plan to return to Neira, but I am afraid I must advise you that, long before we set sail, an alternative had been proposed.'

'An alternative? What, pray, will Walter Haverleigh's reaction be when he hears of this?'

Ambroos Leyn shrugged. 'It was his idea.'

'But . . .' I sank down on to the bench beside him. If I'd got as far as trying to think up possible explanations for our change of course, I really would not have come up with this one. 'But what of the nutmegs?'

Captain Leyn cut and speared another piece of mango. 'Sure you won't?' he asked, waving it at me.

'No.'

'Gabriel,' he said after a chewing pause, 'what are we doing out here in the Eastern Seas? Us, the *Luipaard*'s company? All the other adventurers who have fought their way to a perilous destination so far from home?'

'We're after wealth, of course, which is why we should be heading for Neira and the nutmegs!' I was trying not to shout.

'Wealth,' he repeated, ignoring the rest of the outburst as if he hadn't heard it. 'And are nutmegs the sole source of wealth out here in the East, do you imagine?'

'No, of course not!' My mind leapt to that other cargo hidden away under armed guard at Walter Haverleigh's isolated island manor; the one he kept a very close secret. I was in no doubt that Ambroos Leyn knew of this cargo because I was all but certain it had been he who had sailed home with it, but I decided not to speak of it. 'There's a world of wonders out here that are unheard of back in Europe, any or all of which will make a further fortune or two.'

'Indeed there are,' Ambroos replied. He was smiling openly now; a happy, cheerful smile.

'And?' I demanded.

The smile faded. 'And what, Gabriel?'

'If we're not going to Neira for nutmegs, where *are* we going, and what for?'

With neat, economical movements, he tidied away his breakfast and spread a chart out on the table. Shooting me a doubtful look he pointed at it and said, 'You understand this?'

Of course I bloody do, I wanted to say. I merely gave a curt nod.

With a stubby short-nailed forefinger, he traced our course. 'Atlantic Ocean, Indian Ocean, Sumatra, Sunda Strait, South China Sea.' He let the curve of the line continue. North, and slightly to the east. As he did so, he said, 'You may have observed that some of the company are Portuguese?'

'Yes.'

'Did you wonder why? Well, no matter.' He took my lack of response as a sign that I hadn't. 'I shall explain.' He paused, his finger motionless on the chart. 'The men of several European nations are actively trying to establish themselves in the East, Gabriel. As with a gardener dealing with virgin soil, the man who first breaks up the sod's resistance has the hardest job; it is always easier to follow where others – in particular men of one's own nationality – have led the way. Now none of my countrymen yet reside in the land where we are bound, although it is home to one Englishman that I know of for certain, and there may be more who have visited and stayed for a short time. The people who have settled there in some numbers are, however, the Portuguese, and the first to arrive were a party of merchants who had been blown ashore there by a fortuitous typhoon in 1543. Hard on their heels soon afterwards, as so often happens, came the mighty Francis Xavier, accompanied by three other Jesuits, and together they founded the first Christian mission. He—'

'Francis Xavier was Spanish,' I interrupted.

'He was,' Ambroos agreed mildly. 'Do not forget, though, that Francis Xavier was not there as a Spaniard but as a Catholic. These two groups, the Portuguese merchants and the Jesuit fathers, swiftly turned a trickle into a flood, and forty years later, the Jesuits had established the most successful Catholic mission in Asia and the Portuguese merchants had established a firm trading centre that saw a rapidly increasing amount of trade, regarded as thoroughly beneficial to both parties.'

'And so Portuguese men have been included in the *Luipaard*'s company to ensure their countrymen will give us a welcome?' I asked.

'Of course!' he replied in surprise, as if I had been a fool to ask. 'I am learning the language, and I have become considerably more fluent as our voyage has gone on – as indeed have you, Gabriel – but I am not yet capable of detecting the nuances that without even thinking about it a man recognizes when conversing in his mother tongue.' He paused, watching me closely. 'Our arrival, and more specifically our negotiations concerning what we hope to acquire from this new land, are not matters regarding which there can be any danger of misunderstanding.'

I nodded, interpreting his somewhat convoluted remark and trying to absorb a lot of information in a short space of time. Then, glancing down at the chart, I said, 'You haven't yet told me where this new land is.'

He smiled. 'It is new to us and to other men of the West, Gabriel. Not so to those who belong there, for they claim that their forebears have inhabited the land for thousands, even hundreds of thousands, of years.'

'That is not what the Book of Genesis teaches us,' I remarked primly, 'as no doubt Francis Xavier and his Jesuits explained as they vehemently voiced their objection.'

'I do believe the men we speak of would have been largely indifferent to such an objection,' Ambroos said. 'They would, I expect, have smiled courteously and gone on believing what they have held to be the truth for as long as time.'

I tapped the chart. 'Show me,' I commanded firmly.

His finger moved on to the north-east. The vast land of Cathay bulged out to the east, and there, further on round the vast outward curve, lay a long string of islands. I had the strange illusion that it hugged the great mass of Asia, facing out into the wide Pacific Ocean like a solid reef bravely placed to defend what lay at its back.

'Do you know this land, Gabriel?' Ambroos asked softly. 'Do you recognize it?'

Slowly I nodded. Years ago I had studied its outline on the globe in my study back home in Rosewyke. I had listened to my beloved sister Celia quoting from the endless lessons she received at the hands of our formidable grandmother, Graice Oldreive. Tales of alien lands on the other side of the world had always fascinated Celia the most, and as I stood in that cramped cabin beside a tough Dutchman looking down at his chart, I thought I could hear my sister's voice: *lacquerware, metalwork, swords, fine porcelain, jade, silver, and the most glorious, sumptuous silks*, she was saying, *that's what you find there, Gabe.*

In my memory we were standing together in my study, and I was allowing her a rare and very well-supervised moment with my precious globe.

We had been talking about Japan.

TWO

The *Luipaard* reached Japan in December.

Many of the ship's company had expected the weather to be hot. The Dutchmen among them had been on the run to Neira, and they had come prepared for tropical heat that broiled you alive and rain that beat on your head like a hundred small, vicious hammers. But we were no longer in the Banda Sea; not in the tropics at all but a long way to the north. And in Japan it was winter, and the land was hard and white with frost and snow.

We arrived late in the afternoon in a port near the town of Nagasaki, on the western tip of the southernmost of the islands that made up the country. It had a bowl of a harbour, sheltered by headlands and with the mountains rising up in a protective semicircle. Crowding amongst my shipmates trying to see everywhere at once, Hieronymus's sharp elbow in my ribs, my first impression was of a small but bustling port lined with wharves where craft of all sizes crammed together. And I had a moment's intense disappointment: I'd been at sea for nine months, I'd sailed halfway round the world, and here I was in a place that felt just like Plymouth.

The disappointment didn't last. While it was fair to say that one busy, thriving port feels much like another, I knew that in truth Nagasaki was not like Plymouth at all.

The buildings were surely warehouses and trading houses, with a seasoning of inns, taverns and brothels. My logic told me that was what they were, but they looked like no buildings I had ever seen. They were made entirely of wood, and they had deep open galleries running all the way round, whose low roofs swept down in a graceful curve that entirely covered the space beneath. In heavy rain or scorching sun, anyone conducting their business there would be well sheltered.

The craft jostling for position along the wharves were interesting. Two were trading vessels – Portuguese, I guessed – of a design I knew well. Some were of a type that the man next to me said were junks, and which came from China. These were low in the prow and rose up to a high, square stern, and their sails spread out like a huge fan. There was a fleet of local fishing boats: long, low craft shaped in a curve and rising to a high prow and stern. There were ocean-going sailing ships, clearly created for the same purpose as the European craft I knew, but with a look so unfamiliar that I realized instantly they were the work of Japanese shipbuilders.

In the shallow waters of a bay beyond the fishing boat harbour, I spotted litters, apparently floating on the water. They were being carried, four men to a litter, and in each one sat what I thought were beautifully dressed dummies in silks so brilliant and glossy that they caught the light, and wearing black wigs that seemed to have been painted on. Then one of them moved, and I understood my mistake.

Events had moved fast as I'd stood there enthralled. I heard Ambroos call out to me, and his sharp, impatient tone told me it wasn't the first time he'd done so. I turned to see him standing at the head of the plank that had been run out to rest on the quay. 'Oh, Lord,' Hieronymus muttered, 'he is displeased . . .'

'Come, Gabriel, Hieronymus,' Ambroos said sternly, 'for our host expects us, and in this of all lands, we do not keep people waiting.'

I grimaced at Hieronymus and pulled my heavy coat closer, struggling to fasten it over my padded leather jerkin; I had put on my two thickest garments and still I was cold. I straightened my cap and hurried down the gangplank after the captain and his companions. Other than Ambroos, Hieronymus and me, the party consisted of the four Portuguese, and Flavinho seemed to be their leader.

He hurried to the front of our little procession, courteously bowing to Ambroos as he did so, and set off towards a line of large and well-maintained wooden buildings over to the right that were set into the hillside rising up steeply to the rear. They formed an enclave set apart from the main harbour and its buildings, and faced a separate, small inlet where the stone quays were lined with vessels. We had left the congestion of the big harbour behind now, but the enclave ahead of us hummed with purpose and I could see at least a dozen men going busily about their work. 'It's like a separate little port,' I said to Ambroos.

He made a face. 'It is,' he replied, his voice low. 'The man who founded it runs it as if it was his own fiefdom. And this is not his only trading post – he has many others.'

I thought he was going to say more, but he shook his head and muttered, 'You will see.'

A well-maintained path led to the wooden buildings, which occupied an elevated position above the mud and the detritus of the port. The path ended in a set of steps leading on to the raised area around the middle building, and as I watched a man came out of its door, thumped heavily down the steps and marched towards us.

I had expected him to be Japanese.

He wasn't. He was a European.

There was time to stare as our party advanced towards him. He was perhaps fifty, not tall, barrel-chested and bow-legged, so much so that he appeared to swing each leg round the other as he walked. He was dressed, it seemed, in a series of layered garments wrapped tightly around his stocky body, giving the impression that he was so bundled up that he couldn't bend. His grizzled red-brown hair was close-cut on a spherical skull, he fixed his pale, penetrating eyes on us as if it was vital to assess us comprehensively the very first moment he saw us, and he moved with the utter confidence of a man who knows exactly who he is and is fully satisfied that he occupies the place in the world that was specifically designed for him.

My first impressions were that he was tough, ruthless, and likely to do whatever it took to get his own way. All of which qualities he would have needed, I reflected, to have carved out a thriving string of trading posts in an alien land.

But now we were almost upon him, and he was waiting to greet us.

He bowed to Ambroos, then turned to Flavinho and embraced him. There was a lively flow of Portuguese, of which I managed to make not much sense, and quite a lot of back-slapping between him and his countrymen. Ambroos, I noted, was rather more reserved, embarking on a polite little speech in Portuguese, but the grizzled man interrupted him, exclaimed something in Dutch and then, to my surprise, turned to me and said in accented English, 'I am Romeu Silvestre. You I believe to be Doctor Gabriel, and I am glad to meet you.'

He bowed to me, and, awkwardly, I copied him. 'Thank you.'

He must have seen my surprise at his fluency in my language. 'Here in the nearby port of Nagasaki are the Jesuits,' he said, 'who bravely voyage to take the word of God all over the known world and are relentless educators of men. Only one native English speaker has come with the Fathers, but one is enough.'

'It is a great joy to be greeted in my mother tongue,' I said.

'Then be welcome!' he cried. 'Here in my port quarters are refreshments, which I offer to sustain you for the journey.'

'Journey?' I hadn't meant to speak out loud.

Romeu Silvestre smiled disarmingly. 'Yes! But it is no great distance, and I have provided ponies for myself and my guests, for I make the trip often and I do not care to walk.'

He spun round, hurrying off towards the wooden building and, no doubt, already preoccupied with the serving of the food he had commanded for us. I was watching him closely and I noticed that, as he was turning away, the disarming smile abruptly vanished, to be replaced by a different expression that I sensed was much better suited to his face. For that brief instant in which I observed him, he looked like a man facing a grave challenge and determined to win whatever the cost.

The seven of us followed along behind Romeu on the sturdy ponies. I'd thought I might have preferred to walk; the ponies were small, and, besides the fact that my long legs almost scraped the ground, I feared my weight would be too great. But the pony was tougher than he looked, the steepness of the path increased rapidly as we left the port behind us, and soon I was glad to be mounted. Once I had the pony's measure, I began to look around.

We were climbing out of the bowl in which the little port lay. Around us, hills were turning into mountains, and soon we were negotiating a pass between two peaks, emerging on to a col with steep drops on either side that had one of the Portuguese – Dario, the historian – moaning and crossing himself. The path took to winding to and fro as it found the easiest slope, and then suddenly we emerged from what was almost a tunnel of rock to find ourselves in an open valley up in the mountains with a wonderful view back down to the port behind and below us and the open sea beyond.

The valley contained a small settlement: two large wooden houses with the same overhanging roofs and pillared outside space as the port buildings, and a collection of smaller houses, single-storeyed and low to the ground, that were spread out along a path running beside a little stream, although what might have been a lively flow of water in spring and summer was now bound hard with ice. The snow had been trodden on the tracks that crossed to and fro through the village, but on the slopes soaring up all around it lay white and untrodden.

There was no wind, the sky was a brilliant, cloudless blue, the temperature had steadily dropped as we climbed up from the shore, and I was so cold I could hardly feel my knees, let alone my feet.

Romeu, hurrying on ahead, had summoned servants from somewhere behind the larger of the houses, and as the rest of the party rode up, smiling, bowing men were already hastening to take the ponies and usher us across the covered space towards the sturdy old wooden door. Romeu stood back to let Ambroos and me precede him, and I followed the skipper into the house.

I had no idea what to expect from the interior of a Japanese dwelling. Used to the houses I was familiar with in my own land, I stood for a moment just looking.

The wide timber-floored space was broken up by several screens, and many doorways indicated that there was a maze of other rooms leading off it. It was dominated by a large hearth-stone that stood some two feet high, on which a fire blazed in an iron grate. The heat pulsed out to greet me, and I think I might have groaned with pleasure. The smoke from the fire rose straight up; following it with my eyes, I saw that it filtered out through the thatch of the roof. Around this open area in the centre of the house ran a raised balcony, accessed by a set of wide wooden steps, off which doorways opened. Spaced around the floor in the room in which I stood were a series of thick mats made of some sort of straw, and on the mats were low tables and large, fat cushions.

From somewhere came the smell of food.

The evening that followed was so crammed with new sights, smells and sensations that I wanted to take myself aside to allow my mind to catch up with my senses and assimilate it all. Almost as soon as we were through the door, Romeu had summoned a couple of women to show us to our quarters. To my dismay one of them – she was child-sized to my eyes, thin and wiry, and she moved at a sort of quick trot – seized my kitbag and my medical bag and bore them ahead of me up the steps. I heard Ambroos chuckle; 'Better, my friend, to let them do as they want, because they will anyway,' he remarked.

'But she's only half my size,' I hissed, 'and my bags are heavy!'

'Enjoy it while you may,' he advised.

Ambroos and I were shown to two large rooms off the upper gallery. In mine, I saw through the open door, there would only be room to stand on the side nearer to the passage, for the roof sloped steeply downwards. The woman carrying my bags trotted ahead to deposit them by the bed, and I followed her in. Straightening up, turning to look at me, she was saying something – it sounded like *furo, furo!* – frowning and flapping her hand in front of her face. When I shrugged and looked puzzled, she tried it again a few more times and louder, then added, '*Sento! SENTO!*' with a face that seemed to say, *Surely you can understand that?* Then she said, '*Nanban,*' called out something to her companion, who was waiting for her outside, and with several rapid little bows that resembled small birds pecking at corn, the pair backed away and disappeared.

Belatedly I noticed that there were only two rooms off the upper corridor. 'What about Hieronymus and the Portuguese?' I demanded, striding into Ambroos's room. 'Where are they going to sleep?'

'In the house next door, so I understand.' Ambroos was quickly unpacking his gear, stowing it with the efficiency of a sailor. 'Our host owns both houses. The second one is for guests, this one is his own residence.'

'But—'

'Gabe, this is as new to me as it is to you,' he interrupted. 'Do not expect me to have answers to all the questions that I see are flying through your mind.'

I stood quite still. 'I thought you had been here before. To Japan, to this port?' It emerged as a question.

He grinned. 'I cannot imagine what made you think that.'

'Then what are we doing here? How long will we stay? Do you—'

'*Enough*,' he said firmly. 'Soon we shall be summoned down again. Save your questions for the man we have come here to seek.'

We did not know whether we would offend some rule of local hospitality by descending before we had been asked to, but we went anyway. Another woman – or it might have been one of the first pair – appeared from behind a screen and escorted us to a table on the far side of the hearth. The fire was going well in its iron basket on the enormous hearthstone, and a huge kettle hung suspended over the flames. There were other pots standing ready, and what looked like a griddle. The woman pulled out two of the thick cushions, revealing others set on the floor at right angles so as to form a back support.

'We sit on the floor?' I whispered to Ambroos.

'We do,' he replied, and I watched as he bent his stocky frame, stuck his legs under the table and wriggled around to make himself comfortable. There was a thick padded blanket attached all around the rim of the table, and he pulled it over his lap. An expression of surprise filled his face, then a smile of pleasure.

'That good?' I asked dryly.

But he was busy lifting the thick blanket and peering under the table. 'It's *heated!*' he hissed. 'There is an iron basket attached to the underside of the table and it is full of hot coals!'

Until I sat down and checked for myself, I didn't believe him.

We were still murmuring quietly to each other about the strangeness of it all when our host burst into the room and, beaming happily, drew out a cushion and sat down. I was struggling to get up to greet him, as my mother had always insisted was only polite, but it had taken considerable time and effort to fold my height and breadth under the table and I wasn't nearly quick enough, since before I had even raised my backside off the cushion, Romeu had nimbly seated himself with no apparent discomfort at all.

He called out a long string of instructions in the direction of the screen, then turned to Ambroos and me and said, 'It took long and painful months before I could get up and down from sitting on the floor with any ease, but it is best, I believe, to adopt the customs of the land.'

Ambroos muttered an agreement, but I merely smiled. My legs were cramping already and there was a pain starting up in the small of my back.

A trio of servants came in, and the first of the food was put on the table. Romeu busied himself filling our bowls – rice, fish, vegetables that looked almost raw, sauces whose piquancy made the mouth water – and then a deep pan was placed between the three of us on a trivet over a flame. Whatever liquid was in the pan was soon sizzling and spitting, and swiftly Romeu demonstrated how to put chunks of pork and chicken into the hot oil, then extract them as soon as they were cooked. He used the thin bamboo sticks that he called *hashi*, and for all that Ambroos and I were clumsy and slow, I was so hungry that I managed to shove a great deal of food into my mouth. Several times there was the sound of whispering from the other side of the screen, and quite a lot of giggling, always quickly hushed. The serving women, I guessed, were discreetly watching the visitors, and whatever we were doing was clearly causing considerable mirth.

'And this,' Romeu said, grinning at us while another bowl of meat chunks rapidly cooked in the hot, seasoned oil, 'is *sake*.' He indicated an elegant pottery vessel which one of the servants had just brought in on a beautiful lacquered tray, together with three small matching cups. 'It is rice wine,' he added as he filled two cups, 'and always served at the temperature of the lobe of the ear.' He demonstrated, tugging at his ear. He handed the cups to Ambroos and me.

I waited, then said, 'Do you not like it?'

'I adore it.' His smile widened. 'However, it is not considered mannerly to pour sake for yourself. When you wish to drink, you offer the wine to your companions, put down the carafe and wait, and one of your companions then reciprocates by offering it to you.'

I was already filling a cup for him as he explained.

Soon we had all done far more than take the edge off our hunger, and I, at least, was picking away at the food more out of curiosity than for the satisfying of appetite. The sake was a different matter; I liked it at first taste, and I went on liking it.

Ambroos, I could see, was becoming heavy eyed, frequently having to force himself to sit upright and look interested. I was wide awake, however, and keen to find out more about our host.

'I sense from what you say that you have lived here for some time,' I said. 'May I ask how that came to be?'

He topped up my sake cup, and, the lesson well learned, I did the same for him. 'Of course, Doctor Gabriel,' he replied. 'As I am sure you already know, I am a trader. I found myself in Japan in 1575, when I was twenty-six years old. My companions and I had not the intention to be here; our ship was badly damaged in a typhoon, we were blown far off course, and it was the greatest luck that the inhabitants of Nagasaki, who came to our aid, were as interested in the possibility of doing business with us as we were with them. Soon we had established a trading post in that port, and it was where I spent my first years here. In time I came to see that a measure of – ah – *autonomy* would suit my purposes better.' He smiled, and there was a degree of self-congratulation in the expression.

But before I could ask him to elucidate – I imagined he wouldn't hesitate to explain in detail how clever he'd been, how much money he'd made – he had moved on. 'These inhabitants did not know what to make of us to begin with, my companions and I, and those who so quickly followed us,' he said musingly. 'We were the *nanban-jin*, the southern barbarians' – I recognized *nanban* from what the serving woman had said – 'and we fascinated them, with our long noses and our extraordinary clothing. They put us into their art, you know; into their extraordinary and affecting paintings.' He waved a hand vaguely. 'I have examples, I will show you.' Swiftly picking up the narrative, he went on, 'Not that it would have mattered if they thought we looked like baboons, because they wanted to trade with us and that was that.

Their warlords desired our firearms, and since their traditional armour was no protection against the new weapons, they wanted our heavy armour too, although they adapted it to suit themselves.'

'And which of their goods did you take in exchange?' I asked.

He didn't seem to hear; either that or he had deliberately ignored the question. 'Five years after I arrived, I had already settled here, in the modest port that I have made my headquarters, and I had purchased this village.' He waved a hand around.

'The whole village?' I said.

'It is not so large. Two big houses, many small ones, a couple of farms. Also I have other settlements elsewhere on the southern islands. More of my countrymen have come here to join me, but in addition I provide homes and work for many local people. I treat them well, Doctor,' he said emphatically. 'It is an arrangement of . . .' He snapped his fingers, searching for the phrase.

'Of mutual benefit,' I supplied.

'*Sim*. Thank you, yes. This was always a private house, and belonged to a rich man who liked his comforts,' he continued. I murmured something about it certainly being a luxurious dwelling, but, again, he ignored me. 'The house that stands beside this one, that was an inn, with many rooms but not so large.' He shot me a smirk. 'That is where my countrymen from your ship stay, and the other Dutchman. For tonight only, however, because they set out up the coast early in the morning.' He filled my sake cup, and yet again I reciprocated. 'I hope they will not be imbibing too freely!' he said with a chuckle.

'I would have thought you would have enjoyed talking to them this evening in your own tongue,' I observed.

He frowned – quickly, the expression there and gone – and muttered, 'There will be time. For now, no.'

I studied him, realizing that I had absolutely no idea what he was thinking, what he thought of his influx of visitors, what he expected from us. 'Do you—' I began.

He drowned out the tentative words, saying with gusto, 'But I was telling you the tale of how I came to settle here. I did a wise thing, you see, for I married, Doctor Gabriel, and, if I might be allowed to say so, I married well.' He nodded, as if verifying that he might. 'When I had settled here in my village, when all was made comfortable and ready for a bride, I made my move.

I had noticed a very lovely young woman, although she was closely guarded and I had only caught brief and tantalising glimpses. Kiku she was called, and her name meant chrysanthemum. Her father was a powerful and wealthy man from an ancient family. He not only traded beautiful, costly goods but also manufactured them, as his father and his forefathers had done back into the distant past, and he was not keen on a Portuguese merchant as a son-in-law. Kiku was his only daughter, the one child of her generation.' A slow and not totally pleasant smile spread across his face. 'But I persuaded him, reminding him repeatedly that he very much desired a grandson, and Kiku and I were married in 1580, and two years later she bore a child. The child survived, and the family line was thus ensured for another generation. The mother, however, did not.'

I had suspected he was going to say as much. I'd picked up no sign of a wife's presence. Nor of a child's, I mused, then corrected myself, for a child born in 1582 – this much-desired son who would continue his mother's line – would be twenty-three now. No such young man had been presented to us. No doubt he was away from home, about his father's or his grandfather's business in one of those other enclaves we'd been told about.

I studied Romeu. He was a big man, coarse-featured, rough in his manner, and I found it difficult to imagine him with a delicate Japanese wife.

'I am sorry,' I said. 'It was very sad, to lose your young wife when you were settling so well into your life here.'

He sighed gustily. 'It was sad, yes.' But he said no more.

Perhaps the sudden silence roused Ambroos, for abruptly his eyes snapped open, he sat up straight, and he emitted a grunt of surprise.

Romeu gave an amused guffaw. 'Too much sake, Captain!' he said gleefully. 'Go to bed. All is ready for you.'

Ambroos looked at me, and I realized he was disoriented, not quite sure where he was. 'Up the steps over there' – I pointed – 'and the room is in front of you.'

'But, do you . . . should I . . .' he stuttered.

'Go to bed,' I said firmly.

He made a rueful face and staggered away.

'And now,' Romeu said as we heard him walking unsteadily

across the floorboards of the room upstairs, 'may I introduce you to another of the customs I have adopted?'

'Er . . . yes,' I said tentatively.

He got up, and again the movement looked easy and practised, and held out a hand to help me.

'We must venture to the next house, the one I told you was once an inn, for there is to be found the room that is required.' He grinned to himself, leading the way outside and along under the sheltering eaves to the door of the other house. Even that brief exposure to the night was more than enough; it was intensely cold outside. Romeu must have seen me shiver, for he nodded, muttering something to himself in his own tongue.

I had wondered if I would see Hieronymus or one of the Portuguese, but there was no sign of them. All was profoundly quiet, and the big room was illuminated only by the fire on the hearth and some lanterns set around the walls. Romeu collected one of the lanterns, and by its light led me across to a low doorway that gave on to a long, dark passage leading to the rear of the dwelling.

There was a wave of heat coming towards us. The warm air felt moist, as if water had been boiling. Perhaps we were close to the kitchens . . . There was a delicious fragrance, but it smelt like flowers, or perfume – incense, perhaps – rather than food.

Romeu stopped to push back a sliding screen and a great waft of hot, damp air flowed out. I stared past him into the room beyond. The light was very poor, but I made out what seemed to be a very large stone cistern, and beside it low wooden shelves with jugs of steaming water, stacks of clean towels and a pile of what seemed to be neatly folded garments made of thick, fine wool.

Romeu waved a proud, proprietorial hand. 'Here is *sento*, the bath house!' he exclaimed. 'To be correct, the name for this is *suefuro*, for it is a new variation of an ancient tradition, and was constructed in the inn a short time before I purchased it. It is the Japanese way, to wash, to clean off the dirt of the outside world, most often on returning home after the day's work, but also, sometimes, before bed.'

He was looking at me expectantly.

But I dropped my head, for I was feeling mortified.

I'd already heard that word *sento*. The woman who had shown me to the room had used it, and as she did so she had been glaring at me and waving a hand under her nose.

What she had been saying was: *you stink, you southern barbarian, and you need a bath.*

It looked as though I was going to have one.

THREE

'd imagined it was Romeu who was going to introduce me to the delights of the bath, and already I was feeling deeply embarrassed at the prospect of stripping off before a near-stranger and sharing a bath with him. But it wasn't; it was much worse than that.

He clapped his hands and instantly two women of indeterminate age appeared. They might have been two of the servants who had served our food, but I couldn't be sure. These women too were dressed in the wrap-around garments, every layer giving the impression that it had been arranged with careful precision, but now they wore voluminous white aprons over the garments, whose sleeves ended in gathered cuffs that enclosed the wide sleeves beneath.

It was clear from Romeu's expression that he was enjoying my extreme discomfiture. 'Here are the servants of the bath,' he said, 'and they will show you what to do.'

'But there's no need, I'm sure I—' I began.

Deliberately misunderstanding, he reassured me that it was no trouble, it was the women's main task, they had been very thoroughly trained and they performed the work with skill and enthusiasm.

I was still worrying what he meant by enthusiasm when he said he hoped I'd enjoy my bath, that clean clothes had been prepared for me so that the women could launder my own garments, that he hoped I'd sleep well and would see me in the morning.

I heard the sound of his footsteps echoing along the passage. Then I was alone with two strange women.

I am sure I would have died of embarrassment, except that they went about the job with a practical, businesslike air, and in addition took it for granted that a hot bath was one of the best treats in the world and I was going to absolutely love it. With brisk efficiency they set about unfastening and unlacing my many layers of clothing – coat, padded jerkin, tunic, shirt, hose – and then we were down almost to my skin, and I didn't know if to be more mortified by the fact that I was almost naked or that I stank like an old dog fox. They tutted a bit, and one of them made a face as she bundled up the final layers that I'd been wearing closest to my flesh, but then, seeing that I'd noticed, she blushed, bowed and let out a long string of words that I assumed formed an apology. 'No need to apologize,' I said, although of course she didn't understand, 'it's very brave of you to tackle someone as filthy and smelly as I am, and I am very sorry you have to.'

I hoped very much that I was mistaken, but I thought I heard someone laugh softly from close at hand.

There was no time to worry about that, though. I had been shuffling forward, in the hope of getting into the bath and under the water to hide myself from their very interested eyes, but one of them gave a gasp of horror, took firm hold of my arm to drag me away from the bath, and, with a very effective set of mimed actions, showed me what I had to do first.

I had not appreciated the significance of the bath being communal, which meant, of course, that nobody went into it until they had scrubbed every inch of themselves and were as clean as soap, water, washcloth and scrubbing brush could achieve. In case I had not completely understood, the two women watched me, one of them helpfully pointing out when I missed a bit. I used jug after jug of hot water, washing myself from the crown of my head to my toenails, and at long last one of them abruptly cried '*Hai!*' and, pointing to the steaming, fragrant water, pushed me towards the cistern.

I bent down and put a foot in the water.

It was *so hot.*

I thought afterwards that it must be spring fed from some thermal source; at the time, on that unforgettable first night, it was just one more extraordinary new experience to absorb. The water was far too hot to enter quickly, and, long past shame now, I took my time and lowered myself in gently and slowly until I was sitting on the stone floor of the bath, little ripples were lapping my chin, and my hair, which had grown long in the course of the voyage, was floating like a layer of seaweed.

One of the women put a cushion under my neck. I murmured my thanks. The other handed me an object like a sponge, indicating that I should rub it across my flesh. I nodded, but I was too comfortable to move a muscle. I closed my eyes. I was vaguely aware of movement, and I thought I heard the door slide open and closed again. Perhaps they were going to leave me alone now that they'd finished telling me what to do . . .

I let myself drift into a half-sleep. The sensations felt wonderful. The hot water was working on my tired body, mending the many hurts of a long sea voyage, easing its warmth into muscles worn out and sore with the discomfort inherent in being a big, tall man living for months on end in cramped quarters on a ship designed for speed and not for comfort.

I thought I might have snored.

I rolled my shoulders, appreciating how the exquisite pain of over-used muscles was soothed by the hot, magical water. I slipped into a doze. The few soft night sounds seemed far away, and then near again . . .

I detected the sweet scent of jasmine.

There were hands on my head.

Fingers in my hair, massaging my scalp. The sensations this was sparking off in me were quite extraordinary, and I was starting to relax and simply enjoy them when it occurred to me to wonder whose hands they were.

Their owner must have felt the change in my body; picked up, perhaps, the sudden tension. The fingers ceased their pressure. There was that soft laugh again, and a woman's voice said quietly right in my ear, 'Lie back, Doctor, I have not yet finished.'

Romeu had told me his servants of the bath did their work well. One of them must have returned, I reflected dozily, and knelt down silently behind me to proceed with the next pleasure lined up for me.

But abruptly it occurred to me that I had understood her; she had spoken in my language. A very senior servant, then: a housekeeper, perhaps; someone who, in the absence of a mistress in this widower's house, acted as Romeu's hostess when required. This would explain why she spoke another language. I wondered if she was perhaps Portuguese, like him; maybe the widow of one of his fellow traders.

I moved my head slightly and opened my eyes, trying to see who knelt behind me.

The light was dim; there was only one lantern burning now. I saw dark hair, coiled in an elaborate style. I saw the wrap-around garment, over it the big white apron with the tight cuffs protecting the sleeves. But she wasn't one of the women who had attended me earlier. I had the impression that she was younger, taller, fuller-fleshed; her body was firm and strong, and she held herself with youthful suppleness and grace.

She had noticed me trying to look at her, and she moved slightly so that I couldn't.

When she spoke, it was in Japanese; at least, I presumed it was. It wasn't Dutch or Portuguese, and it certainly wasn't English. As she rattled on, I began to wonder if I'd imagined those few words spoken in English. I'd been on the very edge of sleep, I had drunk quite a lot of sake, I was exhausted; I'd probably been half in a dream.

I started to stand, putting my hands on the edge of the bath and preparing to heave myself out of the water. The woman ducked away, sweeping up a towel and wrapping it around me, draping another one over my head as I stepped out on to the floor. Blinded by it, I heard her moving around the room, still talking. Then she pulled the towel away and, manipulating my arms with surprisingly powerful hands, put one of the wrap-around garments in a soft, white fabric on me, tying it neatly. Quickly I was dressed in another layer, and on top of that went a short-sleeved, heavily padded top layer. In the heat of the bath house, I was instantly too hot. I tried to tell her so, but she was kneeling at my feet, making me lift one and then the other, drying them and putting on strange hose with a gap between the toes. She ushered me to the door, and gave me a pair of wooden-soled shoes raised up on blocks at the front and back. She led the way up the passage, out on to the space beneath the eaves and back to the main house, opening the door just enough to shove me inside before straight away closing it again.

But I took hold of it and stopped her.

In the soft light spilling out of the room, I stared at her.

She was young; younger than any of the other servants. Her hair was dark, although not as intensely black as that of her companions, for it had a sheen of shining chestnut. Her skin was ivory-pale. Her face was lovely, and her hazel eyes were full of light. She strongly resembled the rest of the staff, but there was something about her expression that set her apart. She looked as if she was about to laugh; she also looked as if she didn't take kindly to being told what to do. The consequences of that for someone who had, presumably, been sent by fate to be a rich merchant's bath-house servant for the rest of her life were interesting, to say the least, and I was about to try to ask her name when abruptly she pulled the heavy door out of my grasp and very firmly closed it.

I was left alone.

Smiling – I had the strong sense that this wasn't the last I would be seeing of the young woman – I went up the stairs and stumbled into bed.

Ambroos roused me in the morning. It was light, there were sounds of activity from below, and he was fully dressed.

We descended to find Romeu already tucking into his food. Breakfast was another revelation. He showed us how to beat an egg into a small bowl of rice and flavour it with a savoury, salty sauce, and then demonstrated the technique of spreading some of the mixture on a thin sheet of something dried that tasted of the sea. The result was surprisingly tasty, and when he offered me a second one, I accepted. There were also bowls of a thin, savoury broth; from what I could gather this was called *miso*. Once again we had our invisible audience watching from behind the screen, and they found our attempts this morning as funny as they had last night's. Then one of them said something that had the others going *hai, hai*, which seemed to express agreement.

'They say you learn quickly to manage the *hashi*,' Romeu said.

It was true, for I certainly seemed to be picking it up more easily than Ambroos, who was surreptitiously using his fingers. I could have explained; could have said that a ship's surgeon, who trims and stitches other men's flesh, and who delves into deep cuts to extract splinters of wood, shards of metal and parasitic insects, learns early in his career to wield fine instruments. But, reckoning that I would undoubtedly put the others off their food, I merely nodded.

'And now,' Romeu declared, 'allow me, gentlemen, to reveal the arrangements I have made for your visit.'

It was mid-morning. After our surprising breakfast, our host had taken Ambroos and me on a tour of the bay where he had established his domain. We saw ships of various sizes, some large enough to be ocean-going. We were introduced to a succession of bowing, smiling men, many of whom greeted us in a few words of Portuguese and even one or two of English.

'Your English Jesuit has been busy,' I remarked to Romeu after one of his officials had just faced me with a big smile and a mangled but recognizable version of *good morning, I hope you are well*. 'I expected to hear your language, since it is apparent that you and your countrymen are well established here, but not mine.' Other than this single, very industrious Jesuit priest, I calculated, there surely couldn't be another native English speaker for hundreds, if not thousands, of miles.

Romeu chuckled. 'Ah, but a facility with the tongue of the most determined and ruthless of the trading nations will soon be greatly to our advantage, Doctor Gabriel,' he said. He was smiling, but his eyes had no humour in them; nor even, I thought, any warmth.

I sensed I must be on my guard with Romeu Silvestre.

I sensed he was a dangerous man.

We had ended up in the big building on the quay, where we had seen him emerge to greet us the day before. It appeared to be the headquarters from which he ran his trading empire. He hurried us along a passage and into what he described as his office. There was a table with ink pots and a tray of quills, tied bundles of parchments, shelves of ledgers, and on the floor in a corner a large oak chest bound with iron. Here, as if to differentiate this place of business from the remainder of our host's accommodation, the table was the height that we from the West were used to, and there were heavy chairs with backs and armrests that we drew up to the table.

Comfortably settled, with small cups of a hot drink smelling of jasmine that our host had poured out from a very pretty porcelain pot, Ambroos and I sat back to listen.

As Romeu ran rapidly through the details, I grew increasingly dismayed. I had not given much thought as to how long our voyage would last; initially taken aback at the discovery that we had been bound for Japan and not Neira and the Banda Islands, I had concluded philosophically that it didn't matter much since my role as ship's surgeon was the same wherever we went, and that even if I objected, it would undoubtedly make not a jot of difference. I had expected that the *Luipaard* would put into port, take on the cargo that had been prepared for her and that, after a short spell to effect any repairs, build up our supplies and give the crew some time to rest and recover their full strength, we would set off for home.

Romeu had been detailing our cargo. Porcelain. Precious metals: gold, silver, copper. Lacquerware. Swords. Silk. He mentioned quantities that staggered me: was Walter Haverleigh so greedy? Did he want to buy every last beautiful item that these islands produced?

Even before Romeu told us how long he expected the process to take, I knew. I had been thinking in terms of weeks; Romeu was reckoning in months. Goods destined for the *Luipaard*'s holds and the markets of England had not even been made yet. So vast was Walter Haverleigh's order that it would be the best part of a year before it was complete.

I was very angry, and made more so by the fact that I had no justification for it. Nobody had actually said when the *Luipaard* would return to England. When voyaging so far over such uncertain seas, nobody ever did, as I well knew from my days in Queen Elizabeth's navy. No, if it was anyone's fault that I was suddenly faced with a far longer absence than I had expected, it was mine.

Romeu was still revealing the details of our schedule, Ambroos was nodding, commenting here and there and asking a lot of questions, but I stopped listening. I didn't care about the cargo. I was not a merchant, I wasn't even a sailor; I was there to look after the health and well-being of the *Luipaard*'s company, and where she went, I went too.

Troubled, distressed, I waited for Romeu to finish.

'You look unhappy,' Ambroos said to me as the sturdy ponies took us back up to the village. Romeu had been detained by an anxious-looking Portuguese man pressing for an answer on some problem to do with a consignment of porcelain, and he had urged us to set off without him.

'I had not expected us to be here for so long,' I admitted.

He looked surprised. 'Had you not? It is not done speedily, the preparation of a cargo such as we shall take home with us. But then,' he added kindly, 'why should you know this? Your voyages in your previous years at sea would have been of a very different nature, *nee*?'

I nodded. 'They were.'

'I am sorry,' he said when I didn't go on. 'You . . .' he hesitated, perhaps uncertain if to speak.

'What?' I demanded.

'You are sad for home? I am sorry, Gabe, I do not know the word.'

'Homesick. No, I'm not homesick.' But even as I said it, I knew that it was exactly what was wrong with me.

In the afternoon, Ambroos was summoned back to Romeu's office for more discussion. Hieronymus and the four Portuguese had departed on some unspecified mission to Nagasaki immediately after the midday meal; Ambroos and I had seen them off. I was left to my own devices.

I went back to the port and set about exploring the wider bay that did not fall under the domination of Romeu Silvestre. I went to the furthest point to the south-west, where the density of buildings and people faded away and there was a view along the coast to the town of Nagasaki, a few miles away. I stood and watched as big ocean-going craft edged their way into harbour, and my thoughts went with others as they were hauled out into open water, the sails were raised and they set off on their way. I would have given almost anything, just then, to be sailing with them; away from here, out of these alien waters and on my way west towards home.

My mood did not improve as the short daylight began to fade and I made my reluctant way back to Romeu's village. Inside, gratefully warming my hands and feet, I could hear the pleasant hum of female voices from somewhere at the back of the house, but there was nobody in the room with the big hearth. I went up to my room and flung myself down on the mattress.

I heard Ambroos and Romeu come in. They were talking, their voices loud and animated. They sounded as if they were arguing their way towards an agreement of some sort, and presently Romeu's sudden cheer suggested they had reached it. There were footsteps on the stairs, and a tap on the door. 'Gabe?' said Ambroos's voice. 'Will you come down?'

I wondered how he knew I was there; no doubt one of the servants had seen me come in, even though I had been unaware of it, and told Romeu. The hearty company of two men with something to celebrate was the last thing I wanted that evening but, since there was no excuse I could offer to avoid it, I got up, straightened my clothes and, with very bad grace, stomped down to join them.

My disgruntled mood intensified. I doubt that either of them noticed, for they had indeed come to some sort of conclusion to their arrangements – not caring what it was about, I did not even try to find out – and they were intent on celebrating the signing of the agreement. Fortunately for me, the celebration included the consumption of a great deal of sake, and when the three of us had taken our fill of the rice wine – because I was not going to see them get drunk without me – Ambroos fetched a bottle of genever from his kit and we drank that too.

Ambroos was livelier than I was tonight, and now it was his turn to be offered the delights of the bath house. Romeu asked if I would join them – he was intending to accompany Ambroos – but I'd had enough of their company and grumpily I declined. I went back to my room, where I found that one of the servants had left a big jug of very hot water; it seemed to be a sin in their eyes to retire to bed without a wash, even if you did not elect to have a bath.

I obeyed the unspoken injunction and stripped off. Why not? I thought, and I washed myself all over before putting on the layered garments I had been given last night.

The alcohol was affecting me increasingly now. I almost fell over when standing on one foot to wash the other, and the room was spinning as I righted myself. I helped myself to cold water from the earthenware jug put out for me, downing a large cupful, then fell on to the bed, pulled up the covers and closed my eyes.

I had no idea how long I'd been asleep. I'd been dreaming of

Rosewyke, and the images of home were full of beauty and poignant with memory. I was walking above the river with my sister, and Celia was telling me that I should not have gone away because Tock had a sore arm and expected me to make it better; 'And you cannot blame him for that, Gabe,' she said spiritedly, 'because you have permitted him to become dependent on you and it's all your fault.'

I was in the middle of indignantly protesting my innocence when I woke up.

I didn't know where I was. I thought I was in my room at home, then wondered if I was at sea, then decided I was in a dream world and hadn't woken up at all. That seemed the preferred solution; in my drunken state, being in a dream world was actually very appealing. I closed my eyes. I thought I heard a door open, but the sound was indistinct. I felt rather than heard the footsteps, for they were almost silent, and set off only the merest vibration in the floorboards. I sensed the warmth of another body. I felt soft hair brush against my face. I smelt jasmine. I put out my arms, because if this dream of mine had produced a dream woman, I thought I might as well make her welcome. She lay down beside me, her firm, smooth flesh against mine, and I pulled the covers up over both of us. A warm hand crept inside my layered garments and began to caress my skin.

I'm not sure how soon I admitted to myself that I knew perfectly well I was no longer dreaming. That this was no phantom but a real live woman in my arms. I should have politely told her to leave; I should never have reached for her and drawn her down beside me in the first place.

But I had, and now I found I had no power to reject her. She was no innocent girl, for she knew how to please and arouse, knew how to bend herself to me, to anticipate desires even before they had been hinted at. We kissed deeply, and she whispered to me in words I did not understand but whose meaning was as clear as glass. I was still intoxicated, my judgement was unsound, I was sad, homesick, depressed. She was warm, fragrant, her strong body smooth-fleshed and compliant, and she wanted to give me pleasure. I did not ask myself why; I simply gave myself up to it.

*   *   *

I woke to find the thin early light coming through the shutters. I was alone.

I'd have thought the woman who had materialized from the depths of the night had been a dream after all. Except that there was a long dark hair on the pillow, and the covers smelt of jasmine.

FOUR

Ambroos and I stayed on with Romeu for several more days, although in truth we spent most of the daylight hours on the *Luipaard*, making the preparations for the first of our trading voyages. This time we were going to head along the coast towards the north, and then along the channel between two more of the islands and east to Kobe and Osaka, with a trip inland to Kyoto. The names meant nothing to me: so far they were no more than words on the map.

Since our arrival in port there had been a steady stream of men seeking my attention for a variety of usually minor ailments that had plagued them during the voyage but that they had been too occupied to address. It was, of course, my job to attend to all of them, but the long and dismal parade of muscle strains, boils, ingrowing toenails, piles, and the enduring after-effects of venereal disease (and, as frequently, the harsh remedies administered to deal with it) became quite wearing. As the stream finally showed signs of slowing to a halt, I checked my shelves and realized that I needed to replenish my medical supplies. Accordingly, one bright but bitterly cold morning I went down to the small shop in Romeu's trading post to see what was on offer there. They did not have all that I wanted, but the local man who ran it was eager to help, and in a mixture of mime and Portuguese, informed me that his son – or it might have been his nephew – had a small boat and would transport me along the coast to Nagasaki, where a much grander emporium would have everything I needed.

The obliging son or nephew did as he was bidden, and I spent an entertaining and highly informative morning learning about the traditional healing arts of the land from an old Japanese master. Neither of us spoke the other's tongue, and we resorted to Dutch; there had been Dutch traders in a port on the opposite side of the island since 1600, their population was growing, and enterprising local people had already begun to acquire a working knowledge of the language. After all the months on the *Luipaard* with a crew of Dutchmen, I knew enough to respond, and as I conversed haltingly with my old healer I added considerably to my stock of Japanese words.

The most valuable instruction I had from him, however, concerned the deep knowledge of herbal medicine that had taken him a lifetime to acquire. He introduced me to *kuzu*, a starchy root ground down to make a remedy for inflammation and upset stomach, and to the myriad uses of ginger, a supply of which he sold to me in a beautiful, pale green jar made of almost trans-lucent porcelain. He gave me to understand that no healer could achieve success unless the spirits favoured him, and in order to make sure I appeased them, gave me a small figurine of a *kami*, which I understood to mean a divine spirit. He also presented me with a dried chrysanthemum flower, and told me that drinking dew from its folded petals would give long life. He revealed that he was a shaman, and that this gave him access to the world of the spirits. Through meditation, trance and magic ritual he had penetrated the veil, and he brought the secrets revealed to him there back to this world, where he used them to help those who came to him in need.

He asked where I lived, and when I explained about Romeu and his trading post and his village, his benign expression altered subtly to something rather less kindly and he nodded in a wise way as if to say *I know all about Romeu Silvestre.* He sat in silence for some moments – I had the odd impression that he was listening to some interior voice – and then told me to go to the shrine in the hills above the little bay. He told me to go very early and go alone. As a valediction, he murmured, *You will not be sorry.*

I got up before dawn the next morning. I dressed in every warm garment I could find, for the skies were cloudless, the ground was iron-hard with frost and it was bone-achingly cold. The old healer's instructions had been clear, but he had warned me that the way was difficult, narrow and involved a steep climb over rocky ground. He was right, but I was grateful for the effort it took because it warmed me up.

I had been too busy in the two weeks or so since arriving in

Japan to give much, if any, thought to my spiritual life. My healer friend had told me to seek for a shrine, and I was imagining a small chapel, or a stone altar set into the rocks of the hillside. But, of course, I had been born in a Christian land, and I was conditioned to picture what I knew.

The reality was quite different.

I reached the summit of the first of the successive line of hills that rose up steeply behind the port. These hills swiftly increased in height until, not far above me, they turned into mountains, snow-covered and blue-white in the early light. The narrow path wound on around the shoulder of the slope – there was a steep precipice to my left which I tried not to look at – and then entered a shallow valley, where it descended rapidly, until all at once we were back below the tree line and the skeletons of graceful birch trees, bare of leaves in that winter season, began to appear. Another track came up from below, joining the one I was following, and the two combined into a broader, smooth-surfaced path that straightened out as it went on through the valley. Now the trees stood tall and dense on each side, as if they had been deliberately planted to mark the way.

Presently the path began to climb again, and I went up a long flight of shallow steps, evenly spaced and formed by bedding wide cuts of timber into the earth. The steps had the simple beauty of something well-made. I paused, turning to look around me.

The sun was over the horizon now. It was beyond the wooded slopes over to the right, its long gold rays penetrating the ranks of tall, slim tree trunks to form a dramatic pattern of brilliance against darkness. For a moment I was far away from a hillside in Japan and back in an English town, watching a cart-load of men perform one of the old Miracle Plays from the days of our forefathers. At the back of their makeshift stage on the wagon were several shapes cut out of wood: the outline of a church, a tree filled with birds. And, largest and most dominant, the crude outline of a hand fixed to a big board, thumb at the top, fingers together and outstretched, and, extending from the digits, streams of golden light had been painted on the board. This was the Hand of God, and thus his holy light illuminated the affairs of men.

On that deserted and serene hillside half a world away, I was seeing the real thing.

I stood there for some time. I was entirely alone, there was utter silence, and I seemed to have moved, or been moved, out of time. Staring at those beams of light, I knew I was in the presence of the divine. It was not the God of my childhood and youth; well, it *was,* but it was so much more as well. It was the sky, the earth, the stars and the stones; it was the animating spirit of the entire world and the universe beyond. It was the best of human beings: their capacity to care for each other; the maternal love that makes an exhausted new mother get up yet again from profound and badly needed sleep to tend a crying infant; the comradely love that makes a fighting man give up his life for his friends; the love between a man and a woman that begins in the hot lust of physical attraction and matures over years and decades into a deep and close understanding that makes two minds think as one.

I had the sensation that a window had briefly opened to me.

For the time that I stood there – and I had no idea if it was a few moments or an hour – I seemed to see more clearly than ever before. I had left the realm where we fumbled to understand the meaning of the shadows on the wall of the cave; for that strange time, I thought I could glimpse the origin of the shadows. I knew that I understood but, even as that knowledge came to me, I knew it was only to be transitory.

I sensed the window starting to close. I didn't think I could bear to see it finally shut, so I closed my eyes. I started to pray – to who or what I don't know – and it was a prayer of the most heartfelt thanks.

Then I headed on up the steps.

Presently I came to a gateway. It consisted of a wooden arch built right across the path: two heavy supporting posts on either side and a top beam that had a shallow downward curve. Its simplicity made it striking. I stood for some time just looking at that, too. Then I noticed that offerings had been left, piled up to the left of the gateway. There were sacks of rice, barrels of sake, and I felt ashamed because I was empty-handed.

A little stream emerged from the hillside and set off down a channel beside the path. A basin had been dug out, and there was a long-handled wooden cup on the lip of the basin. I dipped it into the flowing water and drank. The water was icy, and acted like a tonic. Some instinct prompted me to dip again and pour some water over my hands, and then I washed my face.

I went on through the gateway.

Some time later I reached the summit, and the path ended in a smooth pavement and an arch. Beyond the arch was a small wooden building with a steep-pitched tiled roof that opened to a dark interior. Neatly pleated paper decorations hung from the lintel, dancing gently as they were caught by small movements in the air. I moved forward a few paces until I could look inside. Then I stopped.

I could see a few rows of simple wooden benches, and beyond an altar of some sort. There was an old man crouching before the altar, a look of profound bliss on his face. I smelt incense.

I almost went in. I didn't; I had already had a moment of deep spiritual meaning, and to seek another would be greedy.

I went back out to the forecourt beyond the arch and sat down on a roughly made bench.

Where, some time later, the old man came to find me.

He nodded to me, and I nodded back. He sat down beside me, and I felt his utter calm embrace me.

After a while he raised a bent old hand to indicate the trees and the stones, the hillside, the shrine. '*Kami*,' he said.

It was the same word the old healer had used. I nodded. 'Spirits,' I said.

He waved down the hill to the elegant wooden gateway arch. '*Torii*.'

I nodded.

'*Jinja*.' Now he was indicating the shrine.

'*Jinja*,' I repeated.

He stuck a thumb into his chest. '*Kannushi*.' Then he pointed down to the stacked offerings, before pointing to himself again. He meant, I guessed, that he was responsible for tending the shrine and taking care of the rice and wine.

He held up his hand in the universal gesture of *wait a minute!* and scuttled away. He disappeared inside the shrine and emerged a few moments later. Returning to my bench, he held out a small object wrapped in a piece of silk. Unwrapping the silk, I found a thin piece of wood about the length of my forefinger, rectangular in shape and coming to a point at the top, where there was a small hole and a thin thread of ribbon. There were images in black ink inscribed on it, the characters intricate and beautiful.

'*Kanji.*' He pointed at the characters. Then he took the piece of wood out of my hands, wrapped it again and handed it back. '*Omamori,*' he said. '*Fuku. Fukutoku.*' He nodded encouragingly, and dutifully I repeated the words. He grabbed my hand, still holding the silk-wrapped wood, and thrust it deep inside my jerkin, his fingers hard against my skin. I thought I understood: he had given me an amulet for protection, or for luck, and I was to tuck it away and keep it safe.

I stood up and made him a bow.

If I had known how to say *I will return with an offering* in a language that meant anything to him, I would have done. I just said 'Sake,' making the sign for money and pointing to the port below. He nodded, chuckled cheerfully and hurried away, disappearing back inside the shrine.

I took a long time walking back to the village. I felt as if I was leaving an enchanted land; that, even when I went back with my offering, I would not experience the shrine on the hillside in the same way again. Just before the first houses of Romeu's village, I stopped, turned round and said a silent farewell.

I had the amulet safe inside my clothing. But I didn't need it to remember; I knew I had just experienced something that would stay with me as long as I lived.

I returned the next day carrying a barrel of sake on my shoulder. I left it at the gateway, and a different attendant – a much younger man – received it with an indifferent nod and put it with the rest. A group of young men were milling around, chattering brightly, laughing, squealing in mock distress at the chill bite of the water in the basin.

I'd been right; yesterday's magic was not going to reveal itself again.

I left the shrine. I would not go back.

The first and by far the most extensive of our expeditions to collect our cargo went well. We arrived at each successive trading port more or less when we had said we would, we invariably received a polite and sometimes a warm welcome, Flavinho and his fellow countrymen adopted easily to their role of negotiators with the Portuguese traders we dealt with, and, to judge by the hearty, hard-drinking celebrations that inevitably followed a successful transaction, everyone was happy.

It was good to be with Hieronymus again. We greeted each other like old friends, and whenever we could we spent a quiet hour together after supper to catch up with all that we had been doing. I did not tell him about the woman who had come to my bed; I was beginning to think I'd dreamt her after all.

'It was wise to have engaged the services of Flavinho and his friends,' Hieronymus said one evening on the return journey as we sat enjoying pipes of tobacco and cups of sake. 'We would not meet with such success in our trading without the pass that informs everyone we meet that we are acting within the law.'

I murmured an agreement. I was not in truth much bothered about such details. The filling of the *Luipaard*'s holds was really only relevant to me in that the sooner it was completed, the sooner we could go home.

Hieronymus must have picked up my lack of interest. Leaning forward to replenish my cup – even in private we honoured the custom of serving each other – he said, 'Kyoto, eh! What a place.'

I agreed that it was. I'd had no idea what to expect, and the rapidly growing town had taken me by surprise. Its castle dominated the place, awe-inspiring and imposing, and it was surrounded by a complicated network of tightly packed houses and street after street of workshops and craftsmen's dwellings. Knives, fans, items made of paper, gorgeous silk garments, porcelain, exquisite models and statues of bronze, silver and even gold: the entire place buzzed with purpose and activity, and Ambroos Leyn had seemed well satisfied with the many orders we had placed.

Hieronymus was looking out over the water, a frown on his face. Checking that we were alone, he moved closer to me and said very quietly, 'What do you reckon to Aroto Tagauchi?'

I thought before answering. We had visited a number of trading posts that we had been told, either directly or by implication, belonged to Romeu Silvestre. However, it became clear that we had been misled: he might well have owned a warehouse or two here and there, and it certainly seemed that the village where we had stayed and the little port below it did indeed belong to him, but the impression he had given that he owned a great deal more was not true. I could hear him making the boast, the night after our first meeting: *Also I have other settlements elsewhere on the southern islands.* Well, he had lied: the power figure behind this trading empire was a man by the name of Aroto Tagauchi.

We did not encounter him. He did not deal with traders, it appeared; such vulgar matters of business, we were given to understand, were beneath him. The rumour of him, however, was enough to impress. He was an old man now, they said, but still mighty and powerful, and wealthy beyond imagining.

And, as is the way with men of wealth and power, people talked about him. He was Romeu Silvestre's father-in-law; Romeu's wife had been his only child and her death had been a terrible tragedy for her family. Their lineage went back into ancient history, they told us, and we picked up tales of some sort of powerful object which had come to the ancestors via spirits and gods, and whose continued presence among the descendants was essential in order for them to thrive. We heard a whisper of a magical tiger made of some precious substance – one man said gold, another jade – whose claws could metamorphose into chrysanthemums, which empowered the creature to cast terrible spells. This magical figure from out of the mysterious far past contained the full force of the ancestors; the spirit of the clan.

'I don't know what to think of him,' I said now to Hieronymus. 'He seems a man who is both to be envied and pitied.' Envied, I thought, because he had worked hard, made a fortune and created a trade empire; pitied because his only daughter was dead and, with just the one grandson, it was a thin and vulnerable thread to bear the weight of perpetuating the great family name.

Hieronymus was nodding slowly. 'I would like to have met the man,' he remarked. 'People fear him, that is plain, and it seems that there is a mystique about him, as if he had magic powers. That talk of the tiger with chrysanthemums for claws, for instance – the man who told us about that was quaking in dread!'

Hieronymus gave a short laugh, but I sensed that he had been disturbed by the man's fear. I wasn't surprised; it had shaken me too. Even now, sitting apart on the *Luipaard*'s deck as she lay at anchor in a peaceful, night-quiet harbour, my companion was looking uneasily around, as if fearing he might somehow have conjured up an ancient, magical gold tiger because he had dared to speak about it . . .

Dear God, *I* was starting to feel uneasy too . . .

'Nothing to fear from a tiger with flowers for claws, my friend,' I said heartily, refilling his cup.

He shot me a look, and managed a smile.

Back in Romeu's village, settled into his house and with the comforts of the bath house next door, I wondered if I would see the woman again. I fully expected to, and the thought of her set a stab of longing through me that I was more than half ashamed of. I knew I had not seduced her. She had sought me out, had tiptoed into my room and crept into my bed, and she had made it plain from the outset that she had come with one thing in mind. I had not hesitated to oblige.

And that too made me ashamed.

I had said goodbye to Judyth Penwarden before leaving on this voyage. I had made no promises to her, nor she to me; we had exchanged a kiss or two, but we had not become lovers. She was an independent woman, and I was not fool enough to believe that she had been waiting for me to ask her to marry me and heartbroken when I didn't. I think I had left England expecting her to fade from my memory.

But she hadn't.

Which was why I was ashamed of making love to a woman whose name I did not even know . . .

Where, I wondered, had my passionate night-time companion gone?

I saw others who I thought at first were her, and each time I felt the same stab of lust. These young women were the same age, and to my eyes they had the same stature, the same way of moving. Those garments they wore, which I had learned to call *kimonos*, were wrapped around their bodies in a way that made a narrow circumference of fabric at the ankle, so that perforce the women took small steps and walked with their toes pointing

in. The kimonos were fastened with wide sashes tied with large
and elaborate bows, which had the effect of totally disguising
the shape of the woman beneath. There was no way of telling
what her body looked like, whether she was wide in the hips, or
short in the leg, or full in the breasts. I studied the young women
as they served our meals and brought the jugs of sake, listened
to them as they chattered and giggled behind the screen while
Romeu, Ambroos and I sat by the fire in the evening. They were
still fascinated by us, it was plain, still trying to observe us. Now
I was also trying to spy on them.

After some weeks, I thought I knew the group of young women
who regularly attended to our needs in Romeu's house.

The woman who had come to my bed was not among them.

The weeks turned into months. We set off on the *Luipaard* on
more trading missions, and now our goods took up much of the
space in one of Romeu's warehouses. Flavinho and his companions were proving to be excellent traders, especially Flavinho
himself and Dario, the historian. I had accompanied them on
many negotiations with their Portuguese countrymen in trading
posts around the area, and now I could follow the rapid to and
fro of words adequately well. We were becoming well known
in the ports where Romeu's formidable father-in-law held power,
and the fact that we had the favour of both men – particularly
Aroto Tagauchi – must surely have led to many an excellent
deal.

One thing puzzled me.

In the course of our dozens of visits to ports and trading posts
we met and communicated with hundreds of men, many of them
Portuguese but the majority Japanese. I was still unable to
remember Japanese names unless I made a special effort and
asked for several repetitions, but the name I was looking out for
was not Japanese. Returning from what we all hoped would be
one of the final missions, I decided to seek out Hieronymus in
the house next door and consult him.

I waited until the four Portuguese had retired to bed, then
asked him if he had ever met Romeu's son.

He looked at me strangely. 'He has not got a son.'

'He has,' I replied. 'He told me on our first night here how his wife had died giving birth to her son but that the child survived, and thus the family line was ensured for another generation. The boy will be a man now, and I thought we'd meet him,' I added. 'I've been expecting on every voyage we've made that sooner or later we'd turn up at wherever it is he lives and someone would introduce us to him. Either that or he would come here to visit his father, and Romeu would present him with appropriate paternal pride and – *what?*'

Hieronymus had been shaking his head, frowning. 'You are mistaken, Gabe. The child was a daughter.'

But I distinctly recalled Romeu telling me how he had used his father-in-law's deep desire for a grandson to persuade the man to let him marry the daughter named for the chrysanthemum . . .

Desire was all well and good, I thought. But we did not always get what we desired.

'Well, why have we not met her?' I demanded, reluctant to believe I had been mistaken. 'Why hasn't Romeu presented her to us? Does she not live with him in the village?'

Hieronymus was clearly very uncomfortable.

I realized I had embarrassed him. 'Is she dead?' I asked quietly. 'Is that why you're looking so awkward?'

But he shook his head again. 'No. Chiyo is not dead.' He paused, as if considering his words. 'Visitors are not permitted to speak of her, never mind meet her,' he said eventually. 'Especially if they are Dutchmen or Englishmen. You are forgetting who she is, Gabe. She may be Romeu's daughter, and thus half Portuguese through his blood, but she is the granddaughter of Aroto Tagauchi.' He had lowered his voice to a whisper, drawing closer to me. He looked furtively over his shoulder a couple of times to make sure we really were alone. It was plain that he was very uneasy.

'Yes?' I prompted.

'She is the only child of an only daughter,' he murmured, 'and the sole descendant of that ancient and mighty family. Gabe, you've *seen* the extent of the power and wealth of the Tagauchis for yourself, for it is clearly apparent in all the places we've traded! And, in every single port, our presence would have been quite impossible were it not for the fact that Aroto Tagauchi had given us permission to be there.'

'But he—'

Hieronymus ignored the interruption. 'The old man has laid his plans for her, that's what they say. She lives with him, shut away in that great castle of a place that was pointed out to us up above the Island of Shrines, remember?'

I did. I'd thought it was the stronghold of a warlord. It was vast, soaring up in successive storeys and set in its own town, or so it appeared. A series of defences ran all around it, and it had a well-protected harbour in which several fighting ships had been at anchor next to the trading vessels. We had all had the strong impression that absolutely nothing happened there that Aroto Tagauchi did not know about; that he hadn't allowed to happen.

Such was the power of the man.

And when people muttered about him, it was with the sort of awe and superstitious fear that you might find when hearing the fearful whisper of a living legend; a vengeful deity that walked among them . . .

'Why doesn't she live here with her father?' I asked. 'Why does Romeu allow his father-in-law to dictate how and where his daughter spends her life?'

'*Ssssh!*' Hieronymus hissed, looking nervously around. 'It's difficult to explain it to you, Gabe, because you haven't been to Neira or the other spice islands, but here in Japan the Dutch and the Portuguese have found that establishing a working relationship with the indigenous population is quite different. In the islands we have always dictated the terms of the exchange, because the people really want to trade with us and we think we're doing them a big favour by buying their goods so cheaply and selling them for such an enormous profit. It is *not* like that in Japan.' He stopped, again glancing furtively behind him. 'Here we are like the cattle egrets that feed on the ticks on the water buffalo's hide. The buffalo suffers the presence of the bird because it is to his advantage, since through its attentions he is ridding himself of the blood-sucking parasites. The Japanese are a strong and self-sufficient nation, Gabe, with warlords and castles and a fearsome caste of well-armed and extremely well-trained warriors. They will tolerate our presence as long as it benefits them. The moment it ceases to do so, we shall be out.'

I was trying to work out the relevance of Hieronymus's impassioned words to the situation between Romeu, his daughter and his father-in-law. Then I understood.

'You mean Romeu has no choice but to accept?' I asked. Now I was whispering too. Suddenly there was a sense of threat in the room, as if ears were pricking up at our dangerous talk and already a message was on its way to the old warlord in his castle. We had entered his world – been permitted to enter it – because we were in his country to trade with him and he was willing to comply. But he was not only a merchant, he was much more than that. Only a fool would forget it.

'He has no choice,' Hieronymus agreed. 'It is Aroto Tagauchi who makes the rules, and we have to conclude that Romeu knows he must obey. And so his daughter lives with her grandfather. Old Aroto keeps her to himself, well hidden and very well protected, and he will continue to do so until the right man is found to be her husband.'

As if the family were royal, I thought. Like a European king, Tagauchi would place his precious granddaughter where her presence would be most advantageous for him and for the long line of his ancient and powerful family.

'He will naturally insist the fortunate man is Japanese,' Hieronymus was saying. 'The rumour-mongers say he was horrified when Kiku married Romeu, who was lucky to get away with his life. According to the whispers, Aroto's fury that the pure blood of the land should be contaminated brought on an apoplexy.'

'Why did he permit it?' I demanded. 'Why did he not lock up his daughter like he's doing his granddaughter?'

Hieronymus grimaced. 'The gossip-mongers say that Kiku persuaded him she would kill herself if she was forbidden to marry the man she loved. He believed her.'

I nodded. I was thinking deeply.

This granddaughter would be in her early twenties; Romeu told me his only child was born in 1582. She wasn't a daughter, or a granddaughter; she was barely a human being at all, but a card in the hand held by Aroto Tagauchi, to be played at a moment of his choosing, and married off to the man of his choice. In the meantime, she lived within fortified walls in well-guarded isolation, every moment of every day ruled by her grandfather as ruthlessly and rigidly as if he was a king and the castle was his kingdom.

But what if this young woman, this Chiyo, did not agree to the plans made for her by others? What if she had an independent spirit and the courage to arrange her life as she wanted?

What if she had laughter in her lovely face, and a powerful resentment at being told what to do? What if she had inherited some of her father's pluck and determination, along with the chestnut highlights in her dark hair? Might she rebel, and find a way to slip unnoticed out of her grandfather's castle? Contriving by some means to make sure she was not missed, might she make her way to her father's house? Might she then spy on her father's guests, picking out those who appealed to her and slipping into the bath house to attend them as they soaked? Then, if her selection did not disappoint, creep into his bed in the deep rural darkness of the night?

For several moments I let my imagination run with the fantasy I was creating. But it was only that: a fantasy. Of course it wasn't Aroto Tagauchi's pampered and highly valuable granddaughter who had crept to my room when everyone else had retired, made it absolutely clear what she wanted from me, and not left my bed until she'd had it. Because she lived miles away in her grandfather's heavily fortified castle, and there she would stay until she was led out of her luxurious prison to marry the man who had been selected for her.

FIVE

The summer passed. Then autumn was upon us, and still Ambroos, Hieronymus, the Portuguese quartet, the *Luipaard*'s company and their ship's surgeon sailed round the islands amassing Walter Haverleigh's cargo. The crates and boxes steadily stacked up in the warehouse Romeu had set aside for us, and I began to think that very soon now we would be planning our departure.

Between trading trips, we put up at Romeu's house in the village. I became addicted to the nightly bath and was now on friendly terms with the two youngest bath-house servants, who were called Natsu and Shina. I was learning Japanese from them, and teaching them English in return. The two of them were very attentive, never missing a chance to come to the bath house when I was there, and I reckoned the English lessons were valuable to them. Sometimes I caught them muttering and whispering behind their hands when they thought I wasn't looking, their dark heads together, the graceful black eyebrows drawn down in anxiety. On one occasion Natsu became very animated, Shina reached out to shush her and Natsu angrily brushed her hand away. I couldn't begin to guess what these discussions and arguments were about. The girls would always break off as soon as they saw I was watching; not that I could have understood their conversation anyway, because they spoke too softly for me to overhear and my Japanese was far too inadequate for such rapid speech.

I had the strong impression that something was worrying them. The way they kept shooting glances at me when they were whispering suggested that whatever this concern was, somehow it was connected to me. I couldn't think of any way that our lives overlapped outside the bath house, and I soon stopped thinking about it and let them mutter as much as they liked.

We had set our departure date for January of the coming year, 1607. Now Ambroos was in a state of constant anxiety, hurrying down daily to the warehouse and going through his lists again and again, taking Hieronymus with him to check each item against the manifest. I knew Hieronymus was worried about our captain. He told me so more than once and, in the interests of trying to help both of them, I offered to go and join them in the warehouse to see if an independent confirmation that all was in order might help set Ambroos's mind at rest.

Accordingly I accompanied them to the port the next day.

It was the most beautiful morning. I let my two companions go on ahead and stopped in order to enjoy it.

It was intensely, teeth-throbbingly cold. There had been another fall of snow overnight. It was still early, and there had only been half a dozen sets of footprints on the path before ours. On either side of the track, the sloping ground was covered in thick, even, brilliant white, and the low rays of the sun climbing up the sky set off twinkles and sparkles that dazzled and delighted the eye. The sky was absolutely clear, and the deep blue of bluebells. Ahead, the port buildings huddled into the hillside, and soft domestic sounds filtered up in the stillness: the bark of a dog; chickens; the high, clear voice of a mother summoning her children; the musical sound of a deep-toned bell that seemed to linger long on the air before the final echo was gone.

Just for an instant, I was back on the hillside before the shrine, and I could once again see beyond the shadows on the wall.

Then Hieronymus stopped, turned back, and called out to me to hurry up and start moving again or the pony and I would turn to ice.

I smiled. He was right; already my feet and hands were numb.

There was something connected with my memory of that legend of the shadows in the cave that was trying to attract my attention . . . I let the pony walk on, finding a rhythm, and waited. Then it came.

I'd learned about the cave from Jonathan Carew. He was the vicar of St Luke's, our nearest village back home. He was a complex character, with much in his past that he kept to himself. He had told me once he was ashamed. I had wanted to reply that I didn't care what he'd done in an earlier time; I knew the man he was now, and would trust him with my life.

We'd been talking about the mysteries, of the 'beyond things', as he called them, which, he suggested, mankind did not possess the ability to penetrate and understand. It was in this context that he'd told me about the shadows on the wall; it was how one of the ancients had tried to illustrate the problem.

I very much hoped I would find my way home again. There was something I could now add to that conversation.

Down in the warehouse, Ambroos, Hieronymus and I spent an exhausting morning going through the lists. Again, and again, and yet again. I had already picked up that Ambroos was prone to worry, and now, watching the poor man trying to reassure himself for the twentieth time at least that he really did have all that he had been sent to purchase, and that everything was extremely well packed and highly unlikely to suffer damage on the voyage home, I was torn between annoyance and pity.

Either way, it was a relief when he finally accepted he could do no more and agreed we could go back to the village. We had all got very cold in the unheated warehouse; never had the evening bath been so welcome.

Now our departure was the next day. We would be sailing at nightfall.

All our preparations were complete. The cargo was stowed in the *Luipaard*'s holds, and the ship was fully provisioned. The members of the company who professed to have the most accurate weather lore confirmed that the winds were favourable and would remain so for the foreseeable future, and Ambroos's intention was to stock up so well that we would not be driven to make port within the near future because we had already run out of some essential commodity. 'The weather is with us!' he kept saying to anyone who would listen. 'We must *use* it, and not throw this gift back in Providence's face!'

I went over to the bath house after supper. I was on my own; it was clear that others had already bathed, but they had gone now. I went through the familiar routine, removing my clothes, washing all over and then easing myself into the steaming water. I lay back, resting my head on a folded towel, and closed my eyes in bliss. I tried not to dwell on the fact that this was the last time I would do this. I thought of trying to explain to my dear old housekeeper, Sallie, the concept of a deep, hot bath full to the brim with very hot water, and the image of her totally flummoxed expression as she struggled to comprehend made me laugh aloud.

My thoughts wandered on. Maybe Samuel and Tock could make a tub . . . Samuel was the calm, practical man who looked after all outdoor aspects of life at Rosewyke, and Tock was the confused, easily alarmed and gentle boy-man who was his constant companion and probably Rosewyke's most devoted servant. Faced with the problem of making a bath, I reflected, they would . . .

I became aware of little hissing noises, and, coming out of my reverie, realized someone was trying to attract my attention. I looked around, and made out a huddled shape crouched behind one of the screens.

'Who's there?' I said. 'Do you want to speak to me?'

The shape straightened up, and a dark-clad figure emerged. As the shawl over the head was lowered, I saw that it was Natsu.

I smiled in welcome. 'Have you come to say goodbye?' I asked.

She was staring at me, eyes intent, and gave no indication that she had heard. As she advanced into the light of the lanterns, I saw that her pretty face looked haggard, and her eyes were red and swollen from weeping. She looked . . . Yes. She looked like someone who was grieving.

It felt wrong to talk to a woman in such distress when I was lying naked in the bath, so I reached for a towel, got out of the water, quickly dried and dressed. Then, taking her hand, I led her to one of the benches set against the wall and sat her down, settling beside her.

'What is the matter, Natsu?' I asked. 'Why were you crying?'

She looked at me but did not answer. She shook her head, tried to speak, then leapt up and hurried out of the room, quickly returning. Now she was carrying something: a small wooden crate, about as long as my forearm, as tall as my outstretched hand and a little wider than my palm. It was robust and well made, the lid nailed down with twenty nails. She put it in my arms. It was heavy. Whatever was inside had been thoroughly wrapped and padded, and barely moved when I tipped the box gently from side to side.

Natsu saw what I was doing and with a little gasp grabbed my wrist to stop me. Then, her eyes intent on mine, she tapped the crate and whispered urgently, 'Must not open here! Open on boat,' she said. Then – and it was almost a howl – 'Keep secret! *Do not show!*'

I thought, in my foolish, conceited ignorance, that she and Shina had bought me a parting gift, and perhaps included a letter to tell me that they really liked me and would miss me.

But I didn't understand, then.

'Thank you, Natsu,' I said gravely. I said it in Japanese too. Usually my attempts to say the words correctly had her and Shina in fits of giggles, but now she didn't even smile.

'What is making you so sad?' I asked gently.

I thought for a moment she was going to tell me. She leaned closer to me, her soft mouth opened, but then she pulled away, standing up in an uncharacteristically graceless movement and backing away towards the door. She shook her head impatiently, brushed tears from her face and hissed, 'Hide box. *Must* hide. Men want, men *kill* to take.'

Before I could ask her to explain, to give me a hint as to what it was that she had just thrust into my keeping, she had the door open and was outside, drawing it closed. At the last moment she met my glance and said, 'Look out, eyes be busy, when boat go,' and gave several abrupt little nods in confirmation.

Then I heard her small feet hurrying away.

So I was to look out when we sailed late the next day, I reflected. For her? Would she come and wave us off?

As I headed back to Romeu's house and my bed, the wooden crate tucked deep inside my voluminous garments, I realized that Natsu hadn't told me what had upset her.

And, although I told myself it was nothing but a young woman being over-emotional, her alarm seemed to have been infectious.

Romeu threw a farewell feast for us in the evening, immediately before we left, but only Hieronymus and I attended. The ship's company were on board the *Luipaard* already, and although Ambroos had promised to join us for the feast, in the event his nerves overcame him and, having said a formal goodbye and thanked Romeu for his hospitality with a quaintly old-fashioned bow, he had hurried away to his ship. The food was excellent – Romeu and his kitchen staff had surpassed themselves – but I felt uneasy; I kept seeing Natsu's distressed expression. I was impatient to leave now. It was a long way home, and the sooner we were on our way, the better. As we toyed with the last of the food – we'd eaten more than enough already – I leaned over and murmured to Hieronymus, 'Let's not tarry. I want to be away. We'll say our farewells and head on down to the port.'

The alacrity with which he agreed suggested he felt ill at ease too.

Romeu rode down to the port with us. We were as usual mounted on the ponies, just as we had been when we arrived over a year ago. Our bags were already on board the ship.

Romeu became quite emotional as he embraced us in farewell. Hieronymus and I untangled ourselves, thanked him yet again and hurried on board. We sought out Ambroos to announce our arrival – he gave a curt nod but did not reply – and I found a place on the rail from where I could look out for Natsu. If she came, that was; if she hadn't thought better of the impulse now, on this cold night, and elected to stay warmly tucked up at home.

I had done as she asked and hidden the wooden crate. I'd paid a visit to the *Luipaard* earlier in the day to deposit some last boxes of medical supplies in my surgeon's cabin. One more crate among many was never going to arouse anyone's interest, and I made sure to stow it out of sight.

Now, staring out at the quay below, I wondered if there was something else she was planning to give me. If, that was, she turned up. There was not much time left; the ship was prepared for departure, and if she didn't hurry, Natsu would miss us . . .

There were signs of a disturbance. I heard the clatter of hooves from hard-ridden horses, men shouting, someone screaming.

Sailors were unfastening the heavy mooring ropes. Two more of the crew stood ready to bring in the gangplank. Ambroos was distracted, and darting repeated glances to the open water beyond the harbour walls. Following his line of sight, I saw that there was a vessel out there, and she seemed to be signalling.

Then I heard the gunshot.

There were more screams. The crowd milling around down below us suddenly broke apart, a gap opened up and someone came running hard along the quay towards the *Luipaard*.

It was Natsu. She was scarlet in the face, panting, sweating. She saw me, called out, and I shoved a way through the men standing by the rail and hurried back to the gangplank, leaping down it as she ran towards me. She was carrying something – a large bundled-up parcel – and as I jumped on to the quay and held out my arms to steady her, she thrust it at me.

She tried to say something – to offer an explanation, perhaps – but she was gasping for breath and she could not speak.

I thrust the parcel under one arm and put my free hand on her shoulder. 'Steady,' I said, 'slow down, then I will be able to understand you.'

The noise from the end of the quay had intensified. More shots rang out, and now the crowd was starting to panic, yelling, some of them screaming with pain, and as I spun round to look, the mass of people broke apart and began to run away. They left behind them several bodies lying still on the quay. Streams of blood were starting to pool in the gaps between the hard stones.

Ambroos's voice thundered out from above me on the *Luipaard*: '*Gabriel!* Come aboard *NOW!*'

Natsu was gabbling something, nodding, pushing me towards the gangplank, and I ran up it, jumping down on to the *Luipaard*'s deck. Already we were moving, open water now between the side of the ship and the quay.

'What's happening?' I yelled. Hieronymus appeared beside me, shoving a way through sailors working frantically to obey the skipper's increasingly urgent orders. He and I pressed ourselves back against the side of the ship, and I put Natsu's parcel down on the deck. Over our heads the sails were spreading out, catching the evening breeze, and now there was a band of heavily armed men running along towards the *Luipaard* as rapidly she increased the distance between her and the land.

'We're under attack!' Hieronymus cried. 'There's an army of them – *look!*' He pointed. His face was pale, and there was sweat on his forehead.

The warriors on the quay were only the vanguard. Up on the

higher ground behind the port, twice as many men had gathered, mounted on horses and bristling with arms.

I looked back to the spot where I'd just been standing with Natsu. I thought she would have gone. That she'd have fled for cover with everyone else.

She hadn't.

She was just where I'd left her, and she was looking up at me, staring right at me. She was still trying to catch her breath.

She was saying something. I could see her mouth moving, the same words over and over again. Or so it seemed to me. But we were too far away now, and I could not hear her. Now we were at the harbour mouth, moving fast between the two bulwarks that formed the terminals of the great sea walls, and, still staring back at the quay, I could barely make out much detail at all.

But one thing I *could* see: Natsu stood alone, and the foremost of the soldiers were almost on her.

There were two of them. They carried those strangely beautiful, curved swords.

I saw the danger far too late.

I drew a deep breath and as loud as I could I shouted her name. 'Natsu! *Natsu!*' I waved my arms in wild, expansive gestures. 'Look out, *look behind you!*'

She must have realized that I was saying something, but, unable to hear, she shook her head, arms raised in an expression of helplessness.

And it was in that pose – standing on the edge of the quay, her arms outstretched, her palms upwards – that the leading soldier cut her down.

One clean cut.

A savage swipe that took her head from her shoulders.

I saw it bounce twice on the quay before falling into the water.

It seemed to me that her headless body stood there for several heartbeats, the bright blood pumping out of the stump of her neck.

Then she folded like a hinged wooden doll dropped by a bored child.

The warriors had overrun the quayside now and they were lined up, crossbows in their hands. But the *Luipaard* was swift – her speed seemed to take them by surprise – and the few bolts that were loosed in our direction almost all fell short, except for one that struck a glancing blow into the mast behind me and dropped to the deck.

We were out on the open sea now and the ship seemed to gather herself like a fast horse eager to gallop. Ambroos was still shouting, his company were flying to act on his orders even as he gave them, and quickly we began to round the headland that would take us out of sight of the men on the quay.

With a sick dread I remembered the vessel that had been standing off beyond the harbour walls. I grabbed hold of Hieronymus, shouting something about danger, looking round wildly to see where the ship had gone. But with a grim smile he pointed over to port, and I saw her falling steadily behind.

'She cannot catch us,' he said. 'We have made our escape.'

But I remembered that the vessel had been signalling.

I wasn't so sure that we had.

The horror was over.

We had been attacked, although it seemed that nobody knew or cared why. People on the quayside had been injured, perhaps fatally. A young woman had been killed before our eyes. But the company were men of the sea; they saw death, absorbed it, moved on. Now they were back in the practised routines they knew so well, and there was a tangible sense of purpose on board the *Luipaard*.

I wondered if I was the only man on board who felt so drained.

I turned away from the rail at last. I nodded to Hieronymus, heading off towards my cabin.

With a brief grin he called me back. 'You have forgotten your present,' he said, nodding towards the parcel that Natsu had thrust at me.

I bent down and lifted it up from where I'd set it in the angle between the deck and the ship's side.

I knew what it was even as I clutched it close to me.

But I didn't believe the evidence of my senses.

I stood perfectly still. I couldn't work it out; couldn't begin to think how I came to be holding what I had in my arms.

I looked up to see Hieronymus beside me. He was watching

me, his eyes wide with shock. He didn't seem to be able to look away.

Then he muttered a few words in his own tongue.

I understood his dismayed horror.

It was the last thing I'd been expecting, too.

SIX

Celia was only half a mile from the track to Rosewyke. She reined in the grey mare to a sedate walk. She had been right out over the moors, riding hard. There had been a storm – not uncommon at the time of the autumn equinox – but it had now largely gone over, although up there on the high ground the wind had still been blowing strongly and her repeated howls of angry frustration were lost in the general blast of sound. Or so she hoped. She didn't want to return to the house. So much did she not want to that she'd ridden further than she had intended, and it had taken her longer than she'd anticipated to get back.

But she *had* come back; there had been no choice. If she had obeyed the powerful impulse to just keep riding, the burden left on them all because of her brother Gabriel's long absence would fall on the shoulders of the rest of those he'd so blithely and thoughtlessly left behind.

She remembered – far from the first time – what her response had been two and a half years ago, when he said he was going away. She'd remarked that it would be hard to face their parents' opposition, especially that of their mother, serene with happiness to have her wandering son home for good. Then she'd said – she'd actually *said*, fool that she was, 'It's your decision, Gabe, and I will support you.' And she had, so that when finally their mother had turned away to mask the pain in her face and given Gabe her blessing, Celia had felt it was her victory as much as her brother's.

At first she had enjoyed being mistress of Rosewyke. It was still Gabe's house, of course, but it had been her home since she was widowed and, besides, with Gabe away, who else was going to take charge? Celia was used to running the place, she and Gabe's housekeeper Sallie got on extremely well, and the outdoor servants Samuel and the faithful Tock were as loyal as anyone could ask. The household had been a comfortable, smoothly run, clean and fragrant place under Celia's management, and she had persuaded herself that, domestically at least, nobody really felt Gabe's absence at all.

But Gabe hadn't only been the owner of a small, elegant and beautifully constructed Tudor manor house. He had also been a doctor – a particularly devoted and diligent one – and his absence from that role was an awful lot harder to fill. He had not left without making suitable arrangements – naturally he hadn't – and Celia had accompanied him the day he had ridden up to Buckland to call on the old doctor, Josiah Thorn, and ask him tentatively how determined he'd been to stop working entirely when he had retired a year or so ago.

Slowing to a halt under one of the vast oak trees that lined the track, she thought back to that morning. Gabe had first encountered Josiah Thorn soon after he had taken up residence at Rosewyke, and at their very first meeting Dr Thorn had said he was trying to retire but others were unwilling to accept it. Not long afterwards, however, Gabe had quietly taken over as the local physician. Until his past had called out to him and seduced him back to sea.

Josiah Thorn had been willing, not to say eager, to return to work, although he said with a warning frown that he was not prepared to be at the beck and call of the entire neighbourhood at every hour of the day and night, and Gabe had better not go thinking he was. With the assurance that there would be a full-time replacement to do the majority of the work and that Josiah's position would be more in the role of a senior advisor with considerable local knowledge, the two of them had shaken hands and Dr Thorn had wished Gabe well.

Gabe's next mission had been to ride down to Plymouth and engage the services of some suitable doctor, physician or former ship's surgeon willing to take over the care of the patients who regularly summoned Gabe's help among the villages, hamlets and isolated farms down towards the coast. He had found someone he believed to be suitable, for the man's demeanour had exuded competence and trustworthiness, and the fact that he said he had until recently been busy tending the sailors of the King's navy suggested he knew what he was about.

His name was Maudsley Cheverell.

But, Celia reflected now, Gabe's head must have been so full of his plans for the forthcoming voyage, and too overwhelmed by his mounting excitement as the date of departure approached, for there to be much room for his usual highly honed skills of observation and judgement. Because Maudsley Cheverell was not very capable, he didn't know what he was about – indeed, some of what Celia considered to be the basic skills of a doctor were totally absent from his limited range of abilities – and as for being *trustworthy* . . . well, words escaped her.

She had tried to attribute the lapses of judgement, and the insouciant dismissal of those who he considered were wasting his valuable time, to the fact that he was finding his way in an unfamiliar area. Perhaps, given his recent past at sea, he was finding it a challenge to familiarize himself with the ailments and the habits of country people. She told herself that his distressing tendency to bellow at tenant farmers and rural artisans as if they were malingering sailors would soon disappear as his experience grew.

But her misgivings did not lessen; they intensified.

Maudsley Cheverell was a long, lean man of perhaps thirty or thirty-five years. His pale hair hung lankly and it was thin, so that the bones of his bumpy skull were rather too evident. His eyes were an indeterminate shade between light brown and grey, and he had a habit of opening them very widely when he spoke to you, making him look slightly manic, so that instinctively Celia always took a pace back. He spoke in a slow affected drawl, and his light voice had a penetratingly shrill resonance.

Thankfully he did not live at Rosewyke; it was clear, very soon after his arrival, that he expected to, but Celia had been able to inform him with total honesty that another doctor was already in residence. On many occasions since, she had included in her private prayers in church on a Sunday a fervent thank you to God for having inspired Gabe with the foresight to arrange for Jasper Hart's presence, which firmly ruled out any possibility of Maudsley Cheverell installing himself.

For over two years after Gabe's departure, Jasper Hart had been a steady and reassuring antidote to the impulsive and bombastic Cheverell. He was an old friend of Gabe's – Celia recalled that they had studied together in London at the King's College of Physicians – and they had remained friends. With two other physicians, they had formed what they grandiosely called the Symposium, which, as far as Celia could see, was little more than an excuse to meet up when the four of them could manage it, drink a lot, talk over the good old times and occasionally debate something to do with the practise of medicine. There had been a meeting of the Symposium in the December before Gabe went away, the other three joining Jasper in Exeter. Jasper had been staying with relations to recuperate from the deep fatigue brought on by too many months in London trying to help people evade the outbreak of plague, and doing what little he could for those who hadn't. Gabe had come home with the clear impression that Jasper Hart was sick and tired of London and was thinking of a change; he had been the ideal person to approach when Gabe was in need of a replacement.

Jasper Hart, Celia thought, as the mare, sensing her inattention, took the chance to grab a mouthful of grass from the bank beside the road, now *he* was a *sound* man. She had decided she liked him almost as quickly as she'd concluded that she *didn't* like Maudsley Cheverell. Cheverell was lazy, self-important, possessed of the ability to hurl aside his entire burden of work at day's end as if he had been cleaning out cesspits rather than tending human beings in pain, sick, and otherwise distressed, and apparently incapable of listening to a patient as he or she stumbled out the halting words that as a doctor he really *ought* to listen to. Jasper Hart was the opposite in every way. From the outset he had risen early, gone to bed late and thrown every ounce of energy into his work; quite often Sallie would report worriedly that he'd obviously been up since first light because when she went in with the early morning hot water for his ablutions, he was invariably already washed ('With yesterday's stone-cold water!') and dressed, so deep in whatever he was studying that often she had to call his name two or three times before he responded.

Oh, yes, he worked hard. Why, he had even taken on a handful of special cases – three men, a woman and a small child, who were, he had explained with charm and diplomacy, entirely his responsibility – and he gave her his word that these patients would not in any way add to the workload of the other two physicians. He had murmured something about their conditions being relevant to his particular field of study, and Celia had thought no more about it. All five were from wealthy families, and well able to pay for the personal care; if Jasper was making a little extra money for himself, she'd concluded, then good luck to him.

He was modest and self-effacing, and when people praised him for his skill, his kindness and his gentle touch with an agonizing injury, he would drop his head and mutter, 'Please, it is what I am here for.' Quite often he discussed aspects of his cases with her, and with Judyth if she was there, and he frequently retired to bed with a worried frown creasing his brow. And so attentively did he listen to what his patients divulged to him that a visit which would have taken Gabe perhaps half an hour or so occupied most of Japer's morning.

Judyth, Celia thought now, finally realizing what the mare was up to and pulling her head away from the bank. Smiling briefly, she reflected that the strong, unfailing support of the midwife Judyth Penwarden was something else to thank God for. And it was, she reflected, extremely generous of Judyth to wear herself out on Gabe's former patients when she had more than enough of her own, especially considering Celia and her friends had believed there was a romance blooming there and that Judyth must surely be missing him . . .

'But Judyth *knew* Gabe was restless,' she said aloud, reluctantly urging the mare on towards home. 'She suspected he was about to do just what he did do and go to sea again, so she withdrew into herself and gave a convincing impression of indifference.'

She kicked the mare to a trot. It was late afternoon now, and Sallie would be wondering where she was. Dr Thorn would be pacing to and fro across the hall, watching out for her because he always reported to her before riding home for his evening meal. In all likelihood he would be on the verge of some sort of difference of opinion, if not an outright argument, with Dr Cheverell . . .

The two physicians not in residence, Dr Thorn and Dr Cheverell, had developed the habit of discussing their cases with Jasper Hart at Rosewyke at the end of the working day, which had seemed both sensible and practical, even if it did mean that Celia and the household had to put up with Maudsley Cheverell's bumptious presence on a daily basis. Jasper had encouraged the practice; with three of them working together, and Judyth too

when she could spare the time, it was essential to record who
had done what.

Not for the first time, Celia had a moment's grudging admi-
ration for her absent brother, who had done the work of the three
of them by himself. But then, she reflected, Gabe had always
been efficient with his time, and, besides, he had the confidence
in his judgement that Jasper lacked. The wretched Cheverell had
enough for both of them, of course, only his was abysmally
misplaced.

Making up his daily notes had been one of the tasks that made
poor Jasper's days so long and his nights so short. Waking once
from a bad dream and tiptoeing down to the kitchen for a glass
of warm milk, Celia had seen a light under the door of Gabe's
study, and recalled with surprise that the church clock at Tavy
St Luke's had just struck three. Concerned for him, the next
morning Celia had offered to take over the note-making. 'I used
to do it for Gabe when he was particularly busy,' she said. 'You
all talk to me, I know who you've seen each day, and if I am
unsure of the treatment meted out, I'll ask.'

Jasper had taken considerable persuasion, but eventually
accepted her offer. The gratitude in his face was her reward.

Thinking of those months when Jasper Hart had been in residence at Rosewyke made Celia smile. But then, inevitably, she
had to face the fact that he wasn't there any longer. She glanced
quickly over her shoulder, making quite sure she was alone. Then
she let out a stream of curses that would have raised even Gabe's
eyebrows.

Well before the storm broke, Celia, Judyth and Sallie had
sensed an upset brewing. For two years and more, Jasper had
made constant and increasingly desperate efforts to stop Maudsley
Cheverell treating Rosewyke as if it was his home. He had found
accommodation in Withybere, near to where the coroner
Theophilus Davey had his office and his residence, and by all
accounts the rooms were adequately comfortable and he enjoyed
the services of a local woman who cooked, cleaned and washed
for him. Despite this welcoming little home waiting for him at
the end of each day, he persisted in lounging around at Rosewyke,
sprawling in Gabe's chair beside the fire and, as cooking smells
sneaked from the kitchen while whatever Sallie was preparing

for supper neared readiness, seating himself in the carver chair at the end of the dining table that belonged by rights to the master of the house.

The man's presence clearly irritated Jasper profoundly; well, Celia thought now, it deeply irritated all of them. But Jasper, who was very sensitive to the trust Gabe had placed in him by asking him to take over his work and his house, was the most affected. It was, Celia reflected, as if poor Jasper was both resentful that Cheverell was shoving his way into Gabe's house when he hadn't been invited, and fuming with silent rage because it was *he* who should be sitting in Gabe's fireside chair and at his place at table.

All through the spring of this year the tension had increased. Then, as the first hot days of July began, it broke.

There came a day when Judyth was fully occupied with supervising a tricky first delivery and dealing with the results of a twin birth – only one baby of which survived – on a woman whose body was too worn out by hard work and many previous births to undergo such a trial. Judyth had not called in at Rosewyke for two days, and they were not expecting her to do so that evening. Dr Thorn had badly twisted his ankle falling down the river bank where he'd crept out one soft evening for some quiet fishing, and, although willing and able to see people who called at his house, was not yet capable of venturing out. Jasper was in Dartmouth, attending an old friend of Gabe's called Henry Sparre, about whom Gabe had left him very specific instructions, and not expected back until late the next day.

Celia was alone in the house.

She knew full well that Maudsley Cheverell was aware of this. Slipping into the kitchen and closing the door – Cheverell was occupying his usual early evening place, slumped in Gabe's chair in the library – she said softly to the silently fuming Sallie, 'I'll get rid of him. Please don't bring any food, or even a drink, before he goes, or else I'll have him here all night.'

'As if I would, Miss Celia!' Sallie replied angrily. Her patience had long run out where Maudsley Cheverell was concerned. Then, more kindly, she added, 'You just call me, now, if you need me.' And she gave Celia a very knowing look.

Celia braced herself and returned to the library.

Maudsley, turning to grin at her, nudged the chair on the opposite side of the fire with his outstretched foot and invited her to sit down.

In my own home! she screamed silently.

She remained standing, just inside the door. 'No need for you to stay, Dr Cheverell,' she said with a cool smile. 'I believe that you have not made any calls today, and therefore there are no notes for me to write up.'

Cheverell wagged a forefinger at her in admonition. It was so like the gesture of a tolerant parent to a naughty child that she wanted to hit him. 'Now, now, dear Celia,' he drawled. He *would* call her Celia, for all that Judyth and Jasper pointedly referred to her by her married name, Mrs Palfrey, whenever he was present, and Sallie had taken to greeting her with a bobbed curtsey and calling her Mistress Celia. He had implored her to address him as Maudsley, or even The Goat: 'Cheverell is a *very* old Norman-French name and stems from the word for goat, don't you see?' She must have looked unimpressed, because with a straightening of his shoulders and a puffing-out of his narrow chest, he added, 'My forebear came over with William the Conqueror, and he was favoured by the King with a generous estate.' Then, eyeing her closely for a reaction, he had added in an awe-struck tone, 'A later Cheverell was ennobled by King Charles.'

The one who had his head chopped off or the randy profligate one? she wanted to ask. She maintained a frosty silence.

'The Goat is what my best friends call me,' he said smugly.

Celia, totally failing to believe that the wretched man *had* any friends, let alone of the kind to be on the terms of familiarity that give rise to an affectionate nickname, had responded with yet another chilly smile.

'Dearest Celia,' he said now, 'I think you have been gossiping with the yard hands again, haven't you? Give them more work, Celia, then they'll stop spying on me and reporting my movements to you!' He laughed heartily at his own wit. 'That stumbling old man and his idiot lad have too much time on their hands, if you ask me.'

But I'm not asking you, Celia thought, deeply annoyed and distressed by the crude and dismissive references to Samuel and Tock.

With a very obvious gesture, she stood aside and pushed the library door further open. 'Do not let me keep you,' she said tonelessly.

Cheverell affected not to hear. After a brief, awkward silence – awkward to Celia, although she didn't imagine for a moment that he was in the least embarrassed – Cheverell leaned back in Gabe's chair with enough force to make the joints creak and, glancing out of the window, said chattily, 'Rain later, I dare say.' He shot her a sly glance. 'I stand small chance of reaching Withybere before the skies open, and that horse of your brother's always plays up at the merest suggestion of a storm.'

The fact that Cheverell had claimed for himself the use of Gabe's big black horse, Hal, had absolutely no idea how to manage him and as a consequence had raised a very reasonable antipathy in the animal, was yet another grievance to lay at his door.

'The sooner you set out, the sooner you will be home,' she said firmly. 'I suggest you fetch your bag from the hall, Dr Cheverell, and I will ask Samuel to prepare the horse.'

Not for anything was she going to refer to Hal as *your* horse.

Cheverell got slowly to his feet. Thinking he was about to do as she asked, Celia shrank back further against the door frame to give him room to pass.

He came right up to her.

Then he stopped.

He stared at her, bending his thin, lanky body so that he could look into her eyes. 'I had thought, my dear, that I might stay, for it is rare – to the point of never having happened before – for us to find ourselves alone, and I have long sensed that an evening of quiet intimacy is as desirous to you as it is to me.'

She was struggling for the words to express her indignation and her utter fury when he took her by the shoulders, pulled her to him in a hideously tight embrace and pressed his thin wet lips to hers.

She didn't even think about what she did next. She was the younger sister of two elder brothers and she had learned when a small child how to fight and where to land the blow that stopped a member of the male sex in his tracks. Putting her weight on her left leg, she raised her right knee as quickly and as powerfully as she could and drove it into his crotch.

The result was spectacular.

For a few seconds he didn't move, although his face went deathly white and beads of sweat broke out on his forehead. Then he drew a shaky breath and, mouth wide open, let it out again in a great howl of agony. His hands flew to his testicles and he crouched over into a hoop, his greasy hair trailing on the floor.

Before he could speak, or straighten up, or draw breath for another howl, she leaned over him, her mouth close to his ear, and hissed, '*Never* touch me again. Do not even come close enough to touch me. Do not come into this house and sprawl around in my brother's chair or at the head of his dining table. In future you will wait in the porch for me to receive your report, and then return immediately to your lodgings.' She paused, trying to think if there was anything else.

Oh. Yes.

'And tomorrow you will arrange the hire of your own horse,' she finished.

She pushed past him, across the parlour and into the hall, where she was met by Sallie, hurrying out of the kitchen with a frying pan in her hands.

'Are you all right, Miss Celia?' she asked anxiously, 'only I heard that howl, and I thought perhaps the skinny idiot had . . . had . . .' Delicately she refrained from saying what she thought Cheverell had done.

'The skinny idiot tried to kiss me, Sallie, which was an even more unpleasant experience than I had imagined,' Celia replied, starting to grin. 'I . . . er, I defended myself.'

Lowering the pan, Sallie chuckled. 'I'll say you did, miss. Is he . . .?' She paused.

'He doesn't need any medical attention,' Celia replied. 'Presently he will probably skulk away. I have ordered him not to enter the house again and told him I'll receive his daily reports in the porch.'

Sallie nodded her approval. 'Good for you. I *hated* seeing him in the doctor's chair,' she added passionately. 'Made me feel like lamming him with the frying pan even if he hadn't taken a liberty.'

Now Celia was laughing too. 'What is it, miss?' Sallie asked.

'I've told him he'll have to stop riding Gabe's horse, so he'll have to hire one in Withybere.'

'How will he get back there this evening? On his two feet?' Sallie asked.

'No. He can ride Hal, and return him once he's acquired a mount,' Celia replied.

'Hmm.' Sallie sniffed disapprovingly. 'You're too good to him, Miss Celia, I've said it before and I'll say it again.'

Celia smiled. 'I don't think,' she said softly, 'he'll find riding very comfortable for a while. On *any* horse.'

Maudsley Cheverell suffered the new regime at Rosewyke with ill-concealed resentment that constantly threatened to grow to anger. And on a scorching hot day in the middle of August, which came at the end of a week of rising temperatures and was the final blow that drove everyone beyond dumb endurance, the anger burst out of him.

He was infuriated by the fact that Jasper Hart and Judyth Penwarden continued to move freely in and out of the house to which he was now denied entrance. He was driven to fuming rage by the fact that Jasper lived there, as he had done from the start, and enjoyed the comfort of Gabe's bedchamber and study, not to mention the rest of the fine house, while *he* had to put up with miserable rooms in a backwater of a village. Late that hot August afternoon, Cheverell was standing on the front step tersely reporting the meagre tally of his day's work to Celia, busy writing in the big day book, when Jasper arrived home.

He waited courteously for a few moments. Cheverell pretended not to be aware he was there. Jasper said, 'If you please, Dr Cheverell, might I pass? It is very hot out here in the sun, and—'

Cheverell spun round, and before he turned away Celia caught sight of the expression on his face. With a soft gasp she said warningly, '*Jasper!*'

Cheverell had pushed his face into Jasper's, and his hands were clenched into fists. 'Why should I?' he demanded belligerently. '*I'm* forced to stand out here because Miss High Horse in there' – he jerked a thumb rudely at Celia – 'won't have me in her precious bloody brother's house, so I don't see why *you* shouldn't put up with it while I finish what I'm doing!'

He was shouting now, his face contorted in fury, and Celia

was aware of hurrying footsteps in the hall as Judyth and Dr
Thorn came to see what the yelling was about. Thinking that
she'd rather have Sallie and her frying pan, Celia jumped down
the steps and tapped Cheverell smartly on the shoulder. 'Enough
of this!' she said firmly, 'I will not have such behaviour, and—'

At the same time Jasper thrust his hands against Cheverell's
chest, pushing him away, an expression of utter disgust on his
thin face. Before Celia could repeat her command, Cheverell
raised his clenched right hand and with all his anger-fuelled
strength swung a punch straight at Jasper.

Observing, in an odd state of detachment, Celia noted that
unlike her brother, Maudsley Cheverell couldn't punch; his arm
was flailing like a small child throwing a ball, and he had no
idea of powering the thrust from the shoulder and getting his
body weight behind it.

By sheer bad luck, the wildly swinging fist caught Jasper full
on the nose. And Celia didn't think she'd ever seen such a flood
of blood continue for quite so long.

The next day Jasper left.

He expressed his deep regret, he hated leaving Celia to manage
without him, he was ashamed that he had not been able to live up
to the trust that Gabe had put in him. 'But I *cannot* stay,' he
concluded. His face, with the great bloom of his damaged nose
and two incipient black eyes, was creased in distress. 'It's that
man,' he went on, quite unnecessarily. 'Life here at Rosewyke
would be a joy but for him, but *with* him it has turned into torment.'

He confessed that as well as Cheverell's oafish behaviour and
unbreakable self-esteem, from which all of them suffered, as a
fellow physician Jasper also had to endure the wretched man's
laziness, inaccuracy and distressing manner with those who asked
for his help. 'Dear Celia, it is *too* much,' Jasper concluded.

And as waves of distress emanated from him, Celia remembered that Gabe had asked him to take over here in the first place
because the poor man had been in need of a quiet life after the
horrors of London in the plague . . .

'I'm so sorry, Jasper,' she said. 'I do understand.' She hesitated,
for she was reluctant to put pressure on him. 'Perhaps if I were
to dismiss Maudsley Cheverell you might—'

But already Jasper was shaking his head. 'No, Celia, you can't,' he said. 'You do not have the authority, and neither do I. Whatever we may think of him, he was Gabe's choice, and we can only conclude that he had his reasons.'

'Please?' she said in a small voice.

And, his voice anguished, he simply said, 'I can't.'

Now, a month later, life at Rosewyke was at best tolerable, at worse awful. Maudsley Cheverell seemed to think that his continued presence and Jasper Hart's absence – still raw for Celia and, she suspected, for Judyth and old Dr Thorn as well – signified a victory of some sort. Not only did he drop heavy hints about *men not quite up to the task* and *of course, it takes a knowledgeable and dedicated physician to tend such a motley crew with such disparate ailments*, he had also taken to walking with a swagger, his chest thrown out, his arms swinging and a sort of bounce to his step.

And he had helped himself to Gabe's big black horse again, giving the unlikely and self-regarding excuse that hired hacks just weren't sufficiently reliable for a man whose mobility was so important to the community he served.

Now I am nearly home, Celia thought as, without any guidance from her, the grey mare turned on to the track up to the house. Her shoulders drooped, for she had dwelt too long on the various distressing elements of life at Rosewyke without Gabe and it had pulled down her mood.

And she hadn't even begun to think about the aspect that distressed her most.

But she could no longer keep it at bay.

She had known before Gabe went away that she was falling in love with Jonathan Carew; in fact, that she had already done so. She was as sure as she could be that he felt the same, although he had not declared himself. Had Gabe been there, she thought, he probably would have done – no, she corrected herself, he *definitely* would have done.

But Gabe was on the other side of the world.

She knew exactly why Jonathan had not spoken. Once their love was acknowledged, they would surely marry; the sooner the better, she thought with bittersweet anguish. But as man and wife they would, of course, share a house.

Jonathan lived in the Priest's House in Tavy St Luke's, right next to his church. Celia loved his little house; once she had heard it described as a poor sort of dwelling, and she had been angry on Jonathan's behalf at this dismissive description. She had been born in her parents' house, lived briefly as Jeromy Palfrey's wife in another, and on being widowed, moved to Rosewyke; all three dwellings were comfortable, well appointed and roomy.

None of which adjectives could really be applied to the Priest's House . . .

It didn't matter. If she could have been Jonathan's wife, she'd have lived in a stable.

But she could not leave Rosewyke. In Gabe's absence, the house and everyone in it was her responsibility. Jonathan understood this; she knew that without asking. He was required to live in the Priest's House; she had to look after Rosewyke. And since nobody ever heard of a man and wife who did not live under the same roof, the two of them suffered a separation that seemed to have no end.

Summoning up another stream of curses even more colourful than the first, she kicked the mare to a canter and thundered up the track to the house.

SEVEN

Coroner Theo Davey sat at his desk trying to reason himself out of a fit of rage.

The trouble was, he thought crossly, that the small settlement of Withybere was just that, small; and when a newcomer arrived and took lodgings almost next door to the house where you not only lived with your wife and three children but also had your office, it was virtually impossible to avoid him. Theo had tried hurrying past, head down, and muttering, 'Morning, Dr Cheverell, can't stop, emergency,' and more than once he'd ducked into a side alley when he saw the wretched man coming up the road. But unfortunately, he'd stupidly omitted to convey to his beloved wife Elaine just how much he disliked the man. Kind, generous-spirited woman that she was, she had taken pity on Cheverell and invited him to supper one night. 'He's all alone, Theo!' she had protested when Theo, his furious indignation momentarily overcoming him, had angrily thumped a mug down on the board and cracked it. 'Have you no Christian charity?' Elaine cried. 'No *compassion* for a lonely man returning to empty lodgings at the end of a hard-working day?'

Instantly Theo spotted at least two elements of that statement with which to take issue, and that was without even thinking about it. One, he had seen little or no evidence that Cheverell ever did a hard day's work, and two, if his lodgings were empty it was because any friends he might have made in the neighbour-hood had been alienated by the astonishingly high opinion he had of himself and his habit of making patronizing and sometimes insulting remarks to those he considered his inferiors, which was more or less everyone.

What in the dear Lord's holy name, Theo thought now, possessed Gabe to choose the blasted man?

The only answer he had managed to come up with – for this was by no means the first time he'd asked himself the question – was that Gabe's mind had been focused so intently on his forthcoming departure that his normal ability to judge a man's character had deserted him.

'And so we all have to suffer,' Theo muttered.

That, of course, was his main problem with Doctor Maudsley bloody Cheverell.

He wasn't Gabriel Taverner.

Forcing his thoughts away from the subject of Cheverell, Theo reached for the document on the top of the pile awaiting his attention. Unfortunately it was Dr Cheverell's report on a corpse that had been found by fishermen on the banks of the Tavy. He ran his eyes down the page, with its paltry few lines of writing, then, his anger returning in full and with interest, screwed it up and flung it at the wall.

'*Man, age indeterminable but perhaps about fifty, grey hair, brown eyes, thin, ragged clothes. Wet. No discernible wound. Probably drowned,*' he said in a fair attempt at Cheverell's high, drawling voice. 'God alive,' he burst out, '*I* could have written that! My eleven-year-old *son* could have written it, and so could his little sister or brother!'

While Dr Hart resided at Rosewyke, Theo had made sure to seek him out when there was an unnatural or unexplained death to be investigated. But, of course, last month Jasper Hart had left and gone back to London. Not that Theo blamed him, for the poor man had been forced to endure Cheverell on a daily basis, although it was very hard on Celia. Now the only alternative was old Dr Thorn, from Buckland. Theo had no argument with him, for he was thorough and conscientious, and his long years of experience made him a man to trust. But he did not work all the time; he had come out of retirement when Gabe had set off on his travels, and very sensibly insisted on at least three free afternoons a week so that he could go fishing.

Theo sat back in his chair, took a couple of deep breaths, then returned to his work.

Some time later, there was a brisk tap on his door and his best officer Jarman Hodge entered the room.

'Morning, chief. Report of a male body in a ditch in that little lane that winds up from the north-west town gate to the inlet that drains into the Tavy, up beyond Tamerton Foliot,' he said. 'I've been for the doctor, and he's waiting out on the road.'

'Which one?' Theo demanded.

Jarman Hodge grinned. 'Not that Cheverell idiot. I rode up to Rosewyke to ask Mrs Palfrey if Dr Thorn was about, and he was there, just about to set out.'

Theo said a silent prayer of thanks. Then he stood up, flung on the long, sleeveless black robe that he wore when not in his office and followed Jarman out of the room.

It was an isolated spot for a man to meet his death. The ditch was quite full after the recent rain, the hedge on the far side was lush, the ground was muddy. There was a pungent smell made up of the multitudinous substances that had found their way into the inlet further upstream. Stepping forward to peer down into the ditch, Theo grimaced.

The lower half of the body was right in the water, and the upper half was face down on the surface. The thick vegetation of summer was only just starting to die down, and the corpse was almost entirely concealed by nettles and cow parsley.

'Who found him?' Theo asked. 'He's not easy to spot, so I wonder if someone came out looking for him?'

Jarman shook his head. 'Don't think so, chief. It was a local farmer who reported it. He'd been moving stock up the lane and his dog got agitated and wouldn't get his nose out of the ditch when the farmer called him.'

'Dr Thorn? If you please,' Theo said politely.

With considerable grunting and groaning, Josiah Thorn clambered down the steep bank of the ditch, Jarman Hodge clutching on to a heavy fold of his coat to stop him falling in.

'Man's got no clothes on,' Dr Thorn said. Then he cursed, rubbing at the back of his left hand.

'What is it?' Theo asked.

'Nettles,' Dr Thorn said shortly. Jarman tore off a handful of dock leaves and passed them to him.

Theo and Jarman waited in silence as the doctor examined the body. Presently he said, 'Good God. This is *appalling*.'

'What?' Theo demanded. 'Come on, Dr Thorn, what have you discovered?'

He didn't answer immediately. Then, straightening up, he turned to look at Theo and Jarman. 'Someone's gone for him with a very sharp blade,' he said very quietly. His face was pale. 'Stabbed?' Theo asked.

But he shook his head. 'No. Well, he may have been, I can't say for sure until I've turned him over and examined the front of the body. When I said gone for him with a blade, that's exactly what I meant. His back, his buttocks and the backs of his legs are covered in dozens of cuts.' He turned back to the corpse. 'Poor devil must have suffered unimaginably.'

Theo nodded to Jarman. 'Go down and help the doctor turn him over. Go on,' he added impatiently when Jarman hesitated. 'It's all right, you don't need to go on holding on to the doctor – he's steady enough now.'

He watched as Jarman and Dr Thorn took hold of the slippery corpse and eased it on to its back. The water in the ditch, disturbed by their actions, gave off a sudden, powerful stench of foulness and rot.

Then Dr Thorn muttered, 'Oh, dear Jesus.'

Theo shoved Jarman out of the way so that he too could see the face. And he understood the doctor's dismay.

The front of the body had been attacked even more savagely than the back. There were cuts from the thin cheeks right down over the chest and belly to the groin. The thighs were decorated with a crisscross pattern of scratches and shallow cuts that were almost artistic in design.

Checking swiftly, he saw that there were deep welts on both ankles and both wrists where ropes had been tightly tied.

What had occasioned Dr Thorn's exclamation was, Theo suspected, not primarily the horrific manner of the death.

It was because he had recognized the dead man.

Theo knew him too: he was Maudsley Cheverell.

Jarman had ordered the cart to follow the three of them down to the corpse's location, and presently it arrived, lumbering down the lane until the lad drew the horse gently to a standstill. Without being asked – Jarman Hodge had trained him well – the boy leapt down, spread a large sheet of canvas on the ground and hurried over to help Jarman haul the corpse out of the ditch.

Swiftly the dead man was wrapped in the canvas and laid on the flat bed of the cart.

The little procession returned to Withybere. Theo led the way to the empty house along the road from his, where in the office of His Majesty's Coroner he rented the cellar on a permanent basis as a mortuary. It had the dual advantage of being both perpetually cool and some distance from other habitations. Jarman and the lad bore the body down the narrow steps and deposited it on one of the trestle tables. Theo lit the lanterns, and Dr Thorn removed his coat, pushed back his sleeves and said curtly, 'You can go now, Master Coroner.'

Theo didn't need a second invitation.

I might not have liked Cheverell, he reflected as he and Jarman strode back to the office, the lad on the cart right behind. But all the same, I'd just as well not be there to watch the doctor investigate his awful death.

Did it make a difference to a doctor if the deceased was known to him? he mused. Could a man of medicine summon the detachment to treat dead flesh as just that, even when the living being had been an acquaintance? A friend?

He wished suddenly that he'd asked Gabe. Too late now, he thought with a grim smile.

There was something slightly forbidding about old Dr Thorn that made him reluctant to ask the question of him.

It was early afternoon when there was another tap at his door. Thinking it was probably the doctor, he called out, 'Come in, Dr Thorn.'

But it wasn't him. It was Jonathan Carew.

'I apologize for disturbing you, Theo,' Jonathan greeted him, 'I can see you're busy.'

'I'm always busy,' Theo replied. 'I'm sure you are too. What can I do for you?'

Jonathan pulled up a chair and sat down. 'I understand that Maudsley Cheverell has been killed.'

'He has,' Theo confirmed. Then: 'How did you hear about it?'

Jonathan smiled wryly. 'Nothing else very newsworthy along the Tavy valley today.'

Theo reflected that he should have known. He had lived in the area all his life, and he was well aware how word of a dramatic event spread like a blaze in a cornfield among people whose quiet, rural lives were seldom disturbed by the thrilling and the exciting. And it wasn't as if Cheverell's death was going to cause anyone much grief.

Jonathan must have read his thoughts. 'It is sad that he was not a well-liked man,' he said. 'When the body is released for burial, I wonder how many will come to church for the funeral?'

Theo grunted. 'Some from duty, I expect. Mistress Celia, Dr Thorn.' Then he said, 'You haven't asked me how he died.'

'I understand he was found face-down in a ditch, so I assumed it was an accident, and he had fallen in.'

'He was murdered,' Theo said bluntly.

Jonathan's strange green eyes held his. He did not speak for a moment, then said quietly, 'Poor man.'

'Dr Thorn is examining the body now,' Theo said. 'I don't imagine he will be much longer, so if you are not in too much of a hurry, please feel free to stay and wait with me for his report.'

Jonathan inclined his head. 'Thank you. I shall.'

Dr Thorn joined them not long afterwards.

Jonathan took one look at his drawn face and got up to offer his chair and the doctor sat down, waving a vague hand at Jonathan by way of thanks.

'As bad as that?' Theo said.

Dr Thorn nodded. He tried to speak, then gave a brief dry-throated cough. Theo strode out and presently returned with a cup of water.

'Thank you,' Dr Thorn said, taking a sip. Then, as if postponing the revelation of his findings was unthinkable, he said tersely, 'The cuts on the back of the body were fairly superficial, as were those forming the crisscross pattern on the front of the thighs. They were slices, in effect, involving the upper layers of the dermis.' He paused. 'They would have been agonizing,' he added softly. 'The most savage wounds were those to the chest, belly and groin, and here the torturers actually removed pieces of flesh.'

Jonathan made a quiet sound of protest. Theo struggled briefly with nausea.

'I am sorry,' Dr Thorn said. 'I have to tell you of these horrors. It is my job.'

'Of course, Doctor,' Theo said. 'Go on.'

'The most savage wound was the cut across his throat,' Dr Thorn went on. 'It severed the trachea and the left carotid artery, and if the man was not dead already, it would have killed him in seconds.'

Theo was still getting used to Dr Thorn's use of medical terms; briefly he thought of Gabe, who always explained in words that Theo understood.

'The trachea is the windpipe,' Jonathan said, 'the carotid arteries carry blood to the head and brain, and the dermis is the skin.'

Theo nodded his thanks. Dr Thorn, still lost in his thoughts, did not appear to have heard.

Presently the doctor stirred, straightened up and, glaring at Theo, said brusquely, 'Do you need my report right now?'

'No, Dr Thorn. Now that I have heard your verbal account, I have no hesitation in judging that Maudsley Cheverell died by unlawful killing.'

The doctor was struggling to his feet, heading for the door. Turning back briefly to glare at Theo, he gave a snort. 'Fine way you have with an understatement, Master Davey.'

Then the door slammed behind him.

'I once heard tell of a method of execution involving multiple cuts to the body,' Jonathan said some time later. Theo, feeling in need of strong spirits to restore himself after hearing Dr Thorn's account, had fetched a bottle of brandy and two glasses, and the way in which Jonathan had gulped down the first mouthful suggested that his need for restoration was equally pressing.

'Now where,' Theo said, 'would a country priest have come across such information?'

Jonathan smiled briefly. 'I was not always vicar of St Luke's,' he said mildly. Before Theo could demand to know more, he continued. 'The practice of *lingchi* originates, as I recall, in China, and accounts of it have been brought back to the West by travellers to that region, particularly the Portuguese and the Dutch, and of course, our own merchant adventurers of the East India Company.'

Theo's head shot up and he met Jonathan's gaze. The mention of China, of Dutch and Portuguese travellers, of the East India Company, had instantly made him think of Gabe. Judging by Jonathan's expression, it had clearly done the same to him.

'Go on,' Theo said.

'In the ritual of *lingchi*,' Jonathan continued, 'pieces of the body were systematically removed, at first in slices, latterly by the removal of fingers, limbs, genitals. Eyes, too. The purpose was to make a drawn-out death, perhaps to emphasize the severity of whatever crime the victim had committed,' he added, 'and accounts suggest it has a long history in the East; perhaps hundreds of years.'

'Why would anyone inflict that on a man?' Theo asked, disgusted. 'It is barbaric!'

'It is,' Jonathan agreed. 'However, we in the West must not be complacent, for by order of our kings and queens we have inflicted our own ghastly deaths on those we deem deserving of them. Burning at the stake; hanging, drawing and quartering; not to mention what goes on in the deep cellars of the Tower. I have seen—'

But, with a very apparent effort, he stopped.

Intrigued by this window into the vicar's hitherto unsuspectedly dark past, Theo would have liked very much to know more. But, he decided, now was not the time. If ever there would *be* a time . . .

'Why would anyone do that to Cheverell?' he asked. 'Punishment? Making the method of execution fit a particularly awful crime?'

Jonathan did not reply for some moments. Then he said, 'Dr Cheverell was not popular, and I am led to understand that not a few who have gone to him for help with some medical matter of greater or lesser severity have expressed their dissatisfaction with both his treatments and his attitude. In particular, his treatment of pregnant and newly delivered women has caused distress amounting in some cases to outrage, and since Jasper Hart left, Mistress Penwarden has been caring for such women largely on her own.'

'They wouldn't have Cheverell?' Theo demanded.

Jonathan smiled briefly. 'One labouring woman's furious

mother emptied a chamber pot over him when he told her daughter that the agonies she was enduring were God's punishment for Eve's sin. And a blacksmith up on the edge of the moor had to be restrained from punching him when he made a lewd remark about how soon his wife might be able to – er, to resume marital relations.'

'Oh, Gabe, Gabe, what have you done?' Theo muttered.

'I have frequently wondered the same,' Jonathan agreed. Watching him, Theo thought he saw an expression of profound pain cross his face.

Fleetingly he wondered what had caused it.

Then, recalling his question, he said, 'I do not wish to trivialize the degree of offence that Cheverell gave, Jonathan, but surely those are not offences for which anyone would punish him in such an appalling way?'

'No, of course not,' Jonathan said. 'It is unthinkable.' He paused.

'What is it?' Theo asked. 'What is on your mind?'

'There is something else that could make an assailant employ such a method,' Jonathan said quietly. 'Although I have always doubted its efficacy.' He paused, frowning. After a brief pause he went on. 'To assault a man in such a way as to cause extreme pain is a common method of making him reveal information that you believe he holds and that you very much want to know.'

'You doubt its efficacy?' Theo asked.

'I do. The infliction of terrible pain will make a man do anything to make it stop. The obvious thing to do is to tell your interrogators what they want to know, even if you have to make it up and it is very far from the truth.'

Slowly Theo nodded. Then he said, 'What if you do not have the first idea about what they want to know, so that you cannot even blurt out a convincing lie?'

Jonathan sighed. 'You are going to die, whatever happens,' he said. 'If you're unlucky enough to be in the situation you just described, you die sooner.'

Theo reached out and poured more brandy into their two glasses. Sipping thoughtfully, he reflected that they – he – now faced the seemingly impossible question of just what it was that Maudsley Cheverell knew – or was believed to know – that someone else wanted so badly to extract from him.

And he had not the first idea how to set about finding an answer.

Again clearly thinking much the same, Jonathan said after a while, 'Gabe told me that Dr Cheverell was a former ship's surgeon, like himself.'

'Cheverell was *nothing* like Gabe,' Theo muttered darkly.

Smiling faintly, Jonathan went on, 'Perhaps enquiries might be made in the port? It is perhaps unlikely anyone will have anything to tell us, after two and a half years, but if we knew what ship he had lately been on, we might at least be able to discover where he had travelled to make such a deadly enemy.'

'If by using the word *we* you are implying an offer of help, then I shall say thank you kindly and gratefully accept,' Theo said.

Jonathan's smile broadened. Then he said, 'I cannot offer to head down to Plymouth and begin enquiries, because time does not permit it. However, if another mind working on whatever information turns up would be of assistance, I will gladly provide it.'

Solemnly Theo clinked his glass against Jonathan's in confirmation of the arrangement.

That evening, Gabe's horse Hal found his way home to Rosewyke.

The reins were broken and there was blood on the saddle bow.

EIGHT

The winds were consistently fair.
Ambroos Leyn, as was only to be expected, had chosen the time of our voyage well, and we benefited from his knowledge and experience. But as the weeks and months went on and our good fortune held, I began to wonder if one of the two precious gifts that Natsu bestowed upon me as we hastened away from Romeu's trading port did indeed give good luck. I wasn't the only one of the company to wonder; sailors are notoriously superstitious, and quite often I would find small offerings left outside my quarters as if the donors aimed to buy continued favour.

I did not set much store by these little offerings, well meant though they undoubtedly were. If anything was working for us – and try as I might, I couldn't entirely banish the possibility – I thought it was much more likely that it was some power inherent in one or other of my gifts.

Whatever it was, it did not let us down.

We could have made a very rapid escape from the perilous waters of the East China Sea. Thanks to the captain and the company's habitual efficiency, the *Luipaard* was extremely well stocked with enough supplies to see us a long way south before the necessity to take on provisions became urgent. The *Luipaard* ran fast enough to leave behind most other craft, even, perhaps, those manned by men born and bred to the waters around the islands of southern Japan. The ship, with her crew and the countless crates full of Walter Haverleigh's precious cargo that filled her hold, ought to have been well on her way home.

She was not, because as we began our long journey that cold January and swiftly made our way south, I insisted on making repeated stops. Again and again we called in at out-of-the-way ports, all along the line of small islands that curved in a shallow arc from the southern tip of Japan in the north-east to the Portuguese settlement on the big island of Formosa in the south-west. I was driven by the abrupt and devastating change in my circumstances to hunt for commodities that had not been included in our store of provisions. Ambroos, who understood, grudgingly permitted the repeated stops, but they were far from popular with the ship's company. The men were desperate to get as far away as fast as the *Luipaard* could carry us, and their uneasy fear expressed itself in increasingly pointed comments about the ship's surgeon and his selfish demands. First Hieronymus and then Ambroos himself took on the task of trying to reason with me.

In the end I lost my temper. 'Put me ashore, then, if I'm now a pariah and a Jonah!' I yelled at Ambroos. I had heard both these words as members of the company shot covert glances in my direction and muttered under their breath. 'Manage without a surgeon, and see how long it is before you miss me, turn round to find me and beg me to come back!' At that time, fortuitously for me, we had several men sick with a mystifying fever, one with a savagely deep wound in his thigh, another with infected insect bites and one with a broken collar bone, and every one of them was taking his time – and a great deal of mine – over returning to health and full capability.

Ambroos made pacifying gestures with both hands. 'Of course we cannot put you ashore,' he said. 'As you say, we need you. But—'

'*But?*' I repeated softly, glaring at him.

He held my eyes for a moment, then shrugged. 'Perhaps make this the last stop?' he said mildly. And strode away.

It *was* the last stop. By trial and error, I had worked out what I required, and in that pretty little port two-thirds of the way down the long arc of islands, I made sure I stocked up well.

I am not sure anyone of the company ever acknowledged it, but Ambroos confided in me later that our frequent stops had in fact worked to our advantage. Our pursuers, he explained, would undoubtedly have expected us to crowd on sail and leave those waters that were most familiar to them behind us as fast as we could. 'Which of course we would have done,' he added with a grin, 'had you not insisted otherwise.'

'I had no choice!' I protested hotly. 'You know that, you—'

But he held up his hand to silence me. 'Enough, Gabe.'

*　　*　　*

There were three ships on our trail.

One was only slightly smaller than the *Luipaard*, and constructed on the same lines. We decided that she was the mother ship, possibly following a pre-determined course and ploughing her way steadily onwards without any deviation in response to our own movements. The other two were smaller, and appeared to be of the type used by Romeu and probably among the dozens, if not hundreds, of similar craft belonging to Aroto Tagauchi. These two were like a pair of hunting dogs: nimble, fast, and, having picked up a trail, single-minded in their pursuit.

Once I had satisfied my needs and we finally began to maintain a consistent speed, we thought at first that we had lost them. It was now ten days or more since the mother ship or either of the two 'hounds' had been sighted, and I decided Ambroos was right, and that, expecting us to be far to the south-west by now, our pursuers had no idea where we were.

But then a young red-headed lad – called, with a stunning lack of originality, Ginger – claimed to have spotted one of the hounds. His more experienced shipmates jeered at him and one of the older men cuffed him round the ear for having too much imagination. He, and the others, had to eat their words shortly afterwards, however, when Hieronymus made out the mother ship. Ambroos snapped out curt orders, sails filled, arcs of water curved up from the *Luipaard*'s bows, and we were off, in a long, curving course that rapidly put a small cluster of apparently uninhabited rocky islands between us and our pursuers.

But we didn't evade them for long.

They played constantly on our minds. They were like phantoms: there, not there, there again. Sometimes they would disappear for days at a time, and once for almost a fortnight. Times without count the two hunting dogs would suddenly materialize, coming up out of the dawn or at dusk from any of the points of the compass, including dead ahead. They would remain visible for a while – long enough, Ambroos remarked bitterly, for us to be quite sure it was them – and then disappear. Later they would return – perhaps approaching a little closer, as if inspecting us – before finally slipping out of sight. The many anxious, searching eyes on the *Luipaard* always went on staring out to sea for a long time before finally accepting that they had gone.

And they always came back.

It was easy for them, of course. The *Luipaard* and her company had stayed in or around Romeu's trading port for more than a year, and we had made no secret of our business of amassing Walter Haverleigh's cargo. Hieronymus had spread the word far and wide that we wished to purchase costly, luxury goods. It was true that our company included three nationalities, Dutch, Portuguese and myself the sole Englishman, but I did not believe for a moment that this would have confused anybody about where we came from and where we would be returning to.

Our pursuers knew where we were bound.

They did not need to keep us in sight. There were two ways of voyaging from Japan to England: eastwards across the Pacific and around Cape Horn, reversing Francis Drake's infamous circumnavigation of the late 1570s; or westwards, passing to the west of the Philippines, down south through the straight separating Sumatra and Java, and then south-west across the Indian Ocean to the Cape of Good Hope, at last turning north towards home. Those who followed us so relentlessly could have selected the opposite route from that of the *Luipaard* and still ended up at the same final destination, although their arrival would have been unlikely to be anywhere approaching the same time. As it was, the calculations of whoever commanded the pursuit echoed those of Ambroos Leyn: he chose to take the westward route, and so did they.

No, there was no need for them to track us so determinedly. There was no practical purpose to their interminable game of repeatedly letting us go and then seeking us out again. It must surely have been as tiresome for them as it was for us. And you had to admire their skill; or, at least, I did, although I didn't think it would be diplomatic to express the sentiment aloud. For as we left the Eastern Seas and their thousands of islands large and small behind us and sailed out into the Indian Ocean, we ought to have managed to lose our pursuers but we didn't; the game went on. And on.

And, as the weary days continued and amassed into weeks

and then months, we were forced to accept that they knew perfectly well how their pursuit game was affecting us, and that they played it purely to crawl under our skins. Some of the company withstood the constant tension better than others, or perhaps they managed to hide their anxiety. Others had no such inner strength, and their fear was evident in the way they would fiercely deny that they were compelled to keep searching the seas for our pursuers whilst doing precisely that. There was a lot of teasing of the more vulnerable men, and the cruelty was ever-present, sharpening its barbs as it simmered just beneath the surface. I sensed that Ambroos knew exactly what was happening; he would, I was sure, act swiftly and decisively if he had to.

The number of our pursuers' vessels decreased from three to two at some point halfway across the Indian Ocean. We had been out in that vast emptiness for so long, without sight of another vessel for days at a time, that when we did spot the mother ship or one of the two hunting dogs, it was almost a relief.

But then whoever commanded the pursuit decided upon a new tactic, and abruptly the mood changed.

If I had been following a ship and intent on retrieving treasures that I believed had been stolen from me, then an attack out there in the wide empty seas was probably what I'd have done too. But the hunting dog selected for the task cannot have known what she would be faced with, for the *Luipaard* kept her teeth and her claws well concealed. As the smaller vessel raced over the waters towards us, I watched as our ship's company prepared for action. Gun ports opened along each of the *Luipaard*'s sleek sides and the sinister barrels of the ship's culverins nosed out. Up in the bows, immediately behind that fearsome 'beak', two more guns were drawn up.

The great advance in ship design that emerged with the race-built galleons and the absence of a superstructure to the fore was that they could fire straight ahead without blasting away large parts of the ship. The *Luipaard* could fire broadsides as well as any other fighting ship; what those poor sods could not know as they gathered their courage aboard Aroto Tagauchi's hunting dog – looking smaller, less substantial and a great deal more vulnerable as she closed with us from dead ahead – was that our guns were about to fire many pounds of shot straight at her.

I watched Ambroos Leyn as he stood staring at our attacker. The *Luipaard* was slowing. The hunting dog came on.

It seemed to me that we were a sitting duck; that any second now the enemy would open fire and cripple us, come alongside and board us, and those dark-clad men whose faces I could now actually make out would swarm among us. And they wouldn't be alone; suddenly Hieronymus, standing beside me, nudged me sharply and pointed to port, where the second hunting dog was coming up fast.

Then Ambroos gave the order, the *Luipaard*'s forward guns fired, and their load of iron, on a flat and fairly short trajectory, blasted apart the smaller vessel's bows and removed a great deal of her foredeck. As the mortally wounded ship slowed, she began to turn away to her port, and as soon as she was level with us, Ambroos ordered a broadside and our starboard guns fired directly into her guts.

We could see them, those sailors, those poor desperate men who were about to die. Dispassionately I observed that they were a mixture of Japanese and Westerners; Portuguese or Dutch, I guessed. If I'd had any idea that we might have offered our help, I dismissed it. Our port guns fired a round at the second hunting dog – already trying to get out of range – and then Ambroos ordered more canvas and rapidly, ruthlessly, the *Luipaard* left the wreck of the vessel and the drowning men behind.

He stood for some moments looking back. Then he said calmly, 'I do not think they will try a direct approach again.'

As we rounded the Cape of Good Hope, we almost lost the second of the smaller ships. The weather was frightful and the violence of the sea was as fierce as I had ever experienced, if not worse. Aboard the *Luipaard*, with a skipper who was familiar with those southern waters, knew his job and commanded a very well-trained crew, we suffered a nightmare of high peril and extreme discomfort for six days, and although it was hard to dispel entirely images of our gallant ship foundering and hurling us all into the deep, I cannot say honestly, looking back, that I ever really thought we would not survive. Perhaps it was the power of those extraordinary gifts I'd been given, working, always working, to ensure that the ship and those on board stayed safe . . .

I'm not sure I truly believed in magical protection, tempting though it was. However, to judge by the dramatic increase in the number of little offerings that appeared as we battled our way onwards, not a few of my fellow sufferers did.

When at long last we were in calmer waters and had time to think about matters other than how we were going to endure the next half-hour, we took stock and resumed the constant look-out for our pursuers.

The mother ship appeared on our port side three days later. It might have been wishful thinking, but some of the more long-sighted of the *Luipaard*'s company were convinced she had been damaged by the storm; one man even swore she was moving more slowly, although I had no idea how he could be so sure. A week later, the surviving hunting dog took her turn to remind us of the pursuit. Now there was no question but that there had been damage; we could all see it for ourselves.

Standing on the starboard rail one morning with Hieronymus, looking out at the faint and distant dark line that was the west coast of Africa, he gave a sigh and muttered something that sounded like a prayer.

I turned to him questioningly. 'You pray for the men who have haunted us with their presence ever since we left Japan? Who have already mounted an attack? Who, if they caught us, would undoubtedly . . .'

But I couldn't bear to put it into words.

Hieronymus gave me a sympathetic smile. 'I understand how you feel. But for myself, yes, I pray for them. Gabe, think what horrors they have just endured!' he exclaimed. 'The rounding of the Cape was terrible enough for us, in a ship which we know has successfully made the passage many times and under the command of a man of Ambroos's quality. But what of them, the men on that small, insubstantial craft for which such seas, such a tempest, could never have been imagined? Their vessel was not built for the South Atlantic, and I am utterly amazed that they survived.'

He was right. Perhaps I too should have offered a prayer. But, bearing in mind the total lack of mercy they would show if they caught up with the *Luipaard* and sought me out, I didn't.

And so we sailed on.

St Helena, the Guinea Coast, round the great land mass where Africa bulged out to the west. Then we turned north-east for Europe. Portugal, the tip of Spain, the Bay of Biscay, Finisterre. And, at last, we were sailing into my home waters.

The moment of greatest danger was on us.

In intense conference with Ambroos and Hieronymus, a plan had been made. We knew what the pursuers wanted: me, or, more accurately, those treasures that poor, brave Natsu had given her life to hand over into my care.

'We must assume that they know where your home is,' Ambroos said in his slow, solemn way. 'It is not unreasonable to think that a man in your position will wish more than anything to go home. If, therefore, you leave the *Luipaard* and go ashore in Plymouth – or, since it must appear that you are trying to keep your movements secret, at some well-concealed little cove nearby – it is likely that they will follow.'

'Will they not expect such a ruse?' Hieronymus said doubtfully.

'Yes,' Ambroos agreed. 'Yet such is their desire for Gabe and what he bears with him that they will not be able to ignore the possibility that it is *not* a ruse.'

'They still have two vessels,' I pointed out. 'Even if, as we hope, one is dispatched to follow my false trail, the other will remain in post, following the *Luipaard*.'

Ambroos turned his clear blue eyes on to me. 'True,' he said. 'But we shall have lost half of our pursuers. And to deal with the remaining half has to be better than with the whole.'

'They will come hurrying after us once the trick is uncovered,' Hieronymus protested.

'They will have to find us,' Ambroos replied calmly. 'And I am convinced that my knowledge of these waters far surpasses theirs.'

Since that, at least, could not reasonably be disputed, Hieronymus and I shut our mouths and listened to the details of the plan.

*   *   *

It was straightforward, and it depended almost entirely on my having accurately remembered the precise details of the Tamar estuary and a particular piece of the coast to the immediate east of Plymouth.

Under cover of night, I was dropped in the very early morning by the *Luipaard*'s boat on a muddy piece of shore on the eastern side of the river Tamar as it widened out to meet the sea. It was a spot I knew well, and to put my feet on a piece of my home-land after such a long absence would have been a profoundly moving moment, if I hadn't firmly shut my mind to my emotions. The boat did not linger, the four sailors quickly pushing it back into deeper water and pulling hard for the waiting *Luipaard*. They would have a struggle. Coming ashore had been difficult enough, for it was close to the time of the September equinox and the seas were wild. But we had been running with the tide then, and now they would be fighting against it. It wasn't my job, however, to worry about them. I turned and hurried over the mud to where the ground rose gently towards a grassy shore, a narrow belt of trees and, beyond, a very familiar little lane that wound and twisted its way from the estuary to the north side of the town.

The boat had brought me a considerable distance up the estuary, for we were trying to convince the pursuit that I was going home and I had therefore chosen a spot that was only a few miles from Rosewyke. I shut my mind to that, too.

Then the rain started.

It was a tricky task I must do, for I had to leave enough signs of my presence to convince the pursuers that I had come ashore just there, and then *stop* leaving any signs, so that they would not know where I went next. Assuming I succeeded, it would mean, as Ambroos had said, that the *Luipaard* would lose half of her pursuers.

I could only hope and pray that I got it right.

I hid under the cover of a small copse of birch and alder until it was full day. Then, over the next few hours, I made my way around Plymouth. It was tempting to stay on the north side and hurry straight for the place where the boat was going to pick me up, for the thought of the *Luipaard* and what she carried going on without me was unbearable. But I had a task to do. So I

headed down into Plymouth, my hood drawn forward in case I
should encounter someone I knew, and wove a circuitous path
through the maze of alleyways and little streets behind the port.
The rain was coming down harder now, and I was thankful for
the awful weather, since it was keeping most people indoors. I
wanted just enough of Plymouth's inhabitants to be able to say,
if questioned, that they had seen a big man answering my description that day. The almost deserted streets made me bold, and I
even ventured down the alley that went past the tavern in whose
stables I had habitually left my horse Hal when making calls in
that part of town.

I stood between the open gates at the entry to the yard and
stared within. The place seemed deserted. But then I noticed that
someone was peering at me through a narrow gap in a doorway
to the rear of the yard. It was one of the ostlers: a young lad,
nervous and not too bright, and I'd always reckoned he was only
kept on because he was so good with skittish horses.

He opened the door wider, and now his head seemed to crane
forward on his long skinny neck. 'Doctor T?' he whispered, as
if hardly daring to speak the name.

I turned up the high collar of my cloak and, trying to disguise
my voice, grunted harshly, 'You are mistaken.'

I strode off up the alley. There was no sound of pursuing
footsteps, and I hoped the lad's fear of a snarling stranger had
overcome his curiosity. But I decided I'd done enough, and there
was no more need to risk running into someone else who would
not be so easily fooled.

Soaked to the skin, cold, thirsty and hungry, I headed out of
the town, pausing only to pick some urgently needed refreshments. From one of the taverns I caught the aroma of a good
roast dinner being prepared, and I probably moaned aloud with
pleasure; it awoke such a sudden and urgent hunger for the food
of my homeland that it was all I could do to resist and hurry on.
Turning towards the south, I crossed the Plym and then made
my way through little lanes and overgrown tracks over the headland and finally down to the coast.

I stood above a small inlet. I had stood in the same spot almost
three years ago with Theo Davey and Jarman Hodge. There was
a quay: in my memory I heard Theo say, *Is that little harbour*

behind us big enough for a ship? and my own voice replying, *It depends on how big the ship is.*

But Ambroos's plan did not require a deep harbour, for the *Luipaard* would not be chancing her luck by coming to pick me up. She would, after some manoeuvres designed to confuse the pursuit, continue her progress north-eastwards, and the boat that came to collect me would rejoin her somewhere off Heybrook Bay.

There were so many things that could go wrong that, as I sat down to wait for the boat, I had a struggle to go on hoping for a positive outcome.

Three hours later, I stood at the *Luipaard*'s elegant stern, gazing back at Plymouth. The ship's boat had picked me up, and the remaining hunting dog had been seen heading for Plymouth. The plan had worked. My relief was tempered only by Ambroos's smug attitude that said, loud as words, *I told you it would.*

My heart ached at leaving my home behind. We had achieved what we had hoped we would, yes, and now, aided by a strong south-west wind, we were moving swiftly towards our final destination, and the next phase of the plan. Which was far more dangerous than anything we had tackled so far. I knew I must turn all my energy to the immediate future. But I could not fight the urge for this backward look.

I knew I had to go on. Even if the ruse had worked, the pursuit still had two vessels and would likely do exactly what we feared, with one continuing to follow us while the other remained at Plymouth. One enemy ship on our tail was certainly better than two, but there was no escaping the fact that the danger was as pressing as ever.

As if I was telling the beads of an invisible rosary, I went through the list of those I loved who were being left behind. My father and my mother: I sent out a prayer that they still lived and thrived. My brother Nathaniel: stranger to me though he largely was, still he was my flesh and blood. Celia, my lovely sister Celia: even as an image of her came into my mind, I found I was smiling. Jonathan Carew, beloved friend and closer than brother. Theo Davey, his wife and children.

Judyth Penwarden.

Considering the vast alteration in my circumstances that I

would be bringing home with me, if and when I finally got there, I could hardly bear to think about her.

A quiet murmur broke into my contemplation, and I welcomed it. It was a reminder to stop wasting time dreaming and return to my duties.

Our fast progress continued. We sailed out to the south around the Isle of Wight. I thought of Walter Haverleigh, waiting with increasing impatience for the unbelievably costly cargo we were bringing for him, although by now he had probably left his secret and well-concealed manor house and would likely be at our meeting place already. Then we took a straight course that stayed roughly parallel to the south coast. For the time being there was no sign of our pursuers, although experience warned us not to be complacent: without doubt one or even both of them would still be there.

Now I stood up in the bows whenever no pressing task took me below. I had picked some apples as I hurried over the headland to the little quay, and the taste of the sweet fruit of a Devon orchard was poignant. Frequently my thoughts turned to what lay immediately ahead. Unlike the outward journey, when I had believed we were bound for Neira until the *Luipaard* altered course and headed north for Japan, I knew exactly where we were going; Ambroos had told me.

Walter Haverleigh's late sister had been married to a wealthy man who owned property on the south bank of the Thames. From what I could discern, this property was somewhere between the unruly, lawless village of Southwark, where Shakespeare had rebuilt his Globe Theatre, and Greenwich to the east. Ambroos and Hieronymus had clearly been to the place before, and Hieronymus, perhaps realizing that my incessant demand to be provided with every detail concerning our destination was no more than a reflection of my anxiety, described it as well as he could.

'There was a religious foundation there; an abbey of the Cistercians, I believe,' he had told me when he had joined me earlier in my vigil in the bows. 'Elverstone Abbey, if I recall aright, and the church was dedicated to St Thomas, since the ancient pilgrim road to the shrine of St Thomas a Becket at Canterbury passed close by. An inlet served the abbey, although now, to all appearances, it is abandoned and derelict. Where the road crossed it on an ancient bridge there was a place known as St Thomas Watering, for the pilgrims' horses were watered there. They used to hang pirates at St Thomas Watering,' he added thoughtfully.

'But the abbey is no longer there?' I demanded. Surely it had gone, along with every other abbey, as the late Queen's ruthless and single-minded tyrant of a father had abandoned the faith of his forefathers and plundered its precious edifices, and then proceeded to turn his kingdom upside down for the sake of a woman whose head he'd had severed from her body a short year or so later.

'No, naturally not,' Hieronymus replied with a wry smile, 'for an abbey full of monks, not to mention the many visitors, would be too large an audience for an operation such as ours. A house was built among the ruins by a favoured courtier of Queen Elizabeth, and Walter Haverleigh's brother-in-law purchased the place on this man's demise. It is a modest manor house,' he added, 'and I have heard it referred to as Redriff Old Hall.' He looked at me enquiringly.

'Never heard of it,' I said shortly. My mind was still on the derelict inlet. 'Where are we to hide the *Luipaard* if this inlet is silted up?'

He tutted softly. 'I said it *appeared* derelict, but that is because the master of Redriff Old Hall – his name is Gregory Tresham – has arranged it so. The bridge that I mentioned has been allowed to fall into disrepair – the road to Kent now bends to the south of the abbey ruins – and the first few yards of the creek are overgrown. Beyond that, however, it is well maintained.'

'And large enough for the *Luipaard*?'

He gave me a long-suffering look. '*Yes*, Gabe. And, before you demand to know how I can be so sure, she has been concealed there before.'

We sailed on. The *Luipaard* rounded the thrusting bulge of Kent, turned to port into the Thames estuary, passed the mouth of the Medway and at last entered the Thames itself.

And then we were approaching her well-hidden berth, and the end of our long voyage.

NINE

It was evening, darkness was falling and the tide was almost at the full as we approached the inlet. Hieronymus had been right about the place looking derelict. There was a short row of half-ruined buildings on the west side of the old dock, but tall, rampant weeds and wild shrubs grew between the walls, none of the buildings had a roof and it looked as if nobody had lived there for decades. On the east bank there was a thicket of hazel and bramble, and behind, some distance away, could be seen the outline of a substantial house.

The Thames surged on behind the *Luipaard*'s stern as, with infinite care and as slowly as he could contrive, Ambroos nudged her bows into the mouth of the inlet. Standing nervously at the rail, I expected any moment to hear the sounds and feel the lurch as her keel grated on the bottom.

She went on.

Men on either side leaned far out with long poles in their hands, and steadily we proceeded up the ruined dock. Broken stonework indicated where quays had once been, and behind them I could make out among the burgeoning undergrowth the remains of old warehouses.

There was nobody about, and not a light showed.

Then the banks closed in. We had come to a bottleneck, and I could see no way to progress any further. But the men poled on, and after an alarming ten or fifteen yards, the bank on the starboard side suddenly opened out and the *Luipaard*, her way carrying her on, slid serenely into a pool, or basin, that had been dug out of the enclosing land.

I heard the deep metallic clang of machinery from behind us. Hurrying back to look, I saw that four of the company had jumped ashore, two on either side, and they were leaning their weight against the long beams that operated a pair of heavy wooden gates. We had entered the pool at the flood; as the tide turned and the level began to drop again, we would be safe within our reserve of water. I glanced around me, and silently praised whoever had contrived this hiding place, for trees grew densely all around it and, unless you knew where to look, it was almost entirely invisible.

The hour was late now; too late, Ambroos declared, to go and present ourselves to Gregory Tresham at Redriff Old Hall. I joined him and Hieronymus for a scratch supper, after which my two companions went their separate ways to settle in for the night.

I returned to my quarters.

The tiny cabin had become like home during the months spent in it. After so many years in the Queen's navy I was accustomed to maintaining a high level of tidiness, with everything allocated its own place and nothing left out to get in the way. On the outward journey it had been easy, for there had only been myself to think about.

Coming home, however, I'd had my treasures with me.

And not only the contents of my cabin but also my entire life had changed out of all belief.

Now, as the *Luipaard*'s company settled for the night and gradually silence fell, I sat on the hard shelf of my bunk, poured a good measure of brandy, lit a pipe and drew a blanket over my legs. It was a luxury to have some time to myself.

Time to remember what happened when the *Luipaard* sailed for home.

Time to work out what on earth I was going to do.

When I left Japan, Natsu had given me two treasures. The first she had brought the night before our departure. The second she had thrust at me on that terrible day we left Romeu's village.

Even if I had been tempted to abandon them as soon as I discovered what they were (and I'm ashamed to admit I was, although only briefly), I couldn't. Natsu had given her life to deliver them into my hands, and by so doing, she had put a debt of honour on me to look after them no less devotedly than she had done. Which was only fair, I had to accept, certainly as far as one of the treasures was concerned.

Once we were away from Nagasaki, out of immediate danger and relatively safe, other than their being absolutely no doubt that we were being followed, there was time to draw breath. Before Ambroos could start asking questions I could not yet answer, I had hurried below to examine the treasures more thoroughly. I fetched the wooden crate from where I had stowed it in my surgeon's quarters and, in my own cabin, I laid the cloth-wrapped bundle on my bunk. As I began to remove the outer layer of wrappings, a piece of heavy parchment dropped out, folded over neatly and with my name written on the outside. I opened it up and looked at it just long enough to see that all of one page and half of the other side were covered in very small writing in a beautiful hand, and that the language was English.

Something about that densely written page set off alarm and concern deep within me. The obvious response would have been to unwind the rest of the wrappings. But I didn't.

I think I knew, even then, what the bundle was. I sometimes ask myself how I could have set it aside while I inspected the contents of the crate, and the only answer I can come up with is that I chose to preserve my deliberate ignorance just a little longer.

I knelt down on the hard floor and, knowing I must be quick, turned my attention to the crate. It was solid and well-made, roughly the length of my forearm from elbow to wrist, and its lid was secured with a score of neatly spaced nails. I prised them out, putting them carefully in a small pot on the shelf beside my bunk.

The object inside was heavy and hard, made of solid metal. The outer cloth wrapping was bound with carefully knotted string and decorated with red wax seals. I broke the seals with the tip of my knife, untied the string and removed the cloth, to reveal several layers of thick protective padding, which seemed to consist mainly of wood shavings.

I had not yet touched whatever was hidden inside, but already I felt the chill of it. My hands fell away as if it was fire rather than ice that had briefly burned me.

I told myself I could not spare the time to unwrap it just then. But I knew it was an excuse, an evasion. The truth was that I couldn't put the object down swiftly enough. I laid it carefully back inside the crate, replaced the lid, hammered in the nails and slid the crate beneath my bunk.

Even though it was still concealed deep within its padding, I had felt its presence. Its power.

Forcing down my speculation and – I had to admit – my fear, I turned back to the first parcel.

It was wrapped in the thick folds of a soft blanket. It stank of shit and it was emitting the sort of preparatory noises that suggested a full-blown screaming session was imminent.

I took a deep breath and faced up to what I knew I must do.

Enclosed in the blankets was a bundle of soft absorbent cloths, an assortment of towels of greater and smaller size and the long cylinder of a pottery bottle with some sort of teat on one end. The screams were building up momentum, I could hear the voices of inquisitive sailors just outside, so I pushed up my sleeves, laid the infant on one of the towels, removed the soaked and soiled cloths around its loins – it was a girl – and washed off the mess. Then I dried the soft skin and, as best I could, secured a fresh cloth. Wrapping one of the blankets around her again, I took her in the crook of my arm and, praying she was so hungry that the need to feed would overcome her distress, shoved the teat in her mouth.

She gave a sort of sigh, latched on to it and instantly began sucking so hard that her plump pink cheeks turned concave.

My mind was in a turmoil, with a dozen or more questions demanding answers. I didn't know which to address first. Not that I could address any of them just at that moment: I was discovering that when you are feeding a very hungry child, there isn't really anything else you *can* do. Well, I'd seen capable, experienced mothers with a baby at the breast supporting the child with one arm while the free hand cooked the dinner or stoked the fire, but that skill was far beyond me. And anyway I wasn't feeding the child from a breast but from the bottle, which I had to hold in my other hand.

I stared down at the child.

Her hair was dark and glossy, and I thought at first that it was black. But then she moved her head suddenly, and the light caught an auburn sheen. Her skin was pale, the cheeks rosy, and her eyebrows were dark and well-marked. Her eyes were fast shut, the lashes as dark as her brows.

She was, I thought, about five or six months old. She was also quite exquisitely beautiful.

She finished her feed and spat out the teat. I held her against my upper chest – I had a sudden vivid mental picture of Judyth Penwarden teaching a brand-new mother – and gently rubbed her back. Presently a loud burp sounded right in my ear, and I heard a mouthful of regurgitated liquid splatter on my shoulder. A posset, Judyth had called it, and nothing to worry about.

Nevertheless, it didn't smell too good.

I laid the baby carefully down on my bunk and wiped up the slimy curds.

I contrived a nest of blankets on the floor for her and almost instantly she fell asleep. It was the only time she had to sleep on the bare boards, for late the next day the ship's carpenter presented me with a crib that he had spent the morning making.

With frequent glances at the sleeping child, I sank down on to my bunk and unfolded the letter.

I looked first at the signature: Oliver Lambert SJ.

Society of Jesuits.

And I remembered Romeu's words, referring to the Jesuits: *Only one native English speaker has come with the Fathers, but one is enough.*

Enough to explain Romeu's good English, he had meant.

Now this sole native English speaker appeared to have sent me a long letter . . .

I need not have turned to the last page, for he had introduced himself at the top of the first one.

My name is Oliver Lambert and I was born in Sevenoaks, in the county of Kent in the south-east of England. I joined the Jesuit brethren when still a young man, and for the past decade I have worked with them in our mission on the southernmost Japanese island of Kyushu. I speak Japanese and also Portuguese and a little Dutch, and now I am in the service of a Japanese speaker who wishes to address you in your mother tongue.

Recently you will have been presented with two precious parcels. If you are the man that I believe you to be – for I have heard much about you, Doctor Gabriel Taverner, in the months that you have been here – then I am sure that you will have already attended to the urgent needs of the human package. She is constantly in my thoughts and I pray God has kept her safe and hale on her journey to you.

I shall speak first of the other parcel, for all that it is very much the second in my heart. Unwrap it now, Doctor Gabriel.

It was uncanny. It felt as if the priest was in the cabin there with me, and had been watching me intently since Natsu had delivered her packages into my hands.

Staring at the crate, I wondered if he sensed my deep apprehension.

'Go on, you coward,' I commanded myself softly. 'Get on with it.'

Hurriedly, before my nerve failed, I picked up the heavy wooden box and laid it across my legs. Once more I removed the outer wrappings, and now I addressed the thickly padded layers of wood shavings, bundling them up and pushing them under my bunk with my foot.

I stared down at the object standing proud and fierce on my lap. In those first moments I thought that it was trembling gently, and again I sensed the force of its presence. It was . . . it was like trying to hold a heavy and powerful spring closed, and feeling the power of it fighting for release.

It was a beautifully carved model of a tiger. It stood on a rock, one forepaw raised threateningly, long, vicious claws extended, the other clutching at the stone, and its rear legs were tensed as if to propel it into a soaring leap. Its head was turned towards me, its pricked ears were laid back and bright light burst from its intent green eyes as the lantern flame caught them. Its huge mouth was wide open in a roar that I could almost hear. Sharp teeth crowded its jaws, and the curved upper canines hung down like a pair of scimitars.

I had wondered at its great weight, but now I understood. It was so heavy because it was made of solid metal. I thought in that first disbelieving inspection that the metal was bronze, but with a particularly bright golden sheen to it.

Then I realized that it was gold.

The bright green eyes were large emeralds, and the glitter that I had noticed along the row of teeth was a sparkle of diamonds.

It took my breath away. And that was before I had started to wonder what it must be worth.

Then something caught my eye. The animal had been modelled with extraordinary skill, and it was incredibly lifelike; I knew this to be true, for I had seen and feared the living animal more than once in my travels. But there was something odd about the forepaws.

Lifting the tiger – no easy task – I held it close to the lantern.

Yes. It was the claws that were strange. While there was no doubting their ferocious efficiency, they were not true to life; they were shaped like the long, curved petals of a chrysanthemum flower. They were slightly glossy and pale cream in colour – ivory, I later discovered – and the many small diamonds set into them glittered like stars. The scarlet tip of each one was formed from rubies.

Reverentially, I stood the tiger on the shelf opposite my bunk. I picked up the cloth wrapping, intending to cover its shining brilliance, but I didn't. I couldn't.

I was barely able to admit it to myself, but it felt as if some power had stopped me: the tiger didn't *want* to be covered.

Then I picked up Father Oliver's letter.

Once again, it was as if he was watching my every move.

'Beautiful, isn't it?' he wrote.

Or perhaps I should say he, for it is undoubtedly the male of the species. You have before you the Chrysanthemum Tiger, Dr Gabriel. It is a treasure of the mighty and ancient house of Tagauchi, whose origins lie in the deep shadow of the far past, long before civilization began and when the magical and the mysterious entered the world. The treasure's present owner, Aroto Tagauchi, is, according to his own reckoning, the fiftieth patriarch of his clan to possess the statue, for it was made in the first great flowering of the Asuka Period, where the emperors were first established and the ancient practices of nature worship, ancestor worship and the reverence of sacred objects were dominant. Men had begun to create wealth, and with this they patronized and encouraged the skilled craftsmen who flocked to their courts: the jewellers, the silversmiths, those who worked with gold. The House of Tagauchi has long revered its sacred animal. Many myths and legends are attached to this creature. It is said to protect all those who carry the Tagauchi blood in their veins, and they believed it to be a shape-shifter, able in the blink of an eye – and at will – to turn those elegant petal-like ivory claws into blades as sharp and deadly as knives. Men have killed for it, men have died for it, and their numbers are countless, lost in the past. If a Tagauchi were ever asked to justify such a death, he would say, we speak of one short life. What is that against a treasure from the ancient past that will last for all eternity?

The Chrysanthemum Tiger was kept under the protection of many locks and impassable doors and an armed guard of four men who were ever vigilant. Only members of Aroto's immediate family were permitted to venture anywhere near it; for Aroto's single weakness, if indeed weakness it is, is an almost fanatical love of his kin, and in particular his direct descendants. The marriage of his only daughter to the Portuguese trader Romeu Silvestre was a heavy blow, for the Tagauchi clan keep their blood pure; but the deed was done before Aroto could prevent it, and it is said that his fury with his daughter and son-in-law abated considerably when his granddaughter was born, for she was an intelligent and very beautiful child and she captivated him from the start. He indulged her, showered her with costly gifts, granted her every wish and housed her in high luxury. And, as invariably happens, such relentless spoiling made the child headstrong and inclined to her own will and, as she matured and became a woman, Aroto discovered that he had created a character too much in his own image; in short, he found he could no longer control her.

He knew he must marry her off, and he summoned many dozens of men he thought might be capable of the great honour he would bestow upon them by the gift of his granddaughter. All the potential husbands were wealthy – that went without saying – and many came from families almost as ancient as that of the Tagauchis. To a man all were also mature, if not old; some were bald, most were fat, some bore old injuries and the after-effects of long sickness. Aroto's granddaughter, now a grown woman and very clear about the sort of husband she would accept, refused every single one.

She discovered herself to be a prisoner. Her cell was an entire floor of her grandfather's palace, she was surrounded by beautiful objects and indulged with every luxury, she had an entire staff of devoted servants who leapt to obey her least command even before she had uttered it. But it was a prison nevertheless, for she was not allowed to leave it.

She did. Of course she did, for those devoted servants were her servants, and there were ways that she could punish them if they did not obey. By intricate and clever subterfuge – as I told you, she was highly intelligent – she made her escape, and moreover her absence was not spotted until it was too late. Aroto, I believe, was overconfident in the security of his palace, and I do not imagine it even entered his head that his granddaughter could evade his rigid rule or would even desire to. But she was driven: the thought of a marriage bed shared every night with one of those terrible old men repulsed and horrified her, and she assured me that she would die rather than submit to her grandfather's will. She knew of only one way to prevent marriage being forced upon her: she must lose her maidenhood and, if she could work the magic or pray with sufficient fervour, the union would result in her impregnation and the bearing of a child.

I looked up. In my memory I was somewhere quite different, and I could smell the hot jasmine-scented water, feel the enticing, irresistible flesh against mine.

When I was forced to abandon my life as a ship's surgeon and took up the life of a Devon doctor, it had been a not uncommon occurrence for a young girl to come to me in great distress, sometimes accompanied by an equally anxious young man, confessing that she was pregnant, they weren't married, and they were really scared because her father was going to be livid and it wasn't *fair* because they'd only done it once. I always said the same: it only takes once.

Now I had fallen into the same trap.

I had known, I think, almost from the moment the child was thrust into my arms. Perhaps even before that; I was as capable as the next man of working out that January plus nine months and then another five resulted in a child of roughly the age of the one now fast asleep on my cabin floor.

I looked down and stared at her.

My child. My daughter.

As if she felt the intensity of my gaze, she opened her eyes.

I had expected them to be brown, for Chiyo's had been a subtle golden-brown hazel shade. They were not. In the light from the lantern, they were a clear sea green.

And they looked just like my sister's.

'My daughter,' I said softly.

She went on studying me for a few moments. Then the lids drooped closed again and she went back to sleep.

After some time I picked up the letter and, wincing, read what Father Oliver said next.

Chiyo confided every detail of what passed between the two of you, and she was insistent that if seduction took place, it was she who seduced you. Whilst I am naturally not familiar with such matters between men and women, I believe I did both know and understand Chiyo. The two words that leap to mind whenever I think of her are headstrong and truthful; in short, Gabriel, I believed her and do not hold you overly to blame for your careless and unthinking act that resulted in the conception of a child. What I shall hold you to account for is, however, what you do next. I pray that you will be the person Chiyo believed you to be, that you will accept this child as your own, that you will take responsibility for her, as indeed you should, and take her under your care and protection.

I felt as if he was there, speaking to me.

And I knew what he was going to say next.

I went on reading and the sense of foreboding grew.

Chiyo gave birth in secret, attended only by her closest maids, who smuggled the baby out of the palace immediately after the birth. The child was robust and healthy, and thrived from the start. But soon Chiyo grew sick, for she had suffered injury during the birth and in truth should have had someone in attendance more skilled and experienced in delivering babies. She struggled on for several weeks, pining for her child but forced to hide her sorrow, and her maids' reassurances that the baby was well were little help. But then all at once her condition deteriorated rapidly;

she sent for me, and I was taken by night and in secret to see her. I asked immediately after her child, for I saw the instant I entered her rooms that the baby and all signs of her had vanished. 'She is safe,' Chiyo said. 'She is already far from here, for I will not have her live the life I have led and, as Aroto Tagauchi's sole descendant, be forced perhaps to make the same terrible choice as I.' I could see that she was failing, and I rushed to kneel at her side and take her cold hands. 'Where is she?' I whispered. She smiled. 'She is with someone who will take her to her father when the time is right.' Then she gave a feeble jerk of her head, indicating a wrapped parcel whose strings were sealed with wax. 'That will also be taken to him, but for that as for the child, there is need of explanation,' she murmured. 'Write a letter for me, please, Father. Tell him. Tell Gabriel Taverner that she is his, and that I am sending with her the heirloom of which, as my child and my grandfather's great-grandchild, she is the rightful owner.'

I did not need to read more; indeed, there only remained a few lines. I was thinking of poor, courageous Natsu. She had done so well, for, in addition to bringing the crate to me in utter secrecy, she must also have quietly contrived to remove the baby from the palace. And, by extreme skill and cunning, Natsu had managed to bring my child to me in the port below Romeu's village, timing her arrival for the very moment of departure.

She had died for her devotion.

Two women dead, I thought. I could have wept for both of them.

I looked at the final words that Father Oliver had to say to me. He had written:

Her name is Amy. That is how I have translated the kanji of the one bestowed upon her by her mother. It will not sound alien among English-speakers. Take her far away and guard her with your life, for when her great-grandfather learns the truth, as surely he must, he will do his utmost to retrieve her and he will be incandescent with fury when he learns that the Chrysanthemum Tiger has gone with her. You do not need me to tell you, Dr Gabriel, that Aroto Tagauchi has a fleet of swift vessels at his command and a large company of first-rate men to sail them.

These men are warriors; they are skilled in the art of killing, and reserve their most refined agonies for those who have betrayed their lord. No greater betrayal of Aroto Tagauchi could there be than for a foreign devil to abduct his sole surviving descendant and steal his family's priceless heirloom. Have a care, Gabriel Taverner. I will pray for Amy and for you. May God go with you and protect you.

I slumped back against the bulkhead and, dropping the letter on the floor, sank my head in my hands.

It was deep night now in the hidden pool south of the Thames. Everyone else was asleep, my child included. My pipe had gone out and I had drained both the original measure of brandy and another. My reflections had taken me deep into the recent past, and brought vividly to mind those initial days and weeks with Amy, as I struggled to care for her and worried myself sick when I thought she was not thriving.

But between us we seemed to have done all right. She was more than a year old now, walking – well, tottering – and endlessly gabbling in a language that might have been English, Dutch, Portuguese or even a memory of the Japanese of her first few months. Whatever it was, it made little sense in any of them. She was full of laughter, had a quick and violent temper and, once her mind was set on something, utterly determined to have it.

I loved her. Looking down at her as she slept in her simple cradle, I thought I would very probably die for her.

Although I really didn't intend to put that to the test.

TEN

I woke up to a typical autumn morning. There was a mist rising off the water, and not a breath of wind to disperse it. The sun was visible only as a brighter spot among the dense cloud, and gave no discernible warmth. The trees still clung to their leaves where they could, but already the ground was carpeted in shades of bronze and gold.

Ambroos, Hieronymus and I, dressed in our best and as smart as we could contrive after so long at sea, set out for Redriff Old Hall. I had left my child in the care of Piet, my young apprentice, to whom I had entrusted her often enough to know he would ensure her safety. Piet had a string of younger brothers and sisters, so he had told me, and, well used to the antics of small children, he assured me he stood no nonsense from his latest charge. I was not entirely convinced; Amy could be very single-minded, and just recently she had begun to express dislike of the bread soaked in water and goat's milk and the cereals cooked in broth that had comprised her diet over the long months of the voyage. I wished Piet good luck.

Ambroos led us off along a path through the belt of trees that concealed the pool where the *Luipaard* lay. He turned left on the other side of the trees, and crossed the corner of a field to where a humpbacked pack bridge crossed a narrow river that wound in a shallow curve around the end of the derelict dock. Pausing, Hieronymus pointed up the water.

'Where the water once ran into the Thames, before it was diverted by the monks, there was a spot where they used to hang criminals; pirates, mostly,' he said. 'Now they use Execution Dock, over on the north bank. They say this place is still haunted by the ghosts of those who died here, and the practice of leaving the dead hanging for the duration of three tides is a very ancient one.' He grinned. 'Naturally, Gregory Tresham does all he can to perpetrate and encourage these tales of ghostly sounds and visions, for it deters the curious.'

'Are we now on his land?' I asked as we turned sharply to the right on the far side of the bridge.

'We have been since we entered the pool,' Ambroos replied. 'He has been steadily buying up land in every direction. He prefers not to have near neighbours,' he added, lowering his voice.

I absorbed the implications of that.

Presently we saw the vague shapes of buildings looming up ahead out of the mist. A high wall that rose to a graceful arch, and a place where two more low, thick walls met at a gatehouse. We approached it and the sturdy doors opened, a silent and armed man standing at each one.

Within was what had clearly once been the monks' cloister. Now the rows of structures that had formed three of its sides had been rebuilt and turned into stables, storehouses, workshops and what appeared to be fairly spartan accommodation for Gregory Tresham's outdoor servants. The fourth side of the old cloister was filled by a small but beautifully designed manor house. Shallow steps led up to a porched front door, and as we climbed them, once again the door was opened for us.

I spotted the tall, spare form of Walter Haverleigh, dressed in his habitual black, his long silver hair and beard immaculately groomed. His face was creased in a grin, and he gave the impression of excitement barely contained. In front of him, standing with arms spread as if to embrace us, was another man. In contrast to Walter, he was short, broad and running to fat, his heavy leather belt buckled below the burgeoning belly. He was clearly sufficiently wealthy, however, to engage a tailor with the skill to make even a large man look elegant; his dark garments gave the illusion of height, and the gorgeous braid around his high collar drew the attention away from the many chins that a sparse beard barely covered.

He too was smiling widely. 'Ambroos, Hieronymus, welcome and well met!' he exclaimed, slapping both men on the shoulder. Then he held out a big hand to me. 'I am Gregory Tresham,' he said. 'Doctor Gabriel Taverner, I greet you!' He bowed, then, straightening, stood back and waved an arm to usher us into his house. We were shown into a wide hall with a chequered floor, where a long board had been loaded with food and drink. 'Presently to business,' Gregory Tresham said. 'For now, we eat!'

The provender was as good as our host's bulk and cheerful air of bonhomie suggested. After so long on short rations, the three of us from the *Luipaard* fell on it, and Tresham watched us with happy indulgence. Not that he didn't eat and drink as well; catching my eyes on him as he devoured a plump chicken leg, he said through a mouthful of meat, 'My mother taught me that no good host holds back while his guests eat, since it implies the food is good enough for them but not for him!'

I doubted his mother had said any such thing, but it was as good an excuse as any.

I noticed Ambroos and Hieronymus in deep conversation with Walter Haverleigh. Once or twice Walter looked up at me, and I thought I saw anxiety in his expression. As the initial enthusiasm for the food slowly fell away and our host suggested it was time to get to work, I approached Walter.

He reached out a hand and touched my shoulder. 'I hear you have trouble,' he said quietly.

I almost laughed at the understatement. 'I have,' I replied. 'In my keeping there are two items that a certain very wealthy, influential and angry Japanese lord is keen to recover.'

'One of which is your daughter,' Walter murmured.

'Yes.' Ambroos and Hieronymus had not kept anything back, then.

Walter studied me. 'And the *Luipaard* has been pursued all the way home.'

'So we believe, although neither of the remaining two vessels have shown themselves of late.' And I very much hope one of them has remained at Plymouth, I might have added, only I didn't because Walter was the sort of man who would instantly demand elaboration of such a statement and I didn't have anything to offer.

'There are many hiding places along the Thames,' he observed. He thought briefly, shot me a quick, sharp look, then said abruptly, 'You should leave, Gabe. They are aware you are on the *Luipaard*, and even if they do not know her current whereabouts, and I am quite sure they do not, one might suppose they will have little difficulty finding out exactly who is the purchaser of that extremely valuable cargo you have brought home on my ship. Thus they will establish the connection between myself, our host and this house.' He glanced at Gregory Tresham, who was presently laughing long and loud at some jest of his own. Walter winced. 'If you will trust me to look after your interests here, I propose that I receive what is owed to you as your share of our profits and take it with me to Cheverstone when I return there. I will undertake to keep it safe until you come to collect it.'

I did not know what my share would be. I only knew that it would be a very substantial amount of money. I didn't like the idea of riding away and leaving it up to someone else to collect it for me. There were men I would have trusted with my life, never mind the small fortune that was coming to me – Jonathan Carew, for example, or Theo Davey – but Walter Haverleigh was not among them.

He was watching me, the clear grey-blue eyes amused. 'You and I signed a contract before the *Luipaard* sailed, Gabe,' he said softly. 'You may not trust me, but I think it would not be over-rash to put your faith in the law.'

Still I did not answer. I was insulting him, I knew, by the implication that I wanted my hard-won gains to be delivered into my hands and not his, but I discovered I didn't care.

But then, like a slap across the face, I remembered the danger. Had there been only myself to worry about, it would have been a different matter.

I said stiffly, 'Very well.'

He nodded, his face grave. 'I think that is wise,' he said. He was still studying me, and I felt as if he knew exactly what was racing through my mind. After a moment he said, 'Let us agree that at least some of what is owed to you is paid immediately. I will acquire a good horse for you, and dispatch one of the women of Gregory's house to go out and purchase all that will be required by you and your . . . er, your charge for the journey home.' Leaning close, he added very quietly, 'There will also be a bag of gold. A weighty bag, mind, and although it will only be a small part of what I am confident will eventually come your way, it will probably be many times what a country physician normally expects to make in a year.'

'Thank you,' I said.

He grinned. 'Of course, you'll have to sign for it all,' he remarked.

Not for the first time in my dealings with Walter Haverleigh, I didn't know whether to embrace him or punch him.

I hurried back to the *Luipaard*. Having signed for my gold – it was indeed a weighty bag, just as Walter had promised – and arranged with one of Gregory Tresham's servants where and when to pick up the horse and the supplies, I left my companions to it. I had to leave as quickly as I could and I didn't have a choice. I'd known that I couldn't stay where I was, even before Walter had pointed it out.

I wasn't tempted to think he had come up with what I had to admit was a good suggestion purely for my benefit. As I strode back over the packhorse bridge, I decided that he probably hadn't been thinking of me at all; or, at least, only to the extent that if I fled and was followed, I would remove the threat of our ruthlessly determined pursuers from the vicinity of the *Luipaard* and those who would very soon be busy unloading her cargo.

No, I decided as I leapt on to the *Luipaard*. From Walter Haverleigh's point of view, the sooner I mounted my fine new horse and melted away, taking my attendant dangers with me, the better.

I was planning to set out at dusk.

There were matters I must attend to first, however. Walter's offer of his serving woman to carry out some of my commissions was welcome, as it would lessen the time I would have to spend away from the *Luipaard*. However, there were some things to arrange that I was not prepared to entrust to anybody. Accordingly, while Ambroos and Hieronymus were still engaged up at Redriff Old Hall, I went to my cabin to fetch my big old gabardine cloak in preparation for slipping quietly ashore.

Young Piet looked up at me as I entered the cabin, and he wasn't quite quick enough in disguising the relief. Amy was flushed and her small face wore the fearsome frown that invariably resulted when she hadn't got her own way. Piet, aware that I'd noticed, said guiltily, 'I'm sorry, Doctor, but she wanted to go out on deck and you said not to, and when I wouldn't let her she didn't like it.'

'No need for the apology,' I reassured him. 'You did right.'

He hurried away even before I'd dismissed him.

Amy held out her arms to me. The look she gave me as I bent to pick her up suggested she didn't think much of Piet as an entertainer of small children. 'He does his best, little coney,' I whispered in her ear. 'And I came back as soon as I could.'

She waved a clenched fist at me. I didn't think she meant to hit me, and certainly not so hard; it was just that her aim was none too accurate. I arranged the straps of the sling I had fashioned for her when her increasing mobility had meant life on a ship was becoming too hazardous. It consisted of a rectangular piece of soft, supple leather with darts on the long sides to form a pouch, and four long straps, one at each corner. She would sit in the pouch and I would wind the straps over my shoulders and round my waist, pulling them tight so that she was held fast. When she had been small, she seemed more content to be facing me, but now that she was so interested in anything and everything the world had to offer, she preferred to face outwards. Once she was secured to her and my satisfaction, I wrapped my big cloak round us both, leaving just a small gap for her to look out of.

We left the ship in the secret basin and set out upriver for Southwark.

Southwark was a rough part of town. It was growing fast, and it had a reputation as a place for rebels, outlaws, the ungodly, the criminal and anyone else who preferred life not to be as tightly controlled by the government and its many agencies as it was in neighbourhoods on the north of the Thames. There had been much new building since last I was there, I noticed, and it consisted largely of insubstantial tenements let out at a high rent, thrown up cheaply, quickly and carelessly by men who had made a bit of money. The infamous brothels, theatres, bowling alleys, bear pits, cock pits and pleasure gardens still thrived, and the place still stank of the copious amounts of dog and human waste used by the tanneries. The narrow streets were as heaving with pushing, shoving people as ever, and I had not gone five paces down the first of the alleys that made up my route before I'd put a foot in something unpleasantly squelchy that instantly released a stench so foul that it made me heave.

Ah, Southwark.

It was a strange place to look for a man with whom I had done my training, and in any case I did not expect to find him at home. My hope was that his replacement, assuming there was one, would be able to help me. I was not sure what sort of help I needed; it was just that I was hungry for a friendly face. Specifically, and with no disrespect to my companions on the *Luipaard*, a friendly *English* face.

I was heading for a house set slightly apart from the teeming masses, on a street that ran behind an area of gardens that had so far avoided the building frenzy. Here, in the upper storey of a pleasant house at the far end, had once lived my friend and fellow Symposium member, Jasper Hart.

As I raised the brass knocker and banged on the door, I wished I hadn't asked him to take my place in the Devon countryside. I wished he was there now, hurrying down the stairs in answer to my knock, ready and willing to listen to me, to perceive with quick understanding what I needed, and unhesitatingly, like the friend he was, offer his help.

I had only myself to blame for the fact that he wasn't. Which did nothing to improve my mood as, stroking Amy's silky head to soothe her protest at the sudden cessation of movement, I composed my expression into something pleasant to face whatever fellow physician opened the door.

The lock was turned, the bolts were pulled back – I didn't imagine anyone left their properties unsecured hereabouts – and the door opened a crack. Eyes peered out, and Jasper's voice said cautiously, 'What do you want?'

I pushed back my hood and said, 'It's me. Gabe. What the hell are *you* doing here?'

It was no way to greet someone whose help I was about to demand, and I knew I didn't deserve the solicitude with which my friend ushered me inside and up the stairs to his apartments. He took me into a small and cosy room with a good fire going, and pushed me into a comfortable chair. In the first flurry of his astonished questions and my rapid answers, he ascertained that I was on the run and needed to get out of London that very day, and that somehow in the course of my two-and-a-half year absence I had managed to acquire not only an ancient, important and unbelievably valuable item of treasure that its owner very much wanted back, but also a daughter.

He took Amy out of her sling and on to his lap, and, responding to the attention, she treated him to her full range of charms and turned him into an adoring slave within minutes.

I realized, watching him making faces at her that had her chortling with laughter, that he was uneasy. Guilty, even. Thinking that this might have something to do with the fact that he was here, in his old lodgings in one of the better parts of Southwark, and not at Rosewyke looking after my patients, I waited till he fell silent and said, 'Well?'

He shot me a quick furtive look, then dropped his eyes. 'I'm sorry, Gabe. I really am. *But I had no choice,* I'm . . .' The words came out in a rush of anguish, and his desperate eyes pleaded with me. Then abruptly he stopped – it seemed to take an effort – and, in a calmer tone, watching me closely, he said, 'I must explain, must I not, why I am no longer at Rosewyke.' He paused, frowning, then went on, 'I know I've let you down, as well as leaving your dear sister, and Judyth, and Dr Thorn, with the work I should be there to do. But I just couldn't stand that *bastard* any longer!'

He had uttered the word with such vehemence that Amy stopped her chatter and looked curiously at him.

'Sorry,' he muttered.

'When you say that bastard, you mean Maudsley Cheverell, I take it?' I asked.

'Of course!' He shot me an accusing look. 'I can't believe you hired him! What were you *thinking*, Gabe?'

I hadn't been thinking; that was the trouble. I had engaged Maudsley Cheverell when my mind had been almost exclusively engaged with the thrill of imminent departure. He'd been a physician, he'd been young and healthy, he'd been willing. I hadn't looked any further.

'Was he really awful?' I said cautiously. I sensed I was inviting some uncomfortable truths.

My caution hadn't been misplaced. I listened as what sounded like an itinerary of every single instance of Cheverell's poor behaviour, lack of expertise, tactlessness and inconsideration poured out of Jasper's mouth. 'And nobody liked him!' he said in what I hoped very much was his conclusion. 'The sick and the wounded managed to work out how to avoid him – which of course added to everyone else's work – and Theo swore he'd have nothing more to do with the wretched man after the time he summoned him out to a remote farm to view a body!'

I didn't dare ask what Cheverell had done to arouse Theo's animosity.

'I'm sorry,' I said inadequately. 'Thank you for staying as long as you did.' I paused. 'Er . . . how long *did* you stay?'

He made a face. 'I stuck it out till the middle of August. *This* August,' he added with a wry smile.

'Then what happened?' I demanded.

'He punched me.'

'Oh.'

There was an awkward silence. I wondered if I should apologize again, but in view of what Jasper had just said, it seemed rather inadequate.

Then he said, 'Tell me how I can help, Gabe.'

And, looking at him, I sensed that this unexpectedly generous offer – which I wasn't at all sure I deserved – was his way of making amends for having abandoned the household at Rosewyke.

So I told him what I wanted him to do.

Jasper and I returned to the *Luipaard* early in the evening, Jasper mounted on his grey gelding, and he waited while I went on board to collect my bags. I had arranged for the bulk of my gear to go back with the ship and her company to the berth on the island, where I would pick it up when I went to receive my earnings from Walter at Cheverstone. I went to the space under my bunk where I had carefully stowed my doctor's bag, the parcel containing the gold statue and my small pack of personal belongings.

I sought out Ambroos to take my leave, and he greeted me with a wide smile. He was, I observed, more than a little drunk. 'There will be a tidy sum awaiting you at Sir Walter's house when you finally get there,' he said. 'After you left this morning, those gentlemen who know the value of what we have brought home for them calculated a rough estimate of what they expect to make when they sell it.'

'It's a good profit?'

The smile widened and he nodded. 'Oh, yes.'

We shook hands and wished each other good fortune until we met again. He poured out measures of his beloved schnapps and we drank each other's health. I had been looking around for Hieronymus, and as I put down my empty glass, I asked where he was.

'He went down to meet the groom who is bringing your horse,' Ambroos replied. 'Said that it was not wise to leave a valuable animal in isolated woodlands with only one man to guard it.'

As I went ashore to rejoin Jasper, I reflected what a good friend Hieronymus was to me. And always had been, once I had put the manner of our original meeting firmly behind me. He had apologized profusely for deceiving me, drugging me and abducting me; using the age-old excuse, he said he had merely been following orders.

Jasper and I slipped quietly away from the secret basin. Briefly I paused for a last look at the *Luipaard*, and then we were under the cover of the band of trees that surrounded and concealed the beautiful ship. We pushed on down the rough, faint track. It was not far to the place where I was to pick up my horse and the supplies promised by Walter Haverleigh. I hoped he had been as good as his word, and also that whoever had done the purchasing for him understood the needs of a small child on a long journey.

We came to an opening in the trees and emerged into a glade, almost entirely circled with close-growing alder and birch. The horse was there waiting for us. It was a fine chestnut gelding, some sixteen hands, whose blood lines showed in the neat head, the intelligent eyes and the slightly concave nose.

He was all alone.

There was no sign of either the groom from Redriff Old Hall or Hieronymus, and it was clear from first sight that the horse did not like the deep silence of the shadowy, spooky woods. His ears were back, his head was up and there were patches of sweat on his smooth coat. Hoping to soothe his jittery nerves, I walked over to him, put out my hand and spoke quiet, calming words. He studied me for a few anxious moments, then bent his neck and dropped his nose into my open hand. I patted the warm, slightly damp coat, running my palm up under his thick mane, and he gave a soft wicker. He was a fine animal; Walter Haverleigh had been generous.

There were a pair of leather bags attached to the saddle, and, opening them, I found in the first one a generous supply of food – bread, biscuits, smoked meats, a cheese, some fruit – and drink: there was a bottle of brandy as well as a full water bottle. The second bag contained items for my child, and, again, Walter – or whoever had gone shopping for him – had not stinted. I noted in passing that this unknown person had been in haste, for the packing was rough and one of the strap buckles hadn't been fastened. Tucked into a pocket on the front of the second saddle bag I found a note: *The horse is called Spice.*

I smiled as I tucked it away.

I fastened my medical bag and the parcel containing the statue to the back of the saddle, using the leather straps provided. Amy was secure on my chest in her sling, my pack was on my back, and I was ready to mount up and go.

I wondered why Hieronymus had not waited. Did he not want to bid me farewell? The groom had probably gone back to the hall – maybe he thought he could leave the guarding of the horse to Hieronymus – but I was puzzled not to find my friend there. And, I admitted to myself, not a little concerned.

'I thought you said there would be men waiting with the horse?' Jasper said quietly.

'I fully believed there would be,' I replied.

I was torn. The need to get away and be on the road was pressing with rapidly escalating urgency. But then Hieronymus ought to be there . . .

Where was he?

I had been about to loose the reins and untether my horse, but I stopped. 'I'm going to have a quick look round,' I said to Jasper. 'It *will* be quick; I promise.' Maybe, I was thinking, Hieronymus had sat down against a tree and gone to sleep. I began a careful circling of the glade, peering between the trees. Still on his horse, Jasper started to do the same on the other side.

And suddenly Jasper said, 'There's someone over there.' I spun round to look. He pointed. 'Sitting on that seat under the oak tree.'

I turned to look where he was pointing. I made out a wooden bench, simply made, no more than a plank to sit on and a low backrest. It had been placed in the spot where the trees began to thin out, so that anybody sitting there could gaze out at Redriff Old Hall over beyond the grass.

I walked nearer.

The man sat utterly still. The light was sufficient for me to see his face and I recognized one of the grooms from Gregory Tresham's stable yard. He sat upright, leaning against the low back of the bench, his hands in his lap. His eyes were open. He didn't call out.

I went closer.

The man's eyes stared out unblinkingly.

I saw what I thought was a thin ribbon round his neck.

It wasn't ribbon, it was blood, dripping red. It went across his throat in a line that was perfectly parallel to the bench he sat on.

Jasper had dismounted and hurried to join me. I hadn't heard him approach, but all at once he was there beside me. He had come, I guessed, to offer his help. We were both physicians, and we should not blanch and be shocked into impotent horror when confronted by dreadful sights.

But, as very soon became apparent, there was absolutely nothing we could do.

As our combined footfalls caused some small tremor in the earth, the slight motion must have minutely shifted the body.

The head rolled off.

It was a nightmare scene. I heard Jasper give a gasp of pure horror, and then he gave two or three dry retches.

Someone with an unbelievably high level of swordsmanship and an incredibly sharp blade had sliced right through the man's neck with a single strike, severing the head so swiftly and neatly that it had remained where it was on the top of his neck. There wasn't even much blood; the poor man's heart must have stopped almost on the instant.

Filled now with desperate urgency, I said to Jasper, 'We must go. *Now!*' Clutching my child to my chest, I ran back to the chestnut gelding and swung up into the saddle.

Jasper was still staring at the dead man. He was trembling. 'But . . .'

'He's *dead*, Jasper,' I said. 'We will be too if we don't leave now.'

He turned to stare at me, his face chalk white. He began to say something – 'I didn't know, I swear I had no idea they . . .' and then, breaking off, gave a moan of deep horror and fear. Then he ran ahead of me to mount his horse and set off down the shadowy path beneath the trees. I was close behind.

We had gone only a few yards when Jasper's horse stopped so abruptly that Jasper tumbled off. Hastily I drew up the chestnut gelding and dismounted, for as he landed Jasper had emitted an awful sound, and I was very afraid he was badly injured. I crouched beside him, trying to see what he had done to himself, but with a hard push he shoved me away and abruptly I fell over backwards. My hands went instinctively out to either side of me and my right hand landed in something warm and wet.

Blood.

And in a voice that shook with dread, Jasper said, pointing behind me, 'Is that your friend?'

Hieronymus lay on his back, sightless eyes gazing up into the branches. There was an expression of mild interest on his face, as if he'd been reciting to himself the names of the different trees.

In that terrible moment, there was a small comfort in the realization that his death had come to him with such speed that he cannot have known much about it and had probably felt no pain.

Or so I fervently hoped.

He had been struck on the head, and the blow had fallen on the top of his skull and slightly to the rear: he wouldn't even have seen his killer. The weapon must have been fearsome. Something very heavy, wielded with great skill, so that the one strike sufficed. A mace, perhaps? It had crushed poor Hieronymus's skull like a clumsy man attacking a boiled egg, and the repercussions of that deadly blow had collapsed the bone right down to the forehead, which looked slightly dented . . .

'Gabe, *come on!*' Jasper's voice, high-pitched with fear, recalled me. I turned to him; he was up on his horse again. 'I know it is terrible, and he was your companion and you cared for him, but *we have to go* – we *must*, for if we stay here *they'll kill us too!*' The last words were a squeak.

He was right.

I drew out the folds of Hieronymus's cloak and spread the heavy cloth over his face and his ruined head. I placed my hand briefly on his breast and said quietly, 'Goodbye, my friend.'

Then I swung up on to the chestnut's back and followed Jasper off up the track.

ELEVEN

The darkness closed in as night fell down around us.
I had no idea where we were, what route we were taking
away from the abandoned creek, the *Luipaard* and my
dead friend. I noticed that we kept to narrow, out-of-the-way and
largely deserted tracks and lanes as we hurried on, and I spared
a thankful prayer for Jasper Hart and his knowledge of the hidden
paths and byways of the lawless wilderness that made up that
area of London to the south of the Thames.

I had nothing to do but follow where he led and keep as quiet
as I could; Amy, thankfully, had quickly gone to sleep, soothed
by the chestnut gelding's smooth, steady pace. I did not know
the way, and had no suggestions or advice to offer. I wished I
had, for riding in total silence alone with my thoughts was the
last thing I wanted. I tried to halt my speculating; tried to cut
off my powers of reasoning and stop attempting to work out
what could have happened back there in the woods. Without
success; my mind was like a bag of squirrels, and in the end I
gave up and let my thoughts run.

Our pursuers had discovered where the *Luipaard* lay hidden.
I had no idea how. What had allowed them to find us so quickly?
Was one of their two remaining vessels hidden away in some
discreet mooring on the Thames, its dark-clad, secretive company
moving like shadows as they set about their murderous business?
Why hadn't they guessed the horse was for me and waited under
the trees until I arrived? Had they always known where the
Luipaard was bound? No – that was impossible, surely, because
men like Walter Haverleigh and Gregory Tresham did not share
such information and neither did any man in their employ.

The useless thoughts went round and round in my head until
in the end, despairing, I muttered softly, 'Stop.' Our pursuers
had found our hiding place and attacked. Aroto Tagauchi's long
arm had reached out from Kyushu all the way to the south bank
of the Thames. We had escaped. That was enough, for now.

We rode on. The night was advancing – from somewhere a long way off I heard a church clock strike eleven – and we hadn't seen a soul for some time. We were not nearly far enough away from human activity, however. Huddles of houses and ill-con- structed buildings appeared regularly over on our right, between us and the river; there were bursts of drunken laughter and shouting, and once a scream of agony.

Just after that appalling sound had riven the night, Jasper turned to me and said softly, 'We are doing well. Quite soon now we shall leave the inhabited places behind us and head out into the countryside.' He gave me a swift, encouraging smile.

'Good,' I muttered. I tried to return the smile but failed.

We rode on.

I felt deeply guilty that I had involved my friend. He had escaped from my life once when he abandoned his role as my replacement down in Devon, leaving Celia, Judyth and Dr Thorn to cope with the full load of work, *and* the despicable Maudsley Cheverell into the bargain. If Jasper had agreed to come with me out of guilt because of that desertion, then how much more guilt should I bear, first for landing him in a job that he came to hate and second for making him my companion as I fled from ruth- lessly efficient killers?

But I couldn't have travelled alone. There was another, far more vital reason, besides the fact that I could never have got out of London without him: if they caught me they would kill me, and there had to be someone to look after my child.

Signs of habitation were definitely thinning out now. It was too soon for optimism, however; too early to start thinking that our swift and secret flight had thrown our pursuers off our trail. So I told myself, but all the same, my spirits were starting to rise. In the September darkness, the scents of the night were becoming apparent now that the stench of London was fading. There was a sort of magic in the air, and I wondered – irritated with myself even as I did so – whether it was true what the legend said, that the Chrysanthemum Tiger really did bestow protection. I reached behind the saddle and felt the outline of the sturdy wooden box. I gave it a gentle shake, and felt the very slight movement of the Tiger within. I imagined it giving a snarl of protest, the curved, blood-tipped claws extending, the scimitar-shaped incisors gleaming as it tensed to attack . . .

Pushing my folly away (I refused to admit that there was also an element of fear), I thought about how lucky I had just been.

Jasper was meant to be in Devon, I thought. It was by pure good fortune that he'd been back in Southwark when I went looking. Was that simple chance, or was it the Tiger, protecting us? And hadn't it already done so, again and again? All those times when the *Luipaard* had been forced to fight for survival on the seas of the South Atlantic. The countless occasions when we had put into port in search of much-needed supplies and found exactly what we were after in the first place we tried. The badly broken limbs of three members of the ship's company that had healed swiftly and straight. Sudden mysterious fevers that proved to be neither fatal nor infectious . . .

I raised my right hand and, making a fist, punched myself in the head. Hard enough to hurt. Then, forcing my thoughts right away from superstition and whimsy and back to the demands and dangers of the present, I tried to recall what I knew of Jasper's background and whether it was likely that his ability to find a safe and secret route to Devon would extend beyond our southern circumnavigation of London.

I thought hard for some time, but all I could remember was that his kin were farmers. Nudging the chestnut gelding briefly to a trot, I rode up level with Jasper.

'What is it?' he asked anxiously, voice low.

'Nothing.' I waved my arm, demonstrating the utter silence all around and the total lack of light other than that of the bright moon. 'I wanted to congratulate you on how well you've led us out of the city, and . . . er, and . . .'

He chuckled softly. 'And ask whether my extraordinary ability to find the unpeopled tracks will extend as we leave London behind?'

I smiled in the darkness. 'Yes.'

'It will. You see, my father and his forebears have farmed in the North Surrey hills for generations,' he said. 'My mother's kin farmed on the South Downs near Petersfield,' he went on, 'and my childhood was spent exploring the countryside around both these ancestral habitations, so I know both areas well. Once we leave the Thames behind, I'm reasonably confident of finding a route that will wind through woods and along forgotten tracks all the way from Windsor to Winchester, and we'll be unlucky if we encounter more than a handful of people.' He was looking at me closely. 'After that,' he added, 'we'll be getting close to your part of the world, and you will have to be our guide. We're heading for Devon, I assume?'

'Yes, of course,' I muttered absently. I was thinking about what he'd just said. From Windsor to Winchester; it was quite a claim. I was about to remark that it was surely many years since he'd explored those old ways, and how could he be so sure he wouldn't have forgotten them, when he spoke again.

'I take it, Gabe, that you have no idea how we've reached this point?'

'None at all,' I agreed.

He smiled. 'If you'd thought to look up at the stars, you'd have seen that we've been travelling south-west, deviating sometimes but always maintaining that general direction. We cut off a great loop of the river, and now' – he looked around – 'I'd say we were out in the countryside somewhere to the south-east of Richmond. We'll keep to the road' – he pointed ahead to where the track went under trees – 'because although it will lead between many smallholdings and farms, hard-working people go to bed early and they'll have already barred their doors and extinguished their lights.'

Acting on the unspoken sense that we were still too close to the populated regions to risk travelling through the day, we rode until dawn and then began searching for a suitable spot where we could feed and water the horses, eat a much-needed meal, and then sleep through the middle of the day. We had left Richmond far behind us, and the river was away to our right as it made a long, slow bend that had Windsor at its apex. We had reached Bracknell Forest at daybreak, having covered some thirty miles, and now, deep into its tracks and small trails, we felt we'd come across as safe a place as we were likely to find. There was a stream, running at the bottom of a steep bank with a wide strip of gravelly beach beneath oak, beech and alders steadily dropping their leaves. There was plenty of room for our two horses and, after removing their saddles and bridles and giving them a rub-down, we left them down there. Although it seemed unlikely that they would stray, we hobbled them anyway. On the bank above, an ancient yew with a vast trunk offered concealment. Jasper watched with eyebrows raised in surprise as I unfastened the two leather bags and the wooden box from my saddle and lugged them in under the down-spreading branches of the yew, but I merely shrugged. He must have known I had the Chrysanthemum Tiger with me, but something made me reluctant to speak of it, even with him, unless I had to.

I was still wary of it. Sometimes when I stretched out a hand towards it, I could sense the same invisible barrier I had felt at the start, as if the statue itself was keeping me away. But that morning I noticed that there was only a brief initial resistance before I was allowed to pick up the crate. Although I knew it was fanciful, I wondered if the Chrysanthemum Tiger was beginning to adapt to being in my possession.

Not yours. The thought came fast, loud inside my head. *Your daughter's.*

Of course. My daughter was Aroto Tagauchi's great-grandchild. She was of the blood.

I unpacked the provisions that Walter Haverleigh had supplied, and my child ate as greedily as Jasper and I did. She had half a dozen teeth now, and the range of what she was prepared to tackle had increased greatly. I had feared she would be wakeful, that I would have to stay awake with her, and that, so as not to disturb Jasper's well-earned rest, we would have to move away from our camp; Amy had become a chatteret, even if her utterances made little sense, and she was a bright child, with laughter never far away.

Fortunately – for I was exhausted – after a short time of exploring the bank of the stream together and throwing innumerable stones into the water, abruptly she gave a huge yawn and her head started to nod. I realized that, although she had slept for the first couple of hours of our night journey, she had been awake for the remainder of the time; occasionally I'd had to hold her tightly as she spotted something that interested her and tried to wriggle round to keep on looking.

I crept back under the yew tree, lay down among my blankets, clutched Amy's sturdy little body close and spread my cloak over us. Keeping absolutely still, barely breathing, I waited to see if she would settle. Presently her soft breathing began to include a regular little snore, barely audible, and I knew she was fast asleep. Wasting no time – I had no idea how long it would last, how soon this alarming change to her routine would jerk her awake and alert again – I shut my eyes and joined her.

We must all have been more fatigued than we had realized; it was well after noon when I woke, to find Jasper propped up amid his bedding, stretching and yawning, Amy on his lap as he tried to interest her in a crust of bread. I watched them, laughing as Jasper pretended to eat the bread himself, hid it behind his back and then, with an exaggerated expression of surprise, rediscovered it. As Amy batted it out of his hand for the third time he said, 'We need some fresh milk to soften this bread. Babies like milk sops, don't they?'

'We'll stop at the first farm we pass,' I replied. 'Let's hope the farmer's wife has a light hand with a loaf, and that they have cheese and some cured bacon to sell as well. But we'll have to be careful. We're still too close to London to be safe.'

The mood under our yew tree in the beautiful stretch of woodland had been cheerful until I spoke. At the reminder of our continuing peril, however, Jasper's expression straightened and gently he stood Amy on her feet and helped her totter over to me. 'We'd better be on our way,' he said quietly. 'The track goes on under the trees for several miles, and if we reach open country before dusk, we'll wait until dark before moving on.'

The days and nights took on a pattern, and all of us adapted to it swiftly. We would sleep in the day and ride through the night, and I was constantly surprised at how totally alone we were in those hours. My logic told me there were farms, cottages, hamlets and villages all around, that people lived and worked close to the paths and tracks we rode, and that in daytime their presence would be all too evident. At night we could have been the only three humans left alive.

We made our way along the trails of the North Downs, keeping to the high ground. At one point Jasper drew rein and sat for some moments staring down into a pleasant valley where well-tended farmland was interspersed with woodland, and a little river ran through soft green lowlands. I drew up beside him, and presently he said, 'That's my father's farm.' He pointed to a clutch of low buildings forming a square around a yard and said, 'The farmhouse is on the right.'

It was late in the evening – we had only just set out – and I could make out the lighted windows of the farmhouse. I thought Jasper must be full of regret that because of our need for secrecy he could not ride down there, burst in on his surprised parents, introduce me and my child and smile with happy pride as his mother gasped in delight and pressed good food upon us and his father broached a barrel of beer.

I guessed that must be why suddenly he looked so sad.

The weather stayed fair, although even in a few days we noticed that the nights were becoming colder and were glad that we slept in daytime, where staying still for several hours did not risk getting so chilled that it would have been hard to warm up again without a fire. Our progress was good, and after a week that felt like a month, we were looking down on Winchester.

I did not enter a town or even a village on that leg of the journey, for we were still too close to London, and, for all I knew, the long arm of Aroto Tagauchi might have many more than the standard one hand and five fingers and all of them might be scuttling spider-like over the land searching for me. As we steadily increased the distance between us and London, we began our night's journey earlier, in the late afternoon, and we would stop for food at some village or hamlet just as it was beginning to close its doors. I would wait somewhere out of sight with the horses, my child released for once from the confines of the sling and free to crawl on the ground and practise walking, and gradually the few tottering steps she managed before she fell on her bottom turned into a confident trot whose speed rapidly increased.

It was Jasper who hunted for provisions.

The times of waiting for him to return became a sort of torture. I was sure he was as quick as possible. He would be well aware, I reasoned, that even the briefest absence would feel like hours, bearing in mind what was at stake if we were discovered. My thoughts would run away with me, I would imagine someone catching hold of him, saying, *Jasper Hart! You travel with Gabriel*

Taverner, and there is a price on your heads! Wait right where you are, I must report your presence to those who are searching for you!

It didn't happen. Jasper always came back, sometimes with an armful of fine fare and looking cheerful, sometimes looking anxious, and once, returning with only a stale loaf and a jug of milk that was on the turn, looking guilty, although he was not to blame for the little hamlet's lack of decent provisions.

We rode on.

I was quite sure that the pursuers who had followed the *Luipaard* and her precious treasures all the way from Japan had not given up. Even though they gave no sign, they would be hunting for us. One, two, three parties of dogged men, perhaps more, for the master who drove them on had unimaginable wealth and, in my constant anxiety, I imagined our pursuers recruiting local men who knew the roads and tracks of the south of England. Ten, a dozen, twenty, thirty of them, and all of them paid so generously that they followed their orders enthusiastically, efficiently, and without question.

The pursuers knew I would go west. I hoped and prayed that they did not know the country well enough to understand there were so many routes that led to Devon that it would have taken an army to cover every one.

We woke one afternoon in a small copse, situated on the final western shoulder of the South Downs. Winchester was below us to the right. Amy was irritable, and we were unenthusiastically eating a meal of stale bread and some thick slices of over-salty gammon. I was wishing we had a hot meal before us – rich beef stew, or roast pork with crackling, spring vegetables and gravy – and were sitting in comfort at a sturdy old oak table with shining silver and glittering glasses full of fine wine.

Breaking a long and, for my part, glum silence, suddenly Jasper said, 'Do the pursuers know what you look like?'

I thought. 'No-o,' I said slowly. Then, more confidently, 'No. I'm sure they don't.' They were sailors, I told myself, and it was fair to assume they wouldn't have been around when I was living in Romeu Silvestre's house or busy amassing Walter Haverleigh's cargo. 'They could have seen me on the deck of the *Luipaard*,

I suppose, but it was only once that one of the three ships came close enough to make out individual faces, and that was immediately before the *Luipaard*'s guns blasted it to kindling and killed them all. Why?'

He didn't answer straight away. Then he said diffidently, 'Oh, I was thinking about your friend. The man who was killed.'

'Hieronymus,' I said dully. 'His name was Hieronymus Petrarcus. He was a Dutchman.' I closed my eyes, for suddenly my head was full of images and memories. It hurt.

Jasper bowed his head. For some moments he did not speak, and I was grateful for his tact. Then he repeated softly, 'Hieronymus. Yes. You were expecting to find him guarding the horse, you said.' I nodded. 'Well, surely that's what he was doing when they killed him. I am wondering if, coming across him in a place they expected to find you, the pursuers assumed he was you.'

'But why should they kill me?' I asked. Stupidly: in my defence, I was still preoccupied with my memories.

'Because you have what they want,' Jasper said patiently. 'They had to kill the man they thought was you before they could search for what they so badly wanted. *Want,*' he added dryly, correcting himself, 'for I do not imagine that the desire has lessened with the length of the pursuit.'

I barely heard.

For I was remembering the leather saddle bags, the untidy packing, the unfastened strap. Not the result of haste or carelessness by whoever had filled the bags, as I had thought at the time, but because of the unheeding hands of whoever had subsequently searched through the contents looking for a golden tiger.

They had been there. They'd discovered the horse that Walter Haverleigh had left for me and the bags of provisions supplied for the journey. They'd had their hands on everything.

The murderous rage that filled me made me sweat. I waited for my fury to dissipate, because there was no room for logical thought until it did.

We got away, I reminded myself. Thanks to Jasper, we evaded the clutching hands of those who wanted to find me, take back the Chrysanthemum Tiger, abduct my child and dispose of me. I did not dwell on the last, for I was sure those loyal and efficient

foot soldiers in the employ of Aroto Tagauchi possessed a remark-
able repertoire of agonizing and long-drawn-out methods of
snuffing out a life. Especially that of someone like me, whose
perceived insults to their lord were too lengthy, too dreadful, too
unspeakable, to enumerate.

After a while I returned to the gammon and the stale bread.
They tasted even worse than before.

We reached Romsey and the river Test, and went on across the
New Forest. Camping one clear, cold early October day to the north
of Lymington, we could see the Isle of Wight across the Solent.
I wondered if the *Luipaard* was home yet, and if the fortune I'd
been promised for my part in her voyage was now locked up in
some strong box in Walter Haverleigh's manor house.

The Downs of Wiltshire and Dorset, over the river Otter, and
for several hours of one night we took a wide, circuitous route
around Exeter. Devon at last.

Now we were nearing my home, and it was my turn to lead
us on the ancient tracks, as old as England's history, that led up
over the great and sparsely populated wildness of Dartmoor. I
turned to speak to Jasper. 'We should search out a good camp
somewhere up in the middle of the moor,' I suggested, 'and stay
there long enough to move from our present routine of travelling
by night and sleeping by day to something fitting in better with
the rest of the population.'

He had moved up to ride beside me. It was soon after dawn,
the silent moor stretched out around and below us, and it was
cold up there among the high tors.

He frowned. 'Why should we do that?' he asked.

I tried to explain. 'Oh . . . because very soon now we'll be
among my own people. My family, my good friends. Men and
women I trust with my life.' I glanced down at Amy. 'With *her*
life,' I murmured.

I didn't think I needed to say any more. But, glancing at Jasper,
I spotted a strange expression on his face, although it changed
to a wry smile even as I looked. He shrugged, seemed about to
speak and then stopped.

I knew – thought I knew – what was the matter.

'I don't suppose anyone blamed you for leaving as you did,'

I said gently. 'From what you say, Maudsley Cheverell was an unbearable man, and I am very sorry I imposed him on you all. Yes, I expect Celia and Judyth' – my heart gave a lurch as I said their names – 'and old Dr Thorn cursed you as they tried to cope with the extra work, but I'm quite sure they understood that you had to go, especially after the wretched man broke your nose.'

'Not sure he *broke* it,' Jasper muttered.

'I believe that I can confidently promise you a warm welcome,' I said firmly. 'Good God, Jasper,' I added when he did not reply, 'the circumstances have changed dramatically now! You have brought me and my child out of London and all the way across the south of England. You have guided us, found the hidden ways, and most important of all, you've been here and you still are in case the worst should happen and I'm taken or killed, and it would be you who would save my . . .'

I stopped. I hadn't meant to mention that other, vital reason why I'd needed his company.

He was smiling that strange smile again. 'Who would save your daughter,' he said very quietly. 'Yes, Gabe, I know. I realized that as soon as I understood the peril you are in.' Then he drew in his horse and resumed his place behind me.

So that I had no time to question, or even fully to register, the anguish I'd briefly seen on his face.

We found a good camp. It was probably an ancient shepherd's hut, for there were the ruins beside it of low walls that could have once been a sheep pen. It had been placed deep in the lee of a high outcrop of rocks by someone who knew the moors and understood the spite of the winds that blow so hard, so relentlessly and so cold that if you cannot find shelter from them, they will freeze your blood and eventually strip the flesh from your bones.

The hut had three sound walls and one dilapidated one, which we repaired with dry, crackly bracken that had already turned rusty orange. The horses were tethered in the remains of the pen and provided with fodder and water. Once we had shoved the door as close to shut as could be contrived, we felt it was safe to light a fire; there were more than enough holes in the roof to allow the smoke out. We brought in all our luggage and spread out our bedding, and Jasper set out the food while I built a fire. It was not long before I had a blaze going. I let it burn for a while, for we had plenty of wood, there was a great deal more outside, and after so long without the comfort of a fire, I reckoned we needed it. Eventually I tamped it down. Jasper had prepared slices of bread, which we toasted on sticks; while they were still hot we spread them with golden butter, slices of cheese and thin slivers of onion, returning the slices to the heat to melt the cheese and soften the onion. It might not have been the delicious hot meal I'd imagined as we camped above Winchester, but after so long eating cold, indifferent food, it was a feast.

We deviated from our habit of settling down to sleep as soon as we had eaten, and instead spent the middle of the day taking in our surroundings and catching up with repairs to our equipment. After so many days on the road, our garments and belongings were in need of attention, and the horses had certainly earned a careful inspection, a thorough grooming and a rest. We ate again in the early evening, then lay back in our bedding.

Amy, curled up beside me, quickly fell asleep. Jasper was soon snoring gently. It took me a while to get comfortable, and several times I found myself checking to make sure the wooden box containing the Chrysanthemum Tiger was safe behind my head. Perhaps it was that inexplicable need to make sure it was where it should be that led to my dream; maybe the Tiger had been reaching out to me.

I thought I had woken up but I couldn't have done, because the scene that revealed itself to me was very far from the interior of a half-ruined shepherd's hut on Dartmoor. I was in a room with wooden floors and paper screens, one of which had been drawn aside to reveal a beautifully tended garden. There was a sweet smell of sandalwood; smoke curled up from an incense stick. There was little in the way of furnishings. The room's appeal was in its simplicity and lack of clutter, and the small number of beautiful, precious objects spoke all the louder for the lack of competition.

An old man sat on the floor on a thick cushion. He was dressed in gorgeous garments, their folds arranged so carefully around him that they gave the appearance of being pressed in place. His face was lean, the cheekbones high and prominent, and the long, thin strands of hair emerging beneath his black cap were silver grey. At first he sat very still, and then as I watched him he raised a bony hand and beckoned.

A second man came forward on his knees. He bore a large wrapped object in his arms, and from the tension in his body, I knew it was heavy. His head was bent, so that he could not look up at the old man. When he was a couple of paces away, he stopped and bowed low, forehead to the floor, repeating the gesture several times. The old man muttered a single word, and he straightened up. He still did not raise his eyes. The old man said something else, and the man, visibly trembling, carefully laid the wrapped object on the floor and slowly, reverently, uncovered it.

The room was dimly lit, but now it was as if a high, bright, midday sun suddenly beamed down. The light was hard white, and as it hit the object on the floor, a burst of gold fire exploded. I saw movement, and I heard the deep-throated growl of a wild animal. Now the golden fire was twisting and turning, fast, sinuous, and the lean, heavily muscled body was everywhere at once. I tried to cry out, for now the creature was rapidly increasing in size and its brilliant green eyes were sweeping the room and I knew it could see me. Now so dazzled that it was hard to make out the details, I thought I saw it leap towards the raised dais at the end of the room. There it paused, poised as if about to pounce, so vast that it dominated the room, its power so overwhelming that the two men were struck dumb.

Then the old man said a word.

I did not know what it was. It was in a language unfamiliar to me. But my dream self recognized it for what it was: a word of power.

The golden creature heard it too. Slowly it turned its head on the heavily muscled neck and its green eyes met those of the old man. It raised one forepaw and then the other. The long cream chrysanthemum claws extended and their shape began to change subtly. Diamonds dazzled along each one, and the rubies set into the wickedly sharp tips flared like fire.

The old man raised his hand and pointed a forefinger with a long, curving yellow nail straight at the man lying prostrate and sobbing in terror before him.

And the creature sprang.

I saw a great spray of blood curve up in an arc and I heard the crunch of huge teeth on bone. Glittering claws rose briefly, dripping blood. Aghast and numb, horror held me so tight that I could not move. I heard a voice speak words that sounded like a proclamation; the only one I recognized was *Tagauchi*.

I knew I had to move, for very soon the creature would begin to hunt for more prey. But my body would not obey. And then I heard a soft little sound. I looked down and saw Amy crouching beside me.

The gold creature had finished with the man and was stealthily walking towards us. Its tail was twitching slowly from side to side, and its eyes were fierce with intelligence. With *knowing*. Very slowly, hardly moving, I shifted my position so that I was directly in front of my child. I extended my arms to either side, and my body stiffened as if I thought that tense muscles might better resist the powerful jaws and the knife-like claws.

It came on. Its mouth was partly open, and there was blood on its muzzle and dripping from its teeth.

I prayed.

I closed my eyes.

I sensed a huge body right in front of me. I felt its hot breath.

And then I heard my child laugh.

My eyes flew open and I saw her. She was standing up, and her arms were around the creature's neck. It was leaning into her, its great body curving protectively round her. For a few moments they were too fascinated by each other to notice anything or anyone else, but then slowly the huge animal turned its head a little and the green eyes stared straight into mine.

As I waited for it to strike, I thought I would slump to the floor in dread.

I went on waiting.

And presently the creature turned away and nudged its face against my child's little body. She laughed again, a sound of sheer delight.

Then the laughter turned to soft, deep breathing and the Tiger disappeared.

I opened my eyes and my mind flooded with relief as I realized I was back in the shepherd's hut.

Amy was fast asleep, the fire was glowing, Jasper was curled up in his blankets and still snoring. As the wild beating of my heart slowly returned to normal, I wondered what the dream had signified. It *was* just a dream, I thought. How could it be anything else?

But as I turned over and tried to get to sleep again, I couldn't banish the thought that I'd just been given a glimpse into the distant past. I had seen the moment when the skilled craftsman who had made the Chrysanthemum Tiger had presented it to the first of the Tagauchis, only to be fed to the creature as his reward. The horror of that – I kept seeing his dark-haired head inside those huge jaws – was only mitigated by the fact that the Tiger had acted very differently with my child. It had curled its great body around her, as if she had been its own young and in need of its protection. And by the steady way in which it had looked at me and then calmly turned away, I concluded – perhaps more in hope than expectation – that it was showing it accepted me too.

But it was, I reminded myself as sleep took me, just a dream.

I was awake before Amy or Jasper. I slipped outside to answer a call of nature and, looking around, I guessed it was an hour or so before dawn. The ground rose up sharply beyond the rocky outcrop that sheltered the old hut, and now, inspired, I trotted over to its foot and swiftly climbed to the top.

I turned to the west, and the dawn light sent my shadow across the ground in front of me. I could make out the winding course of the Tavy valley in the distance, the white mist rising from the water forming and reforming as it constantly shifted. The river ran close to Tavy St Luke and right past Rosewyke; memories and images of my home and the people I loved filled my mind until they became all but unendurable. Soon, I thought, very soon now I shall be among them, and . . .

Slowly at first, then with the hammer blows of a rock fall, the depths of my folly dawned on me.

God, what had I *done*?

Hieronymus's terrible death back at the Southwark creek had unnerved me, but I could not offer that as an excuse for having been panicked into unthinking flight. Because that was precisely

what it was: my one thought had been to get my child and myself
– and the Tiger – out of danger, and Jasper's knowledge of the
secret ways around and away from London had been the answer
to a prayer. My friend had promised to get us from Windsor to
Winchester along tracks where we would barely meet a soul, and
he had made good his promise. Then as his knowledge ran out
it had been my turn: out of the recent past I heard him say diffidently, *We're heading for Devon, I assume?* and my unthinking
reply, *Yes, of course.*

Great God, did I assume nobody would guess I'd run to the
place I knew best?

And I'd brought us here, to Dartmoor. Nearly home. The last
place in the kingdom where I should have come. For if just one
person knew it was my home – and surely far too many *did* know
– then our situation now was exactly what it had been aboard
the *Luipaard*, pursued by first three and then two of Aroto
Tagauchi's ships.

The pursuers had no need to track our every move because
they knew where we were going.

My anger rising fast, I ran back down to the hut. My child
was still asleep; Jasper, sitting up amid his bedding, looked up
at me and smiled. 'Did you sleep well? It wasn't too . . .' he
began.

Crouching down beside him, I said, trying to keep my voice
down, 'Why in God's name didn't you stop me?'

He looked furtive, then guilty. His eyes slid sideways. 'Stop
you?' The attempt at innocent bemusement wasn't very good.

'We're less than ten miles from Rosewyke,' I said. It was hard
to get the words out. 'If our pursuers know where I live – and I
really can't imagine they haven't the means and the ingenuity to
find out – they are probably already right here.' They could, I
reasoned swiftly, easily have travelled from London via a speedier
and much more direct route than ours, and . . .

But then I remembered the ruse we had carried out at Plymouth.
How I had briefly gone ashore to make the pursuers think I was
heading straight for home while the *Luipaard* sailed on to London
without me.

I sank down beside Jasper. My anger with him had evaporated:
I was blaming the wrong man because I'd led them here myself.

I muttered, 'We shouldn't be here,' and sank my head into my hands.

Presently Jasper got to his feet, and I heard him putting on his heavy cloak. 'I thought it was what you wanted, Gabe,' he said quietly. 'If I am in error, then please forgive me.' He moved towards the door.

'Where are you going?' I demanded.

He smiled faintly. 'Back to that farm we passed a mile or so back to buy provisions,' he replied. 'I'll be a while.'

As he closed the door gently behind him, I realized he was diplomatically giving me time to calm down.

I was very relieved when Amy awoke, since tending to her absorbed almost all my attention. Once she was fed and clean, I took her outside and, holding her hands, helped her to walk a few steps on the short turf. 'This is the earth of your home,' I told her. 'The woman who bore you had a Japanese mother and a Portuguese father, but on my side your family is entirely English, and Devon English at that. You belong here as much as and more than anywhere else, and I will not let anyone take you away.'

Her sea-green eyes studied me intently. Then she held out her hands in an imperious gesture and we resumed our slow walk.

I must have let myself become totally absorbed in my child. It was another grave error to add to the tally, for I should have been constantly on the alert. When the voice from behind and slightly above said quietly, 'Here's a surprise to greet a person on a fine autumn morning!' it made me spin round in shocked surprise. Reaching for a weapon (I had neither sword nor dagger, both of which I could see just inside the open door of the hut), I looked at the dark figure up on the rocks. The sun was climbing up the sky immediately behind him, and I could see no distinguishing feature. All I could make out was an impression of enfolding black garments and a pair of pale, bright eyes.

I bent down and gathered up my child. Then, forcefully, trying to imply a confidence I didn't have, I said, 'Come down and identify yourself.'

And the dark figure laughed.

Relief flooded through me as alarm faded and I recognized Black Carlotta.

She was . . . what was she? Wise woman, herbalist, friend to those in need, especially if they were poor. She was old, and the strands of fine hair visible under the black headdress were pure white. But, just as they had always been, her shining pale grey eyes were as vibrant with life as those of a young woman.

As she jumped down off the rocks, I put out a hand to help her, but she waved it aside with a mocking smile. Then, indicating the hut, she said, 'This is my refuge, and it's one of many. Believe me, Doctor, I was as disconcerted to find you here as you are to have let yourself be taken unawares by me.' It was a fair accusation. 'I saw you last night, when you arrived. Saw that other man, the one who was at Rosewyke doing your work until the other one finally became unbearable.' She gave me a long, steady look. 'You won't be knowing about him, will you?' she murmured.

'Knowing about him? Why, what's he done?'

She didn't answer. 'I've been waiting until you were alone.' She turned to contemplate Amy, who had sat down on the ground and was studying our visitor with fascinated eyes and an open mouth. 'This is quite a surprise, eh?' Black Carlotta went on, grinning. 'I was listening just now when you told her this was her home and you wouldn't let any man take her away. Not that I needed you to reveal that she's yours, because anyone observant can see that for themselves. She's got the Oldreive eyes, just like your sister.'

Oldreive eyes. Yes. I pictured Celia, and our father's mother Graice Oldreive. Our grandmother had always been called by her proud family name, for all that she had been married to my grandfather Ralfe Taverner for much the greater part of her long life.

Both women had the same eyes. And, as I had already noticed, my daughter had them too.

'Her name's Amy,' I said.

Black Carlotta nodded. 'Pretty,' she commented. 'And not likely to raise any eyebrows, now the child's in your care. Reckon there'll be enough to deal with in that one's young life, without having to explain some fancy foreign name to all who ask.'

I stared down at my child. It was a moment of revelation: all at once I was realizing just what was ahead.

'I didn't know you had a regular dwelling right out here on the high moors,' I said in a clumsy attempt to change the subject.

She smiled, and I was sure she knew exactly what I was doing. 'That's the point of a secret refuge, Doctor,' she replied. Then her face straightened and she looked suddenly desolate. 'No choice, not any more. Bad enough when the King' – she paused and spat – 'published that book of his about demons and witches, but now he's brought in a new law, curse him.' She spat again, and muttered words under her breath in an alien language.

'Law?' I asked quietly.

'Yes! *You* know, you must know! Everyone does, or seemingly so.'

'I've been out of England for two and a half years and at sea for most of the last ten months,' I said.

'Aah.' She nodded. 'Well, you'll soon find out, soon as you get amongst your own. Made my life, and that of people like me, all but impossible.' The sun-browned face fell into deep lines and wrinkles, and suddenly she looked very old.

King James, I recalled, was terrified of witchcraft. He had been since the business of the North Berwick witches who, if you believed the frantic garbage spouted by learned men who ought to have known better, had raised a ferocious storm to sink the King's ship as he sailed to Denmark to claim his bride and queen. A handful of women who had done nothing of the sort were tried, found guilty and – marched out to face the full might of Scottish law – were afterwards strangled and burned.

It had probably been only a matter of time before the frightened, superstitious, stupid bloody man who was now our King turned his attention to what he believed to be the threat of strange yet entirely benign old women like Black Carlotta within his new realm of England . . .

'I keep away from people now,' Carlotta said. 'There used to be tolerance for those like me, but all that was doomed in 1602.'

'There's still tolerance at Rosewyke,' I said. 'And there are many thereabouts who are only alive today because of you.'

She shrugged. 'They tolerate me now, maybe. It'll be different when they and their loved ones face some witch-finder giving the option of betrayal or extreme violence.'

'I pray it will not come to that,' I protested.

She shrugged again.

I'd been about to ask her if she had news of Rosewyke, of my kin and my friends. In the light of what she had just told me, I held back.

But she knew what was in my mind.

'They do well,' she said gently. 'Better when you're back there with them, but they are all right.' She eyed me steadily. 'Happen you'd better go and see for yourself.'

'Ah.' I paused, gathering my words. Then I explained that I had been followed home from the East. That my child was the object of a ruthless and brutal search by pursuers who wanted to take her back to where she'd come from. And I told her why I couldn't go home to Rosewyke yet.

TWELVE

In the long days since the murder of Maudsley Cheverell, Theo Davey's attempts to discover who had killed him, and why, had met with failure. The body had been buried, the funeral rites had been read over him and prayers said for his soul. Now, with no progress made in the investigation, Theo was on the point of putting the file to the bottom of the stack and moving on to something that promised a more satisfying outcome.

But the day after he had done exactly that, Jarman Hodge sidled into his office late in the afternoon and, closing the door, said quietly, 'Something you should know, chief. Been on my mind for a while and I ought to share it with you.'

Theo stared at him. Jarman Hodge was his best agent. A nondescript-looking man of medium height with a diffident air, he had a way of simply being present in some tavern or busy street, giving the impression of quietly and modestly minding his own business. He had perfected an absent sort of gaze that hid his bright intelligence as thoroughly as a scarf over the head, yet all the while his eyes, ears and probably his sense of smell too were working away recording and analysing the scene before him. He was his own man, often disappearing for days and sometimes as much as a week, but since he invariably returned with the very information that Theo had been searching for, his absences were rarely punished with anything more than a sarcastic word or two.

'And this evening you've decided to do just that?' Theo replied. 'Decent of you, Jarman, to spare me the time.' He pointed to a chair. 'Sit down.'

Jarman smiled and did as he was told.

'There's been talk,' he began. 'Took it for no more than rumour to begin with. But it came to seem there was a regular pattern, with the same basic facts repeated. Dressed up in different ways, maybe, but then folk with a good story to tell always add their own flourishes.' He paused, frowning.

'Well?' Theo prompted impatiently. 'What were these basic facts?'

Jarman looked up. 'It was round about the time that Doctor Cheverell got done in.' Again he hesitated, as if he couldn't bring himself to go on. 'It's not certain, mind,' he said warningly. 'and you – we – shouldn't necessarily go believing it, and in any case it's not the first time it's happened, and there's like as not no more truth in it this time than in all those previous times, but—'

Theo reached for his ink pot and weighed it in his hand. 'I'm armed, Jarman,' he said. 'And my patience has run out.'

Jarman grinned briefly. 'Sorry, chief. It's just that if it's all no more than gossip, then it'll be hard because . . .' He stopped, took a sharp breath and said, 'Round about the time that Cheverell was killed, people were saying that the doctor had been sighted.'

'But Cheverell *was* a doctor, he was often in the town and he was killed not far out of it, so of course he'd have been spotted!' Theo exclaimed angrily.

Jarman shook his head. 'Not *that* doctor,' he muttered. '*Our* doctor. Doctor T. *Gabriel Taverner!*' The last two words were a sort of suppressed shout.

'Gabe?' Theo said. Then, straight away, 'No. I don't believe it. You're right, Jarman, there have been whispers before, and it'll be no more the truth this time than then, you mark my words.' He thumped a fist on his desk to emphasize the denial.

Jarman sat with his head bent. 'Right, chief,' he muttered.

Then he looked up and met Theo's eyes.

'What is it?' Theo demanded. 'I know that expression, Hodge. What have you not told me?'

There was a pause, then Jarman said, 'Best I tell you exactly what happened, then you can make up your own mind.'

'Very well. Get on with it.' Theo waved a hand in encouragement.

'Well, first off there was this fisherman on the east shore of the estuary,' Jarman began. 'It was very early one morning, and he'd got in from night fishing. Saw a boat row into the estuary, and it went on, up towards where the Tavy flows in, and landed someone on the east shore. A man, he reckoned, only whoever it was got under cover so fast that the fisherman couldn't be sure. Anyway, he thought no more about it – busy with his catch and that – but then later as he made his way home he saw the same figure, or one very like it, emerge from under the trees up ahead in the place the man had come ashore. And it seemed odd, the fisherman said – *odd* was the word he used – for a man to wait so long between coming ashore and heading off wherever he was going.'

'It might not have been the same man,' Theo said. 'You said the fisherman couldn't even be sure it *was* a man, yet he assumed the figure who emerged from the trees was the one who'd come ashore.'

Jarman nodded. 'Like I say, chief, it's all very vague.'

'Go on,' Theo ordered.

'Well, next there was the old man who lives in one of that maze of narrow little streets up behind the port. He said he'd seen a big man in a cloak with a deep hood, and the hood was drawn so far forward that he reckoned the fellow couldn't have seen where he was going any too well. It was raining hard, apparently, which probably explained the hood. Anyway, this old boy watched the big man for a while because – according to the old man – he was weaving around up and down the streets and the old boy wondered if he was lost and looking for somewhere, and he was going to go outside and offer to help but then the big man moved on.'

'A big man in a hood,' Theo said neutrally. 'Anything else?'

'Yes there is!' Jarman said sharply. 'You can say I'm a fool, and that I let myself be carried away into believing something I wanted to be true that wasn't, but I went to that tavern where Doctor T always used to leave his horse when he was in the town.'

'And some half-witted lad with a straw in his teeth said a man in a hood had hidden in his hay loft?' Hearing his own sarcastic voice, Theo wondered why he was pouring such scorn on this tale of Jarman's, when he was every bit as eager for it to be true as Jarman clearly was.

'I spoke to one of the younger lads, skinny sort of a boy and scared to be asked questions by the coroner's agent,' Jarman said, ignoring Theo's jibe. 'Once I'd persuaded him he wasn't in any trouble and I only wanted to talk to him, he stuttered and stumbled a bit and then he told me.'

'*WHAT?*' Theo shouted.

Jarman shook his head. 'Sorry, chief. Trying to bring to mind the exact words. I said to the lad had he seen any strangers about near the time Maudsley Cheverell was killed, especially early one morning when it was raining really hard. And he muttered and stammered a bit more, then said it wasn't a stranger but someone he recognized, someone he knew well because this man had often left his horse there in the yard, and then in a tiny voice the lad whispered, *I says to him, Doctor T?, and he turns up his collar and tells me in this gruff voice that I was mistaken.* I thought the lad was done, but as I turned to leave he grabbed my arm and said, *but it* was *him, I'd swear to it with my hand on the Bible, because he was always kind and you remember the kind ones.*'

Theo waited until the rush of excitement died down. Then he said, 'Did you believe the lad?'

And Jarman said simply, 'Yes.'

There was silence in the office for some time. Then Jarman said slowly, 'Course, if it *was* the doctor, question is, where is he now, and why hasn't anyone seen him since?'

Theo shook his head slowly. 'I have no idea.'

After another silence, Jarman said, 'I'd have put it down to an honest mistake and a bit of wishful thinking, but there's something else.'

'Let's have it, then,' Theo said wearily.

'Should have mentioned it before now,' Jarman said, 'only I needed to be sure, and even now I don't know how many of them there are, not with any sort of precision, and like as not they are here on innocent business and nothing to raise any concern.'

'Who are?'

'There's talk of a group of men, strangers, and maybe half a dozen of them, although they seem to be sort of fluid, if you know what I mean. Some of them are English, although not local, probably from London, and the others are foreign. They dress in black, and keep themselves to themselves, and people say they turn away when you speak to them. Could just be they don't understand what's said, being foreign, but . . .'

'*But,*' Theo repeated thoughtfully. 'So, six men, none of them local and some of them foreign, whose number can't be counted with any accuracy and who have some purpose in Plymouth that they have chosen not to reveal.'

Clearly detecting the sarcasm, Jarman said, 'Well it may be nothing, and I'd say it probably was, except there was no sign of them before that Doctor Cheverell was killed.'

'You think it was these men who killed him.'

'Seems likely,' Jarman agreed. 'Could be they mistook him for Doctor T.'

'But Maudsley Cheverell looked nothing like him!' Theo protested hotly.

'*We* know that, because we know both of them,' Jarman replied swiftly. 'But they'd have seen a man riding Gabe's horse, carrying a doctor's bag, giving the appearance of calling on patients and stabling the horse in the inn that Gabe always used.'

Theo did not speak for a moment. Then he said slowly, 'I think you may be right.'

Early the next morning, Jonathan Carew stood in the silence and peace of the little church of St Luke's, Tavy St Luke. It was a chilly morning, and the early mist was still hanging over the river in its deep valley. He had been there for some time, kneeling before the altar and deep in his own thoughts. Now, pausing halfway down the aisle on his way to the door, he glanced up at the beautiful stained-glass panels let into the top of the wall that separated the little chapel from the main body of the church.

He remembered very well the day that he had fixed them there.[2] And who had been with him.

He said softly, 'It is only rumour. No more than that.'

But the trouble was, it was very hard to dismiss a rumour that you very much wanted to be true.

He left the church and strode down the path to the cottage beside it that had been his home now for nine years. He opened the door and turned to go into the small room beyond. It was dark in there. A little light was penetrating through the gaps in the shutters, but he had not opened them before going over to the church. He was on the point of crossing the threshold when

2 See *The Angel in the Glass.*

he became aware that someone was standing in the room. Nothing
to cause alarm; it wasn't unusual for people wanting a word with
him to go into his house and wait. He did not lock his door
during the day, and he never gave the impression that it was an
unwelcome disturbance even when at times it was . . .

These thoughts were running through his mind, even as he
wondered why all at once he felt full of tension.

Then the tall figure shifted slightly.

And Gabe's voice said, 'I guessed you were in the church. I
didn't want to disturb you, so I came in here. I hope you don't
mind.'

Jonathan shut his eyes, then opened them again. Gabe was
still there. The way he was standing – leaning forward, hesitation
and doubt apparent in the expectant way he craned his head –
gave away quite a lot.

'Of course I don't mind,' Jonathan said. 'I'm—'

But then he couldn't get any more words out because Gabe
had enfolded him in a huge hug. And he muttered, 'Dear *God*,
Jonathan, it's good to see you.'

I quickly released Jonathan, quite sure that my impetuous embrace
had surprised him even more than it had me. 'Sorry,' I muttered.

He smiled. 'No need to apologize,' he replied. 'It's grand to
see you too, Gabe.' He sounded stilted, and the words were the
sort of polite greeting that two distant acquaintances would utter.
As if he noticed this too, the smile deepened and he said, 'It's
far more than grand. Words are inadequate just now, though. Are
you back? Have you come home for good?'

'Yes.' I answered automatically, for I hadn't thought much
beyond the actual return, the peril that faced me, and the fact
that by returning to my home I had brought it right to the door-
steps of all those I loved and cared for. But when Jonathan asked
and I replied, I knew it was the truth. Whatever happened next,
I was home to stay.

He nodded. 'I hoped you would say that,' he said. 'Have you
been to Rosewyke? Does Celia – do your household know?'

'No. I came to you first.'

He looked surprised. 'I am honoured, and it is a joy to see
you, but—'

'Before you welcome me home,' I said quickly, 'if that's what you were going to do, there are things I must tell you.'

He picked up something in my voice. 'Do you wish to go across to the church?' he asked.

He was asking, I thought, if I wanted to confess. Apart from the fact that we were no longer Catholics in England (well, people were very reluctant to say so openly), I wanted to talk to him like a brother, not confess to him as a priest.

'Here will do,' I said.

We sat in his old chairs either side of the hearth. Jonathan had not yet lit a fire, and the room was chill. Amy was asleep in her sling, hidden under the folds of my heavy cloak. Now, seated, I unfastened it and turned it back.

He saw her, asleep on my chest. For some moments his strange green eyes were intent on her. Then he raised his head and looked at me. He did not speak.

'She is my daughter. Her name is Amy,' I began. Struggling for the words – there was something in his silent stare that turned my mouth dry and emptied my head – I explained how I had come to father my child.

'It was while I was in Japan. I went there, you see, not to Neira as I'd been led to believe, and we discovered we were to be the guests of a man called Romeu Silvestre. He was a Portuguese merchant. He was in the employ of a very wealthy man called Aroto Tagauchi, who belonged to a proud and ancient family. Romeu had married Tagauchi's only daughter, and she died giving birth to her daughter, who was called Chiyo. She—'

Jonathan put up a hand. 'Stop, Gabe. Just for a moment, so I can take all that in.' There was a short pause, then he said, 'Go on.'

'Chiyo's life was rigidly controlled by her grandfather,' I went on, 'but in secret she rebelled against his plans for her. I knew nothing of this until much later,' I added hurriedly, 'and when I first encountered Chiyo, I thought she was one of the servants in attendance in the bath house.'

And suddenly, without any warning, I was back there, in the hot, steamy, fragrant water, firm fingers were massaging my scalp and, even at her first touch, I think perhaps I already knew what she had in mind . . .

I forced myself back to the present. To the chilly room, my daughter asleep on my chest and Jonathan's watchful eyes.

I went on.

I tried to be honest; tried to share the responsibility for Amy's conception fairly between her mother and me. Several times I touched Father Oliver Lambert's letter, in the breast pocket of my tunic. I had made sure to bring it with me, and I was planning to show it to Jonathan. He could not speak to Chiyo, could not hear her account, but I hoped that the words she had dictated to the Jesuit would serve to convince Jonathan that I had told the truth.

It took a long time.

At last I stumbled to a halt. There was silence in the little room. Jonathan had quietly lit a small fire as I talked, and now a log collapsed in the hearth, making a shower of sparks.

'Between you,' Jonathan said after what seemed an interminable pause, 'you and the young woman – the daughter of this Romeu Silvestre, the granddaughter of a powerful warlord – have brought a child into the world. You have told me, Gabe, the circumstances of the child's conception, and although I am sure you are keen to prove the truth of your words by some sort of written evidence' – he'd noticed, then, or perhaps even heard the rustle of paper – 'I have no need for it, for I already believe you have told me the truth.'

'I have,' I muttered. 'I swear it.'

He nodded. 'The result of this scheme is that the daughter Chiyo bore to you is now without a mother. Had it not been for the loyalty and selflessness of the servant woman . . . Netsu?'

'Natsu.'

'Had it not been for her courage, your child would not have had a father either, for you would have sailed away, in ignorance of what you had done.'

'I regret Natsu's death bitterly,' I said. 'At the time I thought it might have been unintentional; that those pursuing us as the *Luipaard* sailed away were only trying to stop us. I know better now. They kill with barely a thought, whenever they deem it necessary.'

He did not speak for a few moments. Then he said, 'You do have something to show me? I guessed aright?'

I reached inside my tunic and handed Father Lambert's letter to him.

The movement woke Amy, and I entertained her while Jonathan read.

'I think,' he said eventually, 'that you had very little say in the matter of your child's conception.' It was hard to believe he was smiling, but he was; a faint smile, barely there, but then I knew him well and he hadn't changed at all in two and a half years. 'The plan was Chiyo's, she had what I am sure she believed were sound reasons for it, and I do not imagine she took you into her confidence before she . . . er, before she approached you.'

'No. As I said earlier, I thought she was one of the bath-house attendants. I even wondered if her attentions were a regular part of the experience – the skilful massage, I mean, not afterwards, when she arrived in my room and we . . . er, well, you know.'

'I am familiar with the mechanics of it, Gabe,' Jonathan said dryly. 'It seems clear from what you say, and from what I have just read, that you were – ah – employed by a determined woman as a means of escape from the life that her grandfather had ordained for her. I imagine she hoped you would accept your paternal responsibilities and not abandon her and the child?'

I shrugged. 'I cannot say. It seems she became unwell quite soon after the birth, and died within weeks. She didn't live to see whether or not I would abandon her.' Abruptly I stopped, for all at once it seemed so sad. I hadn't loved Chiyo – of course I hadn't, I'd barely known her – but she had borne me a child. That made a bond. Of sorts.

'You didn't abandon your child,' Jonathan observed. He was staring at Amy. He held out his arms. 'Will she come to me?'

I shifted position and handed Amy to him. They studied each other. I could see from her face and her growing smile that she was happy with him. I sat back, eased the ache between my shoulders – she was getting too heavy to carry in a sling – and watched them together.

'Her eyes are like Celia's,' he said presently.

'They are.'

At the mention of my sister's name, he looked up. 'She will be very surprised,' he remarked.

'She'll be furious,' I said resignedly. 'She'll blast me with all the things I say to young girls and their young men who do exactly what I've done. And her castigation will be totally justified.'

'Perhaps,' he agreed. 'But it will not last. She loves you; she will love your child.' He muttered something else, but his face was against the top of Amy's head and the words were muffled.

I *thought* he'd said, 'She will forgive you, because her heart is full of love.'

Presently he said, 'Will you go there next? To Rosewyke?' He sounded stilted suddenly, as if he had more to say but was holding back. So, for the second time in a morning – and it was still quite early – I explained why my home was barred to me. And all the time I was speaking, I was fighting the fear that was steadily growing colder within me.

I did not dare close my eyes, for I knew I'd see the head of Gregory Tresham's poor groom with the thin red stripe around the neck. And the corpse of Hieronymus Petrarcus, the skull smashed by some fatally heavy object.

The same ruthless intelligence that had guided the hands of the assassins was now sending these brutal men after me, and there was no doubt at all that those precious people I had come home to were in precisely the same peril.

When I had finished talking, Jonathan didn't waste time on either recrimination or sympathy. Instead he said, 'It seems to me that you should tell all this to Theo Davey. He will be very glad to see you, because . . .' He stopped. 'Better that you do not ride to visit him. Will you wait here, while I fetch him?'

There were many things I would rather be doing than sitting in the Priest's House kicking my heels for as long as it took Jonathan to ride to Withybere and back, and then, if he had to leave a message for Theo, the wait would be even longer. But any protest would have been deeply ungrateful, so I just said, 'I will. Thank you.'

Theo heard voices in the outer hall and, recognizing both, called out, 'Jarman, bring him in here!' As Jarman ushered Jonathan Carew into the inner office, Theo stood up to greet him.

'What brings you to the coroner's office on a chilly autumn

morning?' he asked. 'Sit down, and I'll send Jarman for a hot drink and a bite to eat, and—'

'I won't partake of either, thank you,' Jonathan interrupted. 'Nor will I sit down.' Moving to stand closer, he lowered his voice and muttered, 'Forgive me for issuing an order, but you must come with me out to Tavy St Luke's.'

'Why?' Theo muttered back. He glanced at Jarman, who shook his head slightly.

'There is . . .' Jonathan looked at the stack of files on the desk. 'You still have no solution to the murder of Maudsley Cheverell?'

'No, although . . . no.'

Jonathan nodded. 'Then it seems likely that if you come with me, as I ask, the obfuscation may clear a little.'

Theo glared at him. Then, sensing he would only waste time by asking for an explanation, he abruptly put on his cap and his long gown and followed Jonathan out of the office.

They rode up to the Priest's House and round to the shelter at the back to tether their horses. 'Someone's here!' Theo exclaimed. He put a hand to the chestnut gelding's flanks. 'Been here a while, I'd say. I don't recognize the horse. Whose is it?'

'Come inside,' Jonathan said. 'We'll go in through the scullery.'

Theo waited for Jonathan to precede him inside, but the priest stood back. 'He's sitting by the hearth in there,' he said.

Theo blundered on to the small room off the hall. He was increasingly irritated by Jonathan's mysterious manner, and by being called away from his desk when there was, as ever, so much awaiting his attention. Jonathan ought to *know* that and not have forced him to trudge all the way out to Tavy St Luke and—

And then Gabe stood up out of his chair by the fire and said, 'Well met, Theo.'

Theo stared at him. His face was deeply tanned, and his green-blue eyes looked bright in contrast. His hair was even longer, and bleached here and there by the sun. He was well dressed in good-quality garments. And he was armed with a sword and two knives.

'Judging by the weaponry, I'd guess you've brought trouble home with you, Gabe,' Theo said. Then he held out his hands, grasped Gabe's and pulled him forward, embracing him, slapping him hard on the back repeatedly and muttering, 'Can't believe it. Last thing I expected.'

There was a bubble of laughter from somewhere down on the floor beside him, and, looking down, Theo saw a child of a year or so, standing on wobbly legs and holding on to a table, her thick dark hair lit with bronze highlights and her eyes – same colour as Gabe's sister Celia's – staring into Theo's. 'This is my daughter, Theo,' Gabe said. 'Her name is Amy.'

It was not yet noon, but the strong emotions of the morning made me feel I'd lived several long days already. Nothing had changed, I still knew without a doubt what danger I was bringing with me, but being with friends again – and such friends – was so good that I felt like cheering. I watched, an inane smile on my face, as Theo, sitting on the floor and apparently oblivious to the discomfort, indulged himself in a lengthy game of hand-clapping with my daughter.

I was back.

Some time later, after Theo too had been told the long and sorry tale of my journey from the East, Jonathan brought in three glasses and a bottle of brandy and proposed a toast to my safe return.

'Well, you're home,' Theo said as he stood up, wincing, and put down his empty glass. 'From what you've just told me, however, I think we'll have to wait and see just how *safe* it turns out to be.' He paused, frowning, then said, 'Judging by what happened to Cheverell – and always assuming that there's any connection to you, which surely there must be – then I have my doubts it's safe at all.'

I stared at him blankly. He stared back. Then he muttered, 'Dear Lord, you don't know, do you? Nobody's told you.'

'Theo, you're only the third person I've talked to since I returned to Devon,' I said. 'In each case, there have been far more important things to speak of than Maudsley Cheverell. What happened to him?'

He didn't answer for a moment. Then he said gravely, 'You're not going to like it.'

THIRTEEN

'Nobody had any time for the man,' Theo began. 'He was cocksure, lazy, and not much of a doctor. He—'

'I know he drove Jasper Hart away,' I interrupted. 'As I've just been telling you, I met up with Jasper in London and he was our guide for much of the way home. He told me it was Cheverell's awful behaviour that forced him to leave.'

'Aye, and no one blamed him for going, for all that it increased the burden on everyone else at Rosewyke. Trouble was, it made Cheverell even more objectionable. He seemed to think Jasper leaving made his position even more important.'

'I realize I chose badly with Cheverell,' I said stiffly, 'and I can only say I am sorry.'

'Yes, yes, I'm sure you are,' Theo said impatiently. 'But never mind that now – I'm trying to *tell* you something.' He paused, frowning. 'After the incident with Jasper Hart, your splendid sister imposed conditions on Dr Cheverell. He had lodgings in the village here, but he preferred to lounge around at Rosewyke with his fat backside in your chair and his feet on your hearth, but Celia was so angry that she banned him from the house and stopped him riding your big black horse. Well, I don't know if he managed to set foot over your threshold again, although I suspect not, but he did get his way over your horse, complaining so long and so persistently to Celia about the unreliability of hired hacks and the necessity of an important doctor such as himself having a good horse, that in the end she relented, or maybe he took the horse anyway. Whichever it was, Maudsley Cheverell was spotted once more riding a very familiar horse, and the wretched man resumed his habit of leaving him in the stables down behind the port when he had calls in that part of town.'

'My habit first,' I murmured.

Theo ignored the interruption. 'At the end of last month, he set off down that lane leading from the north-west gate out towards the estuary. We haven't found out why. There was no patient waiting for him in some lonely cottage, and the lane only leads to the water. Jarman Hodge wondered if he was looking for a way along above the river, leading up towards where the Tavy flows into the estuary, but, again, why?'

The sense of apprehension was growing. I willed him to go on.

'He was found face down in a ditch,' Theo said. 'And before you ask, it wasn't an accident. He hadn't fallen off your horse, for all that he'd never learned to ride it properly. He'd been attacked, stripped, and he'd suffered a truly appalling death. I'd never heard of the like before, but Jonathan here seemed to know of it.'

'*Lingchi*,' Jonathan said. 'Also referred to as the death of a thousand cuts.'

I spun round to look at him. 'It sounds as if it originated in the East.'

'It did.'

I started to feel cold.

'We had an idea as to why he'd been attacked and killed so brutally,' Theo went on quietly. 'We thought that whoever assailed him was trying to extract information. Unfortunately for Cheverell – assuming we were correct – he couldn't provide the information because he hadn't a clue what they were talking about. They must have realized this, and Cheverell, weak from loss of blood and in terrible pain, was finished off and his corpse dropped into the ditch.'

I knew he had more to say. I also knew what it was going to be.

'They thought he was me,' I said.

I'd done my best to make sure someone in the area knew I was there. I'd laid my false trail, crept through the back streets of Plymouth, let myself be seen by the lad in the stables, in order to divert one of the remaining two ships that were pursuing us and set some of Aroto Tagauchi's killers ashore to hunt me down. Only they hadn't found me, they'd found poor Maudsley Cheverell. Who, as Theo had just pointed out, didn't know one single thing about infant great-granddaughters and Chrysanthemum Tigers and died in agony trying vainly to make his killers believe it.

And Theo said gently, 'You were seen, Gabe. Jarman unearthed three people who spotted a mysterious hooded figure, and one who swore it was you.'

As if that wasn't bad enough, he added, 'There's more, I'm afraid. Jarman told me yesterday that there's word of a shadowy group of maybe half a dozen men, habitually black-clad, some who are assumed to be from London, some of whom are without doubt foreigners. According to Jarman, nobody noticed them lurking around before Cheverell died.'

No, I thought. I knew who they were, and who had sent them.

With an inward sigh, I told my friends exactly what I was facing.

I rode back to the shepherd's hut up on the moor in a sweat of anxiety, trying to look in every direction at once and taking such a roundabout route over the roughest terrain that the return journey took twice as long. And now, in addition to the fear, it felt as if I had a weight on my shoulders. Maudsley Cheverell's death was the direct result of my brief hours in Plymouth. My pursuers knew I'd gone ashore and must have thought I'd remained there, and then it was only a matter of time before some discreet questions asked in a quayside tavern over too much ale elicited the information that Dr Taverner rode a big black horse and regularly visited Plymouth in the course of a day's work.

My mood communicated itself to Amy, and she kept turning round to look at me, her small face creased in a worried frown. So, with a determined effort, I put aside the horror of what I'd just been told and set myself to entertaining her. Bless her, she laughed obligingly and lengthily at my range of silly voices and animal imitations. She particularly liked the pig, which she copied faithfully. By the time we were back, I was already becoming resigned to what had happened.

Jasper must have heard us coming. He came out of the hut and hastened over to the ruins of the animal pen to help me see to my horse. I could sense his unease. It worried me.

The fire was going well inside the hut, and I settled to preparing some food and a drink for Amy. She had almost grown out of the need for a sleep after the midday meal now, but we'd had a long ride and a busy morning, and presently I put her, yawning, eyelids drooping, into her blankets, where she fell fast asleep.

'What's the matter, Jasper?' I asked quietly.

He poked at the fire and did not look at me.

'Jasper?'

Now he raised his head, and just for a moment I thought I saw an anguished expression in his eyes. But then he forced a smile, and said with not entirely convincing cheerfulness, 'I have been busy while you were out!'

'You've certainly managed to find some decent food,' I remarked, indicating the thick slices of cold beef, the fresh loaf and the pat of good Devon butter.

'Yes, and there's a flagon of ale over there.' He pointed. 'But that wasn't actually what I meant.'

'I hope you haven't been seen,' I said. 'I thought we'd agreed that you'd stay nearby?'

'I did venture quite far afield, but I was very careful, I promise you.'

'What were you doing?'

He hesitated, and I had the impression he was working out what to say; how, perhaps, to present what he'd done in a favourable light. 'Gabe, I lived in your house for more than two years,' he began. 'I worked side by side with the people you worked with, I got to know them, and very soon I came to admire them and to like them. I realized they all cared deeply about you. They understood you'd gone away, they didn't know when or even if you would return, they didn't hold it against you that you'd deserted them, but fervently hoped and prayed every Sunday that you'd come back, settle down and start tending them again.'

'I'm not—' I began.

But he didn't let me speak. 'I've ridden a long way today,' he said, leaning towards me, his eyes bright. 'I've taken great care only to speak to people I know are true friends. Dr Thorn, the blacksmith near Tavistock whose wife and newborn son you saved, that lord out beyond Buckland who you treated when he had a grave fever.' He hesitated, and I caught his nervous eyes on me. 'I told them you had made enemies while you were away, that you were in hiding and in grave danger,' he hurried on, 'that you would have need of true friends, that they must keep what

I'd just told them strictly to themselves, and that when the call came, they should make their way in secret and come armed and prepared to help you.'

He was smiling now, as if convinced I would give his actions my approval.

'You ask too much of them,' I said baldly. 'I have been gone too long, and why should any man risk his safety and his well-being to defend someone who, to use your own word, deserted them?'

'I don't know, Gabe,' he said quietly. 'They must be fond of you, I suppose. But I can tell you that to a man – and a woman – they responded. Said they didn't like the idea of men from faraway lands coming right here to Devon, chasing after one of their own who'd had the good sense to come back. Whatever their reasons, they are yours. Somehow, my friend, you have acquired a private army.'

My first instinct was to scoff. To tell him in utter disbelief that people were far too busy with their own lives to care about a doctor who had abandoned them and then returned urgently needing their help. And why indeed should they risk their safety for me? Jasper heard me out, then said simply, 'I could try to convince you, but there is no need, for soon you will see for yourself.'

'What do you mean?' I demanded.

'Those I spoke to undertook to pass the word. They will make for Rosewyke, for your house is strongly built and, set on a rise as it is, a well-organized guard will spot anyone trying to creep up and catch the household unawares.'

'They're all going to *Rosewyke*?' I wanted to shout out in protest, but I managed to keep my voice to a hiss of anger.

'Yes!' He had clearly seen that something was wrong, and his face paled. 'It is wise because—'

I didn't let him finish. 'They don't know I'm back,' I said.

His mouth dropped open and now he looked horrified. 'But I thought that was where you'd been this morning! Where else would you go first,' he added pleadingly, 'but to your home and your household?'

I fought my fury. He was right; it had been a reasonable supposition. Wearily I stood up, gathering Amy in her blanket and gently fastening her back in the carrier. Then I put on my heavy cloak.

'Where are you going, Gabe?' Jasper whispered.

'Home.'

This time I went calling alone.

Before heading for Rosewyke, I went back to Tavy St Luke. Jonathan needed no fulsome explanation: when I said where I was going and asked if he would look after my child, he nodded. 'I won't be away long,' I told him, and he said quietly that I should take what time I needed.

The afternoon was advancing. I left the chestnut gelding tethered in the copse at the end of the track up to the house. I walked slowly, keeping under the trees. The house appeared before me, the mellow old Tudor brickwork rosy red in the low autumn sun. I looked over to the yard beyond the house. I could hear voices, Samuel's low burr and Tock's short, staccato responses. Then the yard gate opened and a big black horse came out. Tock was exercising Hal.

The sight of the two men who comprised my outdoor staff, steadily and conscientiously going about the daily routine just as no doubt they'd done each day since I'd left, was surprisingly moving.

I walked on, moving right in under the trees so as to keep out of sight.

I crossed the open space in front of the house and ran up the steps to the outer door. It opened when I lifted the latch, and I went into the porch. The inner door opening on to the hall was open. Funny, I thought, how you only realize that your house has a distinctive smell of its own when you have been absent for a long time.

Rosewyke – my house – smelt of baking bread and lavender-scented beeswax.

I crossed the hall and peered into the parlour. There was nobody there, and the library beyond was also empty. I could hear Sallie in the kitchen, singing as she worked.

Sallie.

Seeking her out was a pleasure I'd postpone for now.

I went to the rear of the hall and up the stairs. Turning to my left as I emerged on to the gallery, I trod softly along to the pair of rooms at the eastern end of the house. The bedroom led off an anteroom that Celia used as a workroom. The anteroom door stood open.

She was sitting on a low chair with a piece of heavy ivory silk across her lap. She'd been working on it – a pattern of pink, yellow and white flowers was forming under her skilful fingers – but now she sat quite still, needle in hand, gazing out of the window towards the distant village of Tavy St Luke's, down in its shallow valley. She was in profile, but still I could clearly see the sadness in her face.

I stood completely still.

I'm sure no breath or small movement of mine gave away my presence. But she knew; I'd swear she knew.

She folded the ivory silk and laid it aside. She stood up, turning to the door. Her eyes widened for an instant as she saw me, and her face paled alarmingly. Then, before I could hurry to her, for I thought the extreme pallor might indicate an imminent faint, she was in my arms.

Neither of us said anything straight away. There weren't any words, really. I felt her give a couple of deep sobs, and I raised a hand to smooth her shining hair.

Presently she pulled herself out of the hug, shoved me away and said, 'Are you really home? You haven't just called by to wish us a good day before sailing off somewhere else for another two and a half years?'

'No. I'm home.'

She closed her eyes and her lips moved.

'Celia?' I said. 'What is it?'

She opened her eyes and glared at me. 'Relief,' she said shortly.

I smiled. To see her so moved, to watch her utter what I presumed was a prayer of thanks for my safe return, was like a gift.

But then she said – and now she sounded like she always did when I'd done something to annoy her and she was berating me – 'Naturally I'm very happy to see you, and looking very well, I might add. But please, Gabe, don't go thinking that's the reason for my overwhelming relief, because it's not.'

I tried to think what she meant, but failed. I was full of the joy of seeing her, of being in my home again, and I probably wasn't at my intellectual best just then.

'You're back, and you'll take up residence here again and look after the house?' she was saying.

'Of course,' I said. Surely that was obvious.

There was a smile hovering around her mouth. I thought she was probably enjoying this. 'Which means I no longer have to live here,' she went on.

'But I want you to!' I protested. 'I love having you here – it worked well before I went away, didn't it? It will do again!'

She was looking at me expectantly, and when I didn't go on, she sighed. 'Oh, Gabe, Gabe. Do I have to *tell* you?'

Mutely I nodded.

'Who did you imagine would be in charge of Rosewyke while you were away?'

'Well, you, naturally. It was – is – your home.'

'And what if I'd wanted to live elsewhere?'

'You couldn't,' I said firmly. 'Sallie could run the house on her own, that's for sure, but she'd never accept the responsibility, she'd insist it wasn't *decent*, wasn't what was *done*.'

Celia grinned at my imitation of Sallie's deeply affronted tones.

'Quite so, and she'd be right. So, we are agreed, then, that all the time you were away, I had no choice but to live here.' I grunted an assent. 'What,' she said in a small voice, 'if I wanted to marry?'

And then I knew.

And understood what the cost of my impetuosity and my long absence had been to one – no, two – of the people I loved most in the world.

'And if the man you wanted to marry,' I said after a moment, 'was as tightly bound to his own house.'

She looked up at me, her sea-coloured eyes full of tears. 'Yes,' she whispered.

'I'm so sorry,' I said. 'Was there . . . has there been no way?'

'No, of course not,' she said crossly, masking the brief tender moment with sudden irritation. Just like she always did. 'I love him, and for all that he has never said so, I know he loves me too, but he always knew I couldn't abandon Rosewyke, and, as you just said, he is bound to his Priest's House, so both of us have held back.'

I took her in my arms again. 'You don't have to hold back any longer,' I said.

Presently she said, 'Does Sallie know you're here?'

'No. I heard her in the kitchen, but I wanted to find you first.'

'Then we'll go down now and tell her that the wanderer has returned.'

She was heading for the door, but I caught hold of her hand and stopped her. 'Celia, there's something I must tell you.'

She turned round and stared intently at me. I could tell by her face that she knew this was no small thing; no light matter to do with my journey, no deep and philosophical observation on the experience. 'What is it?' she whispered, and I barely heard the words.

'I had . . . an encounter with someone while I was away,' I began. 'A woman. This – she – we slept together, but it was not at my instigation.' Her eyebrows went up, possibly in silent comment on my lack of gallantry in neatly ducking the blame.

'Are you telling me that you have brought a wife home with you?' she asked after a long and painful pause. 'That there is to be a new mistress of Rosewyke? But, Gabe, I just *told* you, I do not plan to *be* here.'

'I have no wife,' I said. 'The woman was called Chiyo, she tended me in the bath house and I thought she was a servant. After we . . . after our one night together, I looked for her but did not see her. She wasn't a servant, she was the daughter of our host and the granddaughter of a warlord who had very firm plans for her future that did not involve copulation with a stranger from the West.'

'You did not love her?' Celia whispered.

'No, of course I didn't. I only met her once; we were only together a matter of hours.'

'Then why . . .' Suddenly the frown on her face cleared. She didn't exactly smile, but she was nodding in an alarmingly knowing way. And her eyes had narrowed. 'She fell pregnant. And since she couldn't present this fearsome warlord of a grand-father with a shameful, illegitimate great-grandchild, somehow she concealed her condition, succeeded in giving birth secretly and then dumped the baby on you. That's it, isn't it?'

I had fully expected her to be angry. But I hadn't anticipated how much it would hurt. It was not so much that I had diminished myself in the eyes of the sister whom I cared for so deeply and whose good opinion I valued beyond rubies. It was the way that hearing those words *shameful illegitimate great-grandchild* and *dumped the baby* aroused in me such fiercely protective and profoundly painful emotions.

And, even as I fumbled for the words to explain that the reality was very different from Celia's bleak analysis, I was thinking how typical it was that it should fall to my beloved sister to make me realize how much I loved my child.

I told her the truth. All of it. How what Chiyo and I had done had led to such terrible danger. I told her Chiyo was dead. I confessed that there was a fearsome and unbelievably wealthy Japanese warlord with apparently endless resources and influence that spread halfway round the world who was utterly and ruthlessly determined to take back what I had stolen. What he thought I had stolen; Amy was my child, and I firmly believed that a father's rights overrode a great-grandfather's. And I had been very firmly informed that the Chrysanthemum Tiger belonged to Amy.

When I had at last finished speaking, Celia looked up and stared right at me for a long moment. Then she said, 'Boy or girl?'

'Hmm?' I was still reliving what I'd just told her; trying to assess how she was receiving it.

She tutted in irritation, as well she might. 'Your child, Gabe. Shall I be welcoming a niece or a nephew?'

'A niece,' I said. 'Her mother gave her a Japanese name, and, although it is spelt differently, it sounds like Amy. When she is baptised, I wanted her to be named Amy Graice.'

'Amy Graice Taverner,' Celia murmured. 'Our Grandmother Oldreive would be delighted.'

We went down together and into the kitchen. Sallie was busy trying to deal with a leg of mutton and she did not turn round as she heard footsteps. 'Dear Lord, Miss Celia, but this was a particularly energetic sheep! I've been struggling for far too long and I'm nowhere near done!'

I moved forward to stand beside her. I put my hand over hers on the handle of the old knife, its blade worn thin with decades of sharpening. 'Let me help,' I said.

I was standing very close, and I felt the tremor go through her. She turned and looked up at me. 'Is it you, Doctor?' she whispered. 'Is it truly you?'

'Yes, Sallie,' I said.

Her face worked and I saw several emotions flood through her. Then she put down the knife and covered her face with her hands. Totally unable to think of anything to say, I gave her a hug.

Some time later, I went outside into the yard. Tock was still out with my big black horse, and at first I didn't spot Samuel. I half expected him to appear from one of the stalls and gape with amazement, but it was another creature who detected my presence. I heard one harsh bark, swiftly followed by a whimper that rose to a howl, and then a big, muscly black shape with ginger eyebrows hurled itself on me and I was engulfed by Flynn.

I knelt down and wrapped my arms round my dog. To be remembered after such a long absence, and to be welcomed home with nothing other than simple joy, with no need to produce awkward and embarrassed explanations, no uprushing sense of shame that I'd let people down, was, just then, particularly sweet.

I was sitting on the hard stone floor muttering foolishly to Flynn when I became aware that someone was watching. Looking up, I saw Samuel in the doorway.

He was less demonstrative than Sallie. In fact, he was less demonstrative than pretty much everybody. He smiled, very briefly, then gave a sort of grunt of acknowledgement and muttered, 'You're back, then, Doctor.'

I got up, dusting myself down, and Flynn took up a position right against my legs. 'I am, Samuel.' We looked at each other. 'Should I stay out here in the yard until Tock returns with Hal?'

Samuel shook his head firmly. 'Best not.'

With a nod, I walked away. Samuel would break the news, in his own way and in his own time. It was better that way.

I went back inside and through to the library, where Celia was standing looking out of the window. 'I can't stay,' I said, 'I must get back to Jasper, out in our refuge up on the moor, and besides I've left my child with Jonathan and—'

She spun round. 'You've seen Jonathan?' she burst out. 'But why didn't you . . .'

She stopped.

I followed her thoughts as if she'd spoken them aloud. *Why didn't you come here straight away?* she'd been going to say. *Why was Jonathan the first person you went to?*

But there was no need for her to ask. She was my sister, we understood each other, and she knew. I'd gone to Jonathan because I was ashamed.

There was quite a long pause. Then she said softly, 'Did he help?'

And I replied. 'Of course he did.'

She cleared her throat, then said in a businesslike way, 'So where is this refuge up on the moor?'

I told her. 'It's all right, it's well hidden and quite out of the way, we're as safe there as anywhere and—'

She couldn't contain herself any longer. 'Gabe, you *idiot!*' she cried. 'Of *course* it's not safe! It's a derelict hut, miles from any human habitation, and you and Jasper are alone there with a *child*, for God's sake! You must see how foolhardy that is?'

'I have no choice!' I yelled back. 'I can't risk coming among people I care about because that will put them – *you* – in the same danger! I'll have to—'

'Have you seen Theo?'

'Yes.'

She managed to restrain her reaction to hearing I'd also visited the coroner before coming home to Rosewyke. 'Well, that was probably wise,' she commented, 'although I'm surprised *he* didn't tell you what a fool you're being in staying out in the wilds.' She was watching me closely. Her frown deepened. 'You didn't tell him about the hut.'

'No.'

'Gabe, if you told him you're in danger he'll have started mustering men!' she cried. 'He has a force at his disposal – he *must* have! – and people, ordinary people, will want to help. Of *course* they will!'

'Jasper's been out this morning talking to people I knew,' I admitted. 'He speaks as if he's amassing quite a force of arms.'

I expected her to smile, even to laugh, at the absurdity of it. But she didn't. She said, 'And why is that so unlikely?'

She said more – quite a lot more – but I barely heard. Something had shifted in my mind. When Jasper had told me what he'd done, I'd thought it was absurd; mere wishful thinking on his behalf, and a great deal of exaggeration. Yet here was my sister, saying the same thing.

I wondered absently if I'd refused to believe it – that people would rally round, that it was safe to return to my home, that we no longer had to stay in the horrible shepherd's hut – purely because I so much wanted to accept that it was true.

'You really think it's all right to return to Rosewyke?' I asked her when at last she'd finished.

Her only answer was to roll her eyes.

FOURTEEN

Jonathan knew exactly what he was going to do that evening. It was very hard to go about the rituals of the daily round, knowing what was to come.

It had been late in the afternoon before Gabe returned. He had stayed only long enough to collect his child and explain that he was going out to the ruined hut as fast as he could to collect Jasper, gather up their belongings and head home to Rosewyke.

'I would leave her with you, if you did not object,' he'd said as he fastened the child in her sling, 'because she's clearly reluctant to leave you. But I know you'll have your usual evening office, and undoubtedly there will be no lack of people wanting to call on you and speak at length to you, and Amy would take quite a lot of explaining.'

Jonathan grinned. 'Indeed.' He reached out and touched the child's cheek, and she laughed. 'I will see you very soon, Gabe, and you must—'

But Gabe was already mounting the chestnut gelding, and Jonathan didn't think he'd been listening.

None of the parishioners would have guessed.

He was as calm, as open and as solicitous as always: the parish priest, courteously seeing his small congregation on their way after evensong with a smile and a kind word; a moment of understanding and of unspoken sympathy for those in need of it, the quiet assurance of support for those who habitually leant on him.

He was determined that not one of them would detect the least sign of impatience.

When the very last of them had gone and there was nobody left to see, he hurried away from the church and round to the primitive little stable behind the house, where swiftly he tacked up his old bay cob with the broad blaze. 'You should be groomed to a state of high perfection and caparisoned with scarlet silk, old friend,' he said as he worked, 'for this day is unlike any other.'

He led the horse outside and mounted. He was tempted to hurry – he'd waited half the day for this moment, after all, and for a very long time before that – but he resisted.

Along the path and on to the track. Up the gentle slope that led out of the little village in its valley, and on to the road. Now he kicked the cob to a trot, and the regular clop of the hooves striking the hard ground masked the sounds of the still evening.

And he did not hear the horse coming fast in the opposite direction until he came to the bend and it was upon him.

A fine grey mare, her flanks sweaty from having been ridden hard. And on her back, tumbling off in an uncharacteristically graceless dismount caused entirely by haste, a young woman dressed in a russet-brown gown that flattered the shining fair hair, uncovered by cap or veil.

Now he too had pulled to a stop and was jumping from the cob's back. Racing to her just as she was racing to him. Wanting to laugh as they ran into each other and he wrapped his arms round her. Wanting to weep at the look in her sea-green eyes.

'Celia, dearest, beloved Celia, I—' he began to say.

But her strong hands were reaching up, taking firm hold of his head, and she was pulling him down towards her. Then he couldn't talk any more because she was kissing him and he was kissing her right back.

It was very late by the time I returned to the ruined hut on the moors. Profound darkness had fallen, and I had been hit with the full eerie strangeness of Dartmoor. In my state of tension I'd seen lurking enemies in every rocky outcrop, and it had only been the presence of my child in her sling, warm and firm against my body, that had kept me from succumbing to the power of dark old tales and luridly terrifying superstitions.

Jasper was standing in the doorway of the shepherd's hut, his silhouette outlined by the lantern light behind him. He was armed with a small knife and a short stick.

'Who's there?' he cried as I slid off the horse's back, and his loud shout made Amy wake from her deep sleep. She gave a squawk of protest, and I heard Jasper's nervous laugh.

'Oh, it's you,' he said, in quite a different voice. Approaching, I saw that he was pallid with dread.

'It is,' I agreed. I glanced at the weapons that he was hastily putting out of sight. 'Just as well, since it's difficult to image Tagauchi's killers taking much notice of a length of kindling and your pocket knife.'

'I thought . . . I thought . . .' he began. He couldn't go on.

I imagined how it must have been. Alone in the hut with its broken walls and insubstantial door. Sounds outside in the night of a rider approaching. Useless to call out for help, useless to search the hut for a decent weapon since I had taken my sword and both my knives. His terror would magnify the threat, as fear always does, and in his mind there would be three, four, half a dozen well-armed, well-trained and utterly ruthless men creeping towards him. They would demand to know where I was, where my child was, where the ancient treasure of the Tagauchis was cached, and they would have gone on asking until his courage gave out in the face of the unendurable pain and he blurted out everything they wanted to know.

Once I understood all that, I saw that to be standing pale and shaking in the doorway with his totally useless weapons, demanding to know the identity of the men about to fall upon him, was an act of very great courage.

I put my arm round his shoulders and said, 'I'm sorry, Jasper.'

I didn't really know what I was apologizing for, and I didn't imagine he did either. He nodded, then said, 'You'd better bring Amy inside and settle her. It's very late.'

'I will, but it won't be for long,' I replied. He shot a swift glance at me. 'We're going to Rosewyke,' I said.

'We . . . but I thought you said we couldn't risk bringing danger to your household, and in any case, it was safer out here where nobody knew our whereabouts!'

Had I said that? Yes, probably. 'I was wrong,' I said. 'My sister has persuaded me of the error of my ways, reminding me that a flimsy hut is no match for a stoutly built house.'

'And people,' he added softly. Then, a smile spreading over his still-pale face, 'We won't have to fight them off alone any more.'

Amy, half asleep, watched as the two of us collected up our

belongings and put the packs on the horses. I left the wooden box containing the gold tiger until last; until immediately before we left, in fact. It would have made sense to put it in place first, with less weighty objects on top, but that would have meant it being left outside in the darkness while I packed the rest of my gear. And, when it came to it, I found I couldn't do that.

I thought at first that Jasper hadn't noticed how I'd taken the crate outside and then come back into the hut with it still clutched to my chest. I was just sliding it back into its shadowed corner when he said quietly, 'You can't leave it untended, can you?'

I spun round to glare at him. 'Of course I can!' I protested. 'I've been away from it all day.'

He nodded. 'Yes, but I've been here much of the time. And you seem to have forgotten that each time you've set off somewhere, you've told me to keep an eye on it and, if I leave it to go out, check on it the instant I return.'

I was about to say hotly that I'd done nothing of the kind, but then, with a distinct sense of unease, I remembered that I had.

I went back to my packing.

In the profound darkness of the desolate moors, Jasper and I set out on our cautious way back to Rosewyke. Neither of us gave the hut a backward glance.

It was a great relief to be on our way. One day had become the next by the time we left; it truly was the dead of night. I rode ahead, and at first Amy was too excited by being out in the thrilling darkness again to go to sleep. But after a few miles I felt her slump against me, her soft steady breathing suggesting she was adequately warm and fed to sleep for some time.

I was aware of Jasper riding close behind me. He didn't speak, and neither did I. The night was still and growing very cold. At first it was too dark to see much more than the faint strip of the path snaking away ahead; our comings and goings had already trodden it to a recognizable track, for which I was very grateful. The sky soared high above us in a great dark bowl, and to begin with I could barely see any stars. But gradually some shift in the impossibly distant upper airs cleared away what mist or cloud had been amassed up there.

And all at once the stars shone down on us.

It was a sight I must have seen many times before, both at sea and on land. But that night as I rode home to Rosewyke, it was as if I was seeing it for the first time. I spotted the old familiar constellations – the Plough, Cassiopeia, and the steady brilliance of the North Star between them; Orion the Hunter, with his belt of stars, and Betelgeuse and Bellatrix on his mighty shoulders. Soaring high in a vast arc, I could see the Milky Way, so many stars visible against the blackness of nothing beyond that they must surely be uncountable.

In an instant of disorientation, I suddenly felt very small. In that strange moment my urgent preoccupations, my present danger, the peril into which I was plunging my family, my friends, those I loved, all seemed distant; no more than shadows acting out a drama that I was witnessing but in which I had no involvement.

Shadows on the wall.

I was back on the island on the other side of the world, staring into the depths of a simple shrine. There was a power, a force, behind all that we were, saw, experienced; it had formed us and our world – all those other worlds soaring high above me – and in a flash of profound insight so fast that it was there and gone before I had properly registered it, I *knew*.

I was shaking.

From right behind me where the wooden box was tightly strapped to my saddle, just for a heartbeat I felt another conscious- ness brush against mine. It was not evil, nor was it benign: it just *was*. And it was *old* – dear God, it was old. With the deep insight with which I'd mysteriously and so briefly been endowed, I understood that the Chrysanthemum Tiger was far, far more than a precious, priceless treasure out of antiquity that a cruel and determined warlord very much wanted back.

The shape in which its powerful presence currently resided contained something else. Which now, it seemed, belonged by right of blood to my child. Which, as quickly as I could, I was taking with me back to my home. My family. My friends, my household.

The strange mood was fading fast.

Before it had entirely gone, it briefly occurred to me that, had there been any practicable alternative, I might just have chosen it.

*   *   *

In his office in the sleeping little village, Theo Davey was still awake.

He was exhausted. It had been a very long day, and he'd been tired as evening drew on, looking forward wearily to locking up the office, climbing the stairs and settling down with Elaine and the children. Eating a good meal, taking a modest glass of port or two with his dear wife once their progeny were asleep, his shoes off and his feet up on the hearth.

But a huge backlog of work kept him at his desk, long past supper time, long past bedtime. Elaine came down with bread, cheese and a mug of ale.

'I am sorry, my love,' he said, pushing his chair back from his desk and scratching his belly. 'I have let myself be swallowed up by all that awaits my attention.'

'Hm,' she said. Then: 'I have brought you something to eat.'

He barely paused to thank her before falling on the platter.

As he drank the last of the ale, she said, 'You feel it too. Don't you?'

He met her eyes. He was tempted to pretend; to ask, *whatever can you mean?* but she knew him too well. 'Yes,' he said.

'Something . . .' she murmured. 'Some disturbance in the very air. Or so I should say, if it did not sound far too fanciful!'

He began to speak, but she held up her hand. He waited.

'Dearest husband,' she said softly, 'every single evening your desk groans with papers you have not yet attended to, and it has done so for as many years as we have been wed. Yet tonight is the first time that I have ever known you to resist the appeal of the evening meal in the company of your family.' She paused. 'Do you know what is amiss?' she asked very softly.

He shook his head. 'No.'

Elaine studied him. 'It is more, I think, than this peril that is pursuing Gabe.'

'It is.' He sighed. 'It is a sort of whisper, and I cannot identify it. But I suspect I soon shall.'

She came round to his side of the desk, bending to drop a kiss on the top of his head. 'I shall be upstairs, and I shall keep watch,' she said. 'There is danger: I can feel it, and so can you.'

'I can,' he agreed.

She went to the door, pausing for a moment. 'I shall pray,' she whispered.

And he sent her a smile full of gratitude and love.

He was tidying up his desk in a desultory manner when at last Jarman Hodge arrived. For once he didn't wear his usual mask of inscrutability. Far from looking as he usually did – as if nothing much had happened and, even if it had, it wasn't going to disturb him – he looked alarmed. Afraid.

And there was fresh blood on his lower legs and spotting his boots.

'What?' Theo demanded as he slid into the inner office.

'Trouble,' Jarman replied. 'Remember those half a dozen men, habitually black-clad, that I mentioned?'

'Yes. Of course I do!' Theo said impatiently.

'Their number has grown. Must have been recruiting locally. There's a great deal more of them now, and there's intelligence behind what they're up to, because it's not the worn-out men of the quay's inns, the angry, the drunk and the hopeless they've been collecting. It's men who can fight.'

Theo glanced at Jarman's bloody boots. 'Fighting's broken out?' he asked urgently.

'It did, but it's over. For now,' Jarman added ominously.

'What happened?' Theo asked.

'Seems quite a lot of the locals down on the quay have heard the rumours about Doctor T being back,' Jarman said, 'and nobody's happy about this talk of men being paid to join strangers planning revenge on him for whatever happened while he was off on his travels. They all seem to remember Doctor T doing something to help them or their wife or their cousin or whoever, and, probably even more important than that, they don't like the idea of a hired band led by foreigners planning to do harm to one of their own.'

'One of their own who has been away for quite a long time,' Theo observed.

Jarman shrugged.

Theo stared at him. 'We cannot have private wars being fought in our town,' he said quietly.

There was a short pause. Then Jarman said, 'Strictly speaking, this is Dr Taverner's fight. Those six men leading the assault are after him, and whatever has come back from his travel with him.'

'It is indeed his fight,' Theo agreed. He thought for some moments. 'So what do we do, Jarman? Do we shut and bar our doors, tell our people to stay safe indoors and let these foreigners and strangers lead their hired fighters out to Rosewyke to take what they want? Leave Gabe to face danger alone? He won't yield without a fight, and he'll fight to the death, and everyone there with him, all those people who grew to like him, to trust him, to love him even, when he lived among us before, will fight with him and possibly – probably – many of them will die too.' He paused, the strong emotion making him breathless. 'Or,' he went on softly, 'do we gather together our own force and go out to join him?'

Very briefly Jarman grinned. 'I was only pointing it out, chief. Course we'll join him, us and everyone else who's already spoiling for a fight.' He was already halfway out of the door, and briefly he turned to say laconically, 'Never thought we'd do anything else.'

FIFTEEN

U ntil I sat in my own study in my own house early the next morning, I don't think I had appreciated just how much I had ached to be back there.

I'd eaten breakfast with Celia and watched as she had taken it upon herself to feed a rusk and milk to her niece. Sallie had been overcome with emotion at the sight of the newest of the Taverners. After a discreet discussion with my sister, we had agreed that it was best to say simply that Amy's mother had died – no more than the truth – and not challenge Sallie's assumption that she and I had been lawfully married. Although I felt ashamed at Sallie's readiness to believe the best of me, I had to admit that it was a relief not to have to make yet another confession.

Celia had been luminous with happiness as we sat either side of the breakfast table. I didn't have to ask why.

Now, up in the privacy of my study, I sat for some time simply taking in the welcome sight of all my familiar belongings, arrayed in just the way I'd left them when I set out for the East. I could have said everything was just the same, but of course that was not true. And, as if to remind me of that, just then my daughter crawled over to my desk, took firm hold of my leg and pulled herself up into a standing position. She pointed an autocratic finger, made the noise that always told me she wanted something and wasn't going to take no for an answer, and then held up her arms for me to lift her on to my lap.

I wondered even as I settled her if she'd known what I was about to do; if somehow she'd been aware that the wooden crate and its precious, weighty contents sat on my desk right in front of us.

'Shall we let him out?' I asked her softly. 'He's probably had quite enough of the inside of that box, and it is time we introduced him to his new home.'

Although I couldn't believe she understood, she nodded.

I had a chisel and a pair of pliers set out beside the crate. I reached out for them.

I thought I could hear a very low, soft humming sound. I dismissed it.

It got louder.

Amy turned to look at me, her expression enquiring. Not afraid: merely questioning.

She was firmly settled on my lap, and I reached round her, put the blade of the chisel under the first of the nails and pushed down on the handle.

The hum rose to a roar.

Amy put her hand on mine, the one holding the chisel, and uttered what sounded just like an order. It wasn't – of course it wasn't; it was no more than her usual flow of experimental syllables.

I found my courage and, forcing myself to be deaf to the increasingly angry sounds that I was quite sure I was hearing, went to work.

A short time later, a row of nails stood on their ends on my desk, the lid was off the wooden box, the wrappings lay scattered on the floor, and the Chrysanthemum Tiger glared out at us.

The morning sun was shining in through the window, and the deep yellow light struck the Tiger's golden body so that the creature seemed to shimmer with subtle movement.

I felt its formidable power.

I stared at it, at the full length of it from its open, snarling mouth to the tip of its twitching tail. I was fascinated by its paws: by those long, curving claws that extended like blades. I realized they were bewitching me, for in almost the same glance I seemed to see them both as the graceful petals of the chrysanthemum flower and as fierce and terrible weapons. The cream of the ivory seemed to sparkle as the light caught the facets of the diamonds, and the red rubies at the claws' tips seemed to be liquid . . .

I watched my hand stretch out to touch.

I tried to pull back, for it was folly to test out the substance of the claws in so risky a manner. But my hand moved on, and I had no power to stop it.

I extended my fingers and ran them the length of the most prominent claw on the tiger's left paw. At first it felt cool and smooth – just as I'd expected ivory to feel – but then suddenly it was a long, curving petal: soft, flexible, vibrant with the life within it.

And then the claw was neither hard and diamond-studded ivory nor a flower petal. It was worked metal – what metal I had no idea – and its edge was as sharp as freshly knapped flint.

I felt a sudden sharp, deep pain in the pads of my forefinger and middle finger.

I stared at the claw.

Its tip was still ruby red, but now the ruby dripped blood.

The Chrysanthemum Tiger had taken my libation.

I might have continued in my trance state for some time. But Amy was as interested in the golden figure as I was, and in horror I watched as she copied my movement and put out her chubby hand towards those deadly claws.

The impulse was there to stretch out and grasp her wrist, but my body would not obey. I fought, I felt the sweat break out as I struggled, but I could not move.

Could not even cry out a warning to her, for I was struck dumb, my mouth stopped up.

So I was a mute and helpless witness to what happened next.

I must have imagined it. I must have slipped briefly into a doze – I was exhausted, after all, so it was not impossible – and what I saw was no more than a dream.

I watched as my daughter, the last of the ancient line of the Tagauchis, stared in fascination at the formidable gold creature that was her heritage and hers by ancient, absolute right. She was smiling, she laughed once or twice, and the Tiger twitched his tail in response. Her hand was on him now: patting his heavily muscled shoulder in a clumsy gesture typical of the small child that she was, as yet not in full control of her limbs and incapable of a subtle touch.

I winced as her probing fingers explored him, stabbed against his eye, pushed inquisitively into his mouth, among that ferocious array of teeth. I waited, totally helpless, for him to respond. For the powerful jaws to snap shut, and for my child's hand to be savaged, perhaps even detached. I heard myself give a suppressed moan of terror.

She laughed again. And then – now I knew I was dreaming – I saw the Tiger's green eyes sparkle in delight.

She leaned forwards across my desk, her head and her soft

hair brushing against the Tiger's side, her busy little fingers now exploring the paws as if she wanted to hold hands with him.

I knew what was going to happen. It had just happened to me. My fingers were throbbing with pain and I could hear my blood drip-dripping on the floor.

She touched the biggest of the claws. The one that had just opened up two deep cuts on my hand. Clutched it, wrapping her hand right round it. Then she grabbed another one, and another.

She laughed.

She was not wounded, not deeply cut, not even scratched.

The Tiger shimmered brightly, and I thought he turned to look at me. He was vibrant with power; his presence pulsated through my study, and I could almost see the golden beams flowing off him and dancing around the room, filling it right up into the far corners, pushing out through the partly open window to join the brilliance of the sunlight outside.

He had just declared that he was Amy's creature.

He had veiled his might, turned his devastating claws from blades to petals, twitched and glittered as he felt her attention on him.

And as the paralysis eased and I could move again, could think once more with some sort of logic, I remembered that moment when the Tiger's noble head turned and his eyes stared into mine.

He had made me bleed, yes. He had accepted my unwitting offering; yes, surely he had. Did he know, then? Was some sort of enchantment at work, that this magnificent and priceless creature out of the deep, mystical past was aware that I was Amy's father? That henceforth it – he – would include me under the banner of his protection?

I found myself praying it was true.

I should not have even entertained such a thought, for I was a man of science, a physician, and I dealt in facts, in learning, in the slow and painstaking acquisition and accumulation of human knowledge. Superstition and myths of magic from the dawn of time had no place in my world.

Yet here I sat, so affected by what I had just witnessed – what I thought I had just witnessed – that I still felt shaken, and more than half still in the dream world. And, however I tried to explain it away, however much I battled to impose logic on fantasy, I could not escape the hard fact that I now had two severe cuts in the pads of my fingers that had been inflicted by a claw made of ivory that could not have inflicted even the mildest scratch.

Back downstairs, I sought out my sister.

'Do our parents know?' Celia said.

'No. Not yet.'

'Then you have to tell them. Straight away, before anyone else does. There's a strange mood about this morning,' she went on, her expression moving from curious to anxious, 'and I have the sense that something will happen . . .' I was about to ask her to explain, but she hurried on. 'You think you've been so discreet and secretive, Gabe,' she said crossly, 'but I'm quite sure a great many people know you have come back, even if they don't know about – er, about the rest. It can only be a matter of time before someone tells our mother or our father. And *you* ought to be the one who does that!'

She was right. 'I will,' I muttered.

Taking pity on me, she came over and hugged me. 'You must screw your courage to the sticking place,' she told me.

'Sticking place?'

She grinned. 'Trust you to ignore the huge matter of explaining to our parents that they have a granddaughter and no daughter-in-law and focus instead on the trivial detail. Asking me about an obscure expression!' she added, impatient with my lack of comprehension. 'If you must know, screwing your courage to the sticking place comes from a new play about a Scottish king and his murderous ways. The wife,' she added, 'is rather a memorable character.'

I rode to Fernycombe along the faint, insignificant and rarely frequented tracks of my childhood. I had left Hal in the stable; everyone locally knew he was my horse and there was enough gossip already. For now I could at least try to keep my movements secret. The chestnut gelding was a good horse, but I knew what a great pleasure it would eventually be to ride Hal again.

My mother was out in the yard feeding the chickens. She looked up and saw me. She dropped the pail and the grain scattered, to the delight of the hens. Then she simply stood there, her mouth open. I dismounted, hitched the reins to a post and walked towards her.

'Your hair's grown,' she remarked.

'Yes,' I said.

She frowned. 'And you still have that silly earring.'

'Yes.'

Then, at last, she smiled, although in truth the expression on her lined old face deserved a better word. 'Come inside.' She took my arm and we walked into the house where I was born. 'Your father's in his study. I expect he'll be pleased to see you.'

The calm understatement struck me as funny. I smiled, then I chuckled, and my mother joined in.

My father said not a word. He rose slowly to his feet, walked round his desk, held out his right arm and shook my hand.

Ah well, I thought, *we all show emotion in our own ways.*

They took the news that I had brought a daughter home with me surprisingly well. My mother assumed I had been married to Chiyo, and made a few remarks about the dubious wisdom of swift and impulsive decisions to marry, and how tragic it was for a young wife to die and a child to lose her mother. My father said little. But, as I got up to leave, he gave me a long, steady look and I was quite sure he knew what I'd kept back.

There was one last call I had to make.

Again I took to the unpeopled byways, and much of the route went along beside the river. The water was high, but the chestnut horse was not disturbed by wading along flooded paths and did not protest.

Too soon, I was approaching Blaxton, and the little house beyond the settlement near to where the ferry goes across the Tavy. I remembered the first time I'd seen the cottage. It was as well-maintained now as it had been then, and the diamond-paned windows sparkled in the sun. I tethered my horse in the shelter at the end of the row and strode up to the stout oak door with the heavy iron door-knocker in the form of an angel. I was about to knock, when all at once I knew that she was not inside the house but out in the yard at the back, in her still room. I followed the path that went around the house and emerged into the garden.

Autumn was well advanced, there had been a lot of heavy rain and some violent winds, but in this magical spot the plants still flourished, and the well-remembered mixed scents of mint, citrus, cloves, lavender and rosemary burgeoned in the soft sunshine. The door to the still room was like a stable door, and, as on my first visit, the top half was open.

I leaned on the lower half and stared into the room.

She was standing with her back to me, busy at the workbench with pestle and mortar, pausing frequently to chop with a small, sharp knife on a wooden board more of whatever she was pulverizing. She was making a fair amount of noise. I studied her. Perhaps it was my intense gaze that warned her I was there; slowly she put down the knife and turned round.

She looked just the same. She was as striking as ever, her tanned skin setting off the pale silver of her wide eyes. Her thick dark hair had a small streak of pure white, but that was the only change I could see. She still held herself with the same grace.

'Queen Mab the fairies' midwife,' I murmured. It was how I'd once heard her described.

Judyth stared at me. 'I heard a rumour you were back. I wasn't sure if I believed it.'

Her toneless voice gave nothing away.

'I have brought trouble back with me,' I said. 'I managed to enrage a very powerful merchant in Japan. I fled with two very precious items that he believes belong to him, and he is trying very hard to regain both of them and have me killed, as brutally and as savagely as can be contrived, to punish me for my impudence.'

Her mouth twisted in a wry smile. 'Well, it was never going to be likely you'd just walk in the door and say *here I am*,' she observed. She paused. 'Have you come to tell me about it?'

'If you will listen, then yes.'

She nodded. 'Come into the house.'

I stood back from the doorway and she emerged into the garden, turning to open the rear door of the little house. Closing and bolting it, she led the way along the passage and into a tiny, bright room whose small window admitted the golden light of late morning. It was an enchanting space. A settle stood beside the hearth, in which a small fire glowed beneath an iron pot suspended above it. Water in the pot steamed gently, and there was a sweet, citrus-tinged smell in the room.

She sat down on a stool and, pointing to the settle, said, 'Sit down and tell me, then.'

I gave her a more earthy version of the tale I'd now told several times. I held nothing back, for this was Judyth, and I felt in my guts that I owed her the full truth. I told her that I hadn't even tried to send Chiyo away when she came to my bed, that I'd made love to her willingly and more than once in the course of our night together and that, although I'd kept an eye out for her afterwards and hoped we might repeat the experience, I'd hardly been heartbroken when we didn't.

'I didn't grieve when I was told she was dead,' I added. 'I was sorry, of course I was, and I lamented the loss of a young woman with so much of her life ahead. Also, I was sorry because I was a doctor, and – arrogantly no doubt – I thought I might have been able to save her if I'd known she was becoming so sick and weak.'

Judyth nodded. 'It's a temptation to us all, to think we could have done better,' she said softly.

Until that moment, she had given no sign of what she was thinking or feeling. I hoped very much that what she'd just said was a positive sign.

I waited.

Presently she came out of whatever thought was preoccupying her and looked at me. 'She sounds like a woman who had firmly made up her mind what she wanted,' she remarked. 'You said she was determined to foil her grandfather's plans to marry her off to a man of his choice, and the only way she could achieve this was to make herself unfit for marriage by giving herself to some other man.'

Some other man. Judyth was quite right, but still it hurt my pride to be dismissed in this way. Even if it had been exactly what Chiyo had thought . . .

'Do you think she expected you would marry her?' she asked.

I shrugged. 'I don't know. I don't think so,' I added, 'because she sent no word, even when she knew she had conceived. The first I heard of her pregnancy and our child was when Natsu

arrived at the quay carrying Amy, and even then, I only understood the truth when I read the Jesuit priest's letter.'

Judyth smiled faintly. 'Then one might conclude that her sole
aim was to lose her maidenhead and thus render her grandfather's
scheme unworkable, that the pregnancy was a bonus, that she
had no more use for you after that and she would have been as
happy to wave farewell to you as you were to sail away.'

It was harsh, and I opened my mouth to protest.

I didn't.

Judyth's summation might well have been harsh but it was
also totally accurate. So I just said, 'Yes.'

She studied me in silence for some time; long enough for me
to start feeling awkward under her scrutiny. Eventually I gave a
stupid grin and said lamely, 'Say something, won't you?'

She smiled. 'What would you like me to say, Gabe?'

That you forgive me, I thought. That what I did with Chiyo
and what it led to have not turned me into someone for whom
you now could not ever contemplate having any feelings.

It was true that I had not thought about her all that much while
I'd been away. For sure, I hadn't let any sense of loyalty or
fidelity to her hold me back when Chiyo crept into my bed. But
now that I was back, now that I was in her wonderfully welcoming
house and sitting so close to her that I could have reached out
and touched her, she was filling each of my senses.

Both of us waited for me to speak. When I didn't, her smile
returned and now intensified. Then, her face straightening, she
said, 'Gabe, I believe I knew that you would be going away, even
before you told me. Even before *you* knew, perhaps, because I'd
always realized that a large part of you wanted to go back to the
life you'd had before. All the time you believed it was barred to
you because being on board a ship would bring back the terrible
nausea, you made the most of your life ashore, because you
thought it was the only life you could have. But it was, I think,
always second best, and—'

'*You* were never second best,' I said. The words burst out of
me, but it was the truth.

She gave me a very tender look. 'Thank you, but I was. Of
course I was,' she said over my instinctive protest, 'because as
soon as you'd been on a ship and didn't become ill, all you

wanted was to go to sea again. And you accepted the offer of a doctor's job on a ship going as far away as any ship can go.'

She was right. I'd left just as quickly as I could.

I made myself keep silent while I thought. What I said next was very important, and it had to sound right.

'It's true that I did indeed resent the abrupt curtailment of my life at sea,' I said eventually, 'and also that I went back to it as soon as I knew it was possible.' I leaned closer to her and took hold of her hands. She didn't pull them away. 'But I want to come home. People have asked me if I'm back for good, and each time I've heard the question my instant answer has been the same: yes. When they then ask if I'm quite sure, I say yes to that too.' I paused. 'I can choose, now. I'm not forced into a life I didn't plan. And I choose to stay here.'

She stared at me, the pupils in her pale grey eyes wide and dark. Then she let go of my hands and very gently put them back on my lap.

'Good,' she said gently. 'That makes me very glad.'

'Judyth, I have no right to—' I began. But she held up her hand and put her fingers to my lips.

'Don't say any more,' she whispered. 'You are in danger, as you've just told me. You have your child to care for, and her safety and security must be your priority.'

'Of course, but—'

Again she stopped me. 'I will be here,' she said simply. 'When it is over, I shall be here. And in the meantime, if I can help you in any way, I am here for that too.'

I wanted to shout. Wanted to hug her. Wanted to kiss her, thank her, tell her I did not deserve her generosity. But she was getting up, her expression had closed in, and she led the way out of the room and along the dark little passage to the front door. I rose and followed her.

She was at the door, at the tiny window beside it. She glanced out, and then suddenly she ducked, hurried back towards me and threw herself against me, pushing me against the wall.

The feel of her body, the fragrance of her hair, her very nearness, affected me like a strong drink and I put my arms around her and hugged her tightly to me.

'*No!*' she hissed. 'Gabe, I want to hold you more than anything, although not now! There are *men* outside, a group of them, and to judge by the way they're skulking in the shadows and the fact that all are very well armed, I'd say they *really* don't wish you well.'

I leant forward and kissed her on her beautiful mouth. Then, gently but firmly, I set her back against the wall and crept forward, crouching down, until I was beneath the little window. Very cautiously I straightened up and peered out of the bottom corner of the glass.

Then there was a thunderous noise as the man standing not two feet away from me raised the door knocker shaped like an angel and thumped it down against the door.

I heard Judyth's muffled gasp. Spinning round, I saw her holding her hands in front of her mouth. She looked very frightened. I put my finger to my lips, and briefly she cast up her eyes as if to say, *do you really think I'd cry out and let them know there's someone here?*

I pictured the rear door. Had she closed and secured it? She must have had the same thought, for she touched my arm to make me look at her and mimed shooting a bolt home. I nodded, feeling huge relief. Her eyes widened and she mouthed, 'Hal!'

I shook my head. 'Riding another horse,' I said, as quietly as I could.

The door knocker banged again, then twice more. I heard someone mutter a curse, and someone further away asked something in a language I did not know. The man at the door answered. After what seemed an hour, we heard him stride away.

I counted to a hundred, then looked out of the window again. There was nobody there.

SIXTEEN

'You cannot stay here,' I said to her urgently.

She had run off along the passage and I'd gone after her.

'Judyth, I know you're an independent woman, I know you need no man's protection, but just now no one with any connection to me is safe and I'm not safe either!' She was kneeling on the floor reaching inside a recess and I was talking to her rump. 'We have a chance – a very good chance – if we stay together, but here, on your own . . .' I couldn't bear to think about it. 'They know where you live!'

She straightened up, flushed. She stared right at me, and her eyes were alight with fear but also with high excitement. 'I know, Gabe,' she said. 'I'm coming with you.' She indicated the large bag she held in her hand. 'Why do you think I've got this?'

It was her medical bag. I almost said, but nobody's having a baby, then, fortunately, remembered in time that she was a nurse as well as a midwife. People were going to be hurt; in more ways than one, it would be very good to have her near.

'Come on,' I said, grabbing her hand and heading for the door. 'We should go while they're not there.'

But she held me back. 'Not that way,' she said. 'We know they were at the front of the house, but they may not have gone round the back.' But they would, I thought, of course they would. And if there were enough of them, they'd have left one man, even two men, to watch the house. If that was the case, however, we were doomed already. We'd just have to hope it wasn't.

'Very well!' I said, far too brightly. She shot a quick look at me, one eyebrow raised. 'Lead on.'

She led me to the rear door. All was quiet. She unbolted it, opened it a crack and said, 'Clear.' We slipped outside and she locked the door with a big key while I peered out round the side of the still room. Nobody there.

'Where's your horse?' I asked.

She shook her head. 'Too far away. In a stable, up by the ferry port. Yours?'

'In the shelter at the end of the row.'

We ran down the garden, out through the gate in the high wall at the end, along the path to the shelter. I led the chestnut gelding outside and was about to mount and pull Judyth up in front of me but she said, 'You came up the main track from the river, along the road?'

'Yes.' I was taut with impatience.

'People know that track. There's another path, very narrow, just there.' She pointed. 'I often use it when I'm on foot, but I've never tried my horse on it.' She eyed the chestnut gelding. 'How's his temperament?'

'Fine,' I said firmly. I'd ridden him the breadth of southern England without incident, but I'd never tried him on a steep and narrow path above a full and fast-flowing river. Surreptitiously I crossed my fingers.

I'm not sure I'd even have attempted the path if I'd understood the danger.

Judyth handed me a long, soft scarf. 'Put this over the horse's eyes, maybe?'

I nodded, speaking quiet words to the gelding. 'I'll go first,' I said. 'If we . . . if it doesn't go smoothly, I don't want to fall on you.'

She smiled. 'You won't fall.'

Blindfolding the horse might have hidden the hazards of the path from him, but it meant I had to guide him every step. By the time we were halfway down to the narrow strip of shingle beside the rushing water, I was soaked in sweat and my heart was thumping with dread.

The path was very narrow, it bent sharply to and fro across the steep slope, it was rock-strewn and gravelly, and the gravel slid away alarmingly under our feet. It provided a secret and swift way down to the track along the river, but it was perilous, and to attempt the descent with a horse was foolhardy in the extreme. As I led the horse on to the strip of beach, I was saying a silent prayer of thanks.

Judyth jumped down beside me. 'Said you wouldn't fall,' she murmured.

I handed back her scarf. 'So you did.'

We looked at each other. Then I swung up into the saddle and reached down for her. She settled astride, in front of me, and I reached round her for the reins. It was around half a mile to the path I'd ascended earlier, and it was clearly apparent that this first stretch of track was never used by people on horseback. While not as terrifying as the steep descent, it was alarmingly narrow, and on several occasions the gelding put down a fore or a hind foot that started to slip away down the muddy bank. I sensed his fear, and constantly spoke calm words to him.

And then we were approaching the foot of the wider, far less steep path that I'd used before, and I knew we were going to be all right.

It seemed to take an age to reach the path up to the woods below Rosewyke. Judyth was so close, her back pressing tight to my chest. I wanted to talk to her; wanted to let the words that were crowding around in my head spill out. But I held back. She barely spoke. Three or four times she pointed out a dwelling up on the right, high above the river, as if ticking off the markers that were leading us to our destination. She sounded restrained, as if we were strangers thrown together by circumstance and forced to endure each other's company and make it bearable with polite conversation.

I wished she wouldn't. I made increasingly brief responses, and soon she ceased.

We reached the path. We climbed it, rode up through the woods, crossed the orchard and emerged on the open ground to the west of the house. I urged the chestnut on and headed round to the yard. The gates were tightly closed and I counted at least four men on lookout on the far side. One of them was Tock. He called out something in his strange voice, and I who had known him so long recognized it as: 'The master! Doctor's here!'

The gate opened, we rode through and the men on watch closed and barred it behind us.

They ran towards us, helping Judyth down, several voices talking at once. I recognized two of Theo's men and a farmer friend of Josiah Thorn's who I'd once treated for severe bronchitis.

There were a lot of horses about, and Tock had run off to tend one which was restless with fear.

'Samuel, what's happening?' I demanded.

'Well, now, let's see,' he said calmly. He was unperturbed; he might have been discussing the progress of the fruit picking. 'The coroner came and said we needed to prepare. Said there'd be people arriving, many people, and he left this pair' – he indicated Theo's two men – 'to say who could come in and who couldn't.' He leaned closer, dropping his voice. 'Seems we're likely to be attacked, Doctor. Men from far away, who want to steal something from you.' He looked embarrassed, as well he might. 'That was all they said, so I can't tell you any more.'

'It's all right, Samuel, I know.' The guilt hit me. Again.

'Tock insisted on watching out for you,' Samuel went on. 'Said he knew you were on your way, and he was right, seemingly.' He glanced at me, quickly looking away.

It wasn't the first time that Tock's strange intelligence had picked up something unknown to the rest of us.

'Is he all right?'

Samuel nodded. 'Better now you're here. I sent him to look after the horses. One or two are nervous.'

'Good. Yes.'

'Gabe?' Judyth was right beside me. 'We should go in.'

Briefly I touched Samuel on the shoulder, then followed her.

The house was loud with people. Through what seemed like a huge crowd in the hall, Sallie came pushing towards me.

'Sallie, what—'

But she didn't let me speak. 'First things first, Doctor.' She was pale, and there was blood on her cuff. She saw me looking at it. 'Not mine,' she said. 'But you're needed. Morning parlour.' Then she shoved several people out of the way and headed off to the kitchen.

I saw Josiah Thorn, talking to a group of half a dozen men standing around him. Jasper Hart was beside him. They all carried weapons – a pike, a lethal-looking broadsword, knives, cudgels – and Josiah seemed to be telling them how the land lay around the house.

Staring at them, I recognized each one. They had turned out to give their help. Gratitude rose up in me, and the guilt increased.

Judyth was right behind me and she gave me a hard shove, 'Morning room,' she said firmly.

I was just going to tell her that I wasn't going anywhere until I knew my sister and my daughter were safe when I heard Celia say, 'Away, now, Amy, there's blood on the floor,' and Amy's yell of protest.

I ran towards the sound, down the short passage to the morning parlour. And bumped into Theo's wife Elaine, who held her younger son's hand and was clutching an angry Amy in her free arm. 'Your daughter's quite a handful, Gabe,' she said with a small smile. 'Celia suggested I take her and my Benjamin here up to her room, where three of the farmers' wives are caring for a handful of other children.'

'Yes, fine, thank you, Elaine,' I said.

Then I went into the parlour.

A man was lying on the floor, on a straw mattress. Celia was kneeling by his head, Jonathan right beside her, and they were both leaning down hard on a pad of white linen pressed to the man's upper left chest. Celia looked up and said, 'I'm glad you're here, Gabe. You too, Judyth. Jonathan and I are applying as much pressure as we can, but we haven't stopped the bleeding.'

I knelt down and stared into the pale face and closed eyes of Jarman Hodge.

'He's hanging on,' Jonathan said very quietly right in my ear, 'but it's a grave injury.'

I nodded. He and Celia sat back and I removed the blood-soaked pad. Someone had taken a lump out of Jarman's flesh. The memory of what they'd told me about Maudsley Cheverell's awful death crashed into my mind. Was this the same? Had someone begun on that frightful torture?

'I need hot water and my bag,' I said as I took off my jerkin and rolled up my sleeves.

'Your bag is here,' Celia said – of course it was, she'd have known I'd want it as soon as I arrived – 'and Sallie is fetching hot water.'

As soon as I leaned over my patient, I felt myself detach. This was what I did; this was what I was good at. It was calming to return to a job I knew I could perform. Although it was indeed a grave injury, it did not go very deep; it was a slicing wound and not a stabbing one. Which was just as well because if the blade had been driven down instead of across, he would have died straight away.

Swiftly Judyth mixed herbs and poured hot water to make a strong potion, and she managed to get most of it down Jarman's throat. Then I began. I closed my mind to the fact that this was Jarman Hodge, a man I had known for a long time and who I liked and trusted. All the time I worked on him he was a body, and I was the person trying to stop the bleeding and save him.

Finally the stitches were all in place and the bleeding had first slowed to a seep and was now almost stopping. At last I could straighten up. My back gave a great stabbing pain in protest.

I looked round, noticing now that Theo stood in the corner of the room and his daughter Isabella was huddled against him.

She was about nine or ten, I recalled. She had long fair hair like her mother's and Theo's bright eyes, although hers were more silver than blue. She was as pretty as a picture, and I wondered what on earth they'd been thinking of to allow her in here with a badly wounded man in urgent need of treatment.

I glanced at Theo and raised my eyebrows. He nudged Isabella, and she came shyly over to where I still knelt on the floor.

'Have you saved him?' she asked.

'For now, yes, I believe so,' I replied. 'You . . . er, did it not make you feel queasy, Isabella, to be close to him when he was so poorly?'

'No,' she said firmly. 'I want to look after people like you and Mistress Penwarden do, and I'm not scared of blood and messy bits.'

I glared up at Theo. This was not the time and the place for his child to have a lesson in wound-stitching.

But he said, '*Listen*, Gabe. She needs to tell you.'

I met Isabella's shining eyes and waited.

'I was at home, and I went down to Daddy's office because I heard someone there,' she said. She was speaking very quickly, her fingers twisting together. 'I thought it was Daddy or Jarman, and I wanted to see if there was any news. But as I went into the office there was a man hiding behind the door and he was all in dark clothes and he had a face with narrow, cruel eyes and he clenched his teeth, and then we heard the street door open and he grabbed me and held me very tightly right in front of him and he put his hand over my mouth and dragged me behind the door.' She stopped, panting slightly.

'Go on, sweetheart,' Theo said. She reached up and grasped one of his hands, so tightly that her knuckles went white. Theo winced.

'This time it *was* Jarman,' she said, the words tumbling out, 'and he came on into the office and then he sensed someone was there and he turned and the man had a knife on my neck and he said *do not approach or I will kill her* and he had a strong accent and the words came out funny and Jarman put his hands out from his sides and said no, he wasn't coming any nearer, and then the man drew a *huge* blade that was thin and curved a bit and he was aiming it right at Jarman, at his heart, and he twisted his wrist and brought it down in a sort of curve that cut *right* through Jarman's clothes and his leather tunic and everything and Jarman went *uuurgh* and fell on his knees and the man had the sword up again and I *knew* what he was going to do and he still had his hand over my mouth and I opened my jaws and I *bit* him as hard as I could and a lump of his hand was in my mouth and there was blood and I was spitting and then the man grabbed his bitten hand in the other one and sort of crouched into himself and Jarman was half on his feet and he'd grabbed the big heavy stick that Daddy keeps beside the door and he hit the man over the head with it and the man fell on the floor and he didn't move.' She stopped, and at last gasped in some air.

I sensed Theo's reaction as the tumble of words abruptly ceased. I glanced up at him and saw he was desperate to sweep up his daughter in his arms, hold her, hug her, comfort her.

But not just yet.

I reached out and held her by the shoulders. Stared into her eyes. 'Isabella, how brave,' I said. 'You must have been very scared, but you fought the man. You bit him and distracted him, and you saved Jarman's life.'

She stood very still. 'But the man died,' she whispered. 'Daddy told me. You shouldn't kill people. It says so in the Bible and it's against the law.'

Jonathan was behind me, and I heard him give a quiet exclamation. 'Yes it does,' I agreed. 'But the man had threatened to
hurt you, he'd already really hurt Jarman and he was about to
do so again. To hurt or kill someone who is going to hurt or kill
you or someone else is not against the law, and if you told a
priest about it, I believe he would say that God would understand.'

I turned and met Jonathan's watchful eyes. He said calmly, 'It
is true, Isabella.'

She looked at Jonathan, then back at me. 'Really?'

'Really,' we said together.

Isabella glanced at Theo. 'I think I'll go and find Carolus and
Benjamin now, if that's all right.'

'Of course,' he replied. She hugged him – I could see what it
cost him not to cling on to her – and then calmly walked out of
the room.

I looked up at him and smiled. 'You have a fine daughter,' I
said.

And he replied, 'I know.'

I left Celia and Judyth in the morning parlour, watching over
Jarman and making preparations for whatever they would have
to deal with next. I washed my hands, picked up my jerkin and,
with an inclination of the head to Theo and Jonathan, left the
parlour and went across the hall, up the stairs and into my study.
I'd hoped that the sudden influx of people in the house would
be largely confined to downstairs, and so it was. As Theo and
Jonathan followed me inside and shut the door, we could hear
women's and children's voices from along the passage in Celia's
room, but the study was empty.

'Tell me,' I said.

Jonathan went first. He had not needed to seek out men to
rally to my cause, he began, because they started coming to him.
'It's always the way,' he went on, 'news travels fast, and a great
many people, on hearing you were facing a threat with only your
household and Jasper Hart to help you, started to remember how
you had come to their aid when they were in need and decided
they'd like to return the favour. Yes, I know,' he raised his voice
as I tried to speak, 'you'll say you're a physician, it's your job
to care for people and they don't have to show their gratitude

by coming to stand shoulder to shoulder with you. However, they're here, they don't like what's happening down in Plymouth, they resent the idea of outsiders paying local people to take up arms against one of their own – that's you – and they'll stop them if they can.'

I nodded, momentarily too moved to speak.

'I've come with a private army too,' Theo said after a short pause. I spun round to look at him: that was what Jasper Hart had said, when we were still in the hut. *Somehow, my friend, you have acquired a private army.* 'We had to, Gabe!' he said when I still did not speak. 'That band of half a dozen men has grown rapidly and become a formidable force. The original six have been offering a very generous reward, and there are always men who will do just about anything for money.'

'Yes, the one thing their master has in abundance is money,' I said bitterly. I thought of Aroto Tagauchi. His wealth was so vast that it was almost certainly impossible to count. I was suddenly angry; more than angry.

For a moment I was barely able to breathe as I thought of that cold, ruthless man and his single-minded determination to mould his descendants into the creatures he wanted them to be. Creatures who would mindlessly do his bidding, perpetuate his great family line. A line which probably had its own creation myth, so charismatic that its history was almost a religion, so ancient that it could have come into the world at the time the gods were born. And what had this ruthlessness achieved? A daughter who foiled his plan to marry her into another ancient family and fell in love with a Portuguese merchant; a granddaughter who escaped his gold-lined, luxurious captivity and crept into a stranger's bed, only to die in the aftermath of the birth of the child she bore to that stranger. A great-granddaughter who had cost a loyal and devoted young serving woman her life, and was now on the other side of the globe.

What was all the wealth in the world when set against that rebellion?

It can buy men to fight your cause, I reflected bitterly.

Which was exactly what it had done.

I came out of my thoughts and listened to Theo.

'. . . vast sums of money must indeed have been spent,' he

was saying testily. He glared at me. 'But you have something too, Gabe. You have the loyal support of your friends. There they all are, downstairs and outside, manning the gates, waiting to be given their orders. Your brother Nathaniel's outside with three of his household checking the outer boundaries, and your father's in the library trying to persuade your mother that she doesn't need to go into the kitchen and help Sallie.'

My brother. My parents. 'My parents shouldn't be here!' I exclaimed. 'Not my mother, anyway.' It would, I reflected, have been impossible to keep my father away. But for my mother to put herself in peril was intolerable.

Jonathan said quietly, 'Gabe, they are safer here. Yes, I understand that you're the target, that what these men are after is here, under your roof, and so this is where we expect the threat to materialize. But they are clever, those men who are on your trail, and I doubt that they would have needed to rely on local knowledge to inform them of the whereabouts of your family and your friends.'

And I remembered Judyth. They'd known about her, known she was important to me, known where she lived. Come to hunt her down, to use her as leverage to make me give up what they wanted so badly and had come so far to claim.

They could have done the same with my brother. My father. My mother. Would I have held out, if my mother had been facing a dreadful death? Given them the Chrysanthemum Tiger, yes, of course. But surrender my child?

I closed my eyes and said a brief, fervent prayer for the good sense of all of them, family, friends, former patients, for they had known better than I and they were here, all of them, and we'd fight together.

SEVENTEEN

Evening was coming down.

As Theo, Jonathan and I made our way downstairs, I thought I should check on everybody. I found my father in the library; my mother wasn't with him. Apparently he had lost the argument over whether or not she should join Sallie in the kitchen, but again, as so often throughout their lives together, he was reluctantly having to admit that he'd been wrong.

'It's hard to credit it,' he muttered to me, 'but she and your Sallie are chatting away like old friends!' He looked amazed. 'I was always led to believe you can't have two women in a kitchen,' he remarked. He shrugged. 'Still, it's been a day full of surprises, and from the appetizing smells creeping through your house, son, I'd say we were in for a decent meal tonight.'

Nathaniel was standing by the window, peering out at the gathering darkness. 'We should close and secure the shutters throughout the house,' he announced. 'We don't want them creeping up and spying on those within.'

'You're staying, you and your friends?' I asked.

'They are my outdoor staff,' he corrected. Ever the pedant, my brother, I thought, smiling. 'No, we'll not be staying, if by that you mean remaining in the house. I've organized a rota and we shall be on watch on the boundaries during the hours of darkness.'

I thanked him, trying to match his grave tone.

Celia hurried in as he finished speaking, cast me a brief commiserating look, then began to tell my father that she had made up her bed with fresh sheets for him and my mother and prepared a shake-down bed for herself in her workroom.

I slipped away.

I crossed the hall, dodging a huddle of Theo's men, and headed out into the cold night air in the yard. I was heading for the stable block to speak to Samuel and the group of men making themselves at home in the barn when someone hurried up behind me.

'Gabe?'

I turned and saw Jonathan.

'Have you come to take the air?' I asked, smiling.

'No.' He paused, and I suddenly realized he was nervous.

'What is it?'

'I . . .' He stopped, drew a breath, then said in an oddly toneless and formal voice, 'I would like to marry your sister. We
have come to respect and care for one another, and—'

'Jonathan, stop, for goodness' sake!' I interrupted. I wanted
to smile, to laugh, to embrace him and slap him on the back.
'First, if you're asking me for my permission, you don't need it
because although she lives in my house she is in fact a widow
and her own woman, and anyway, if you *were* asking it ought
to be my father and—'

'I'm not asking,' he said quietly.

'Oh. Er . . .' I tried to remember what I'd been about to say.
'Second, you don't have to be so restrained, not with me. Respect
and care for each other! Good God, Jonathan, you've been in
love with her for years, and I've known for a long time that she
loves you.'

'Yes,' he said simply.

I remembered my recent conversation with Celia.

'I didn't think of the two of you when I went away,' I said
quietly. 'If I had, if I'd paused in my headlong dash when I
answered the call of the wide world and went back to sea, I'd
have realized the effect that my absence would have on you.'

'You did what you had to do, and—' he began.

'Jonathan, Celia told me with her usual bluntness that while
I was away, she had to stay at Rosewyke and you couldn't leave
the Priest's House, so you had no choice. I *gave* you no choice.'

'No,' he said.

We were both silent for what felt like a long moment. Then
I took his arm and said, 'I'm sorry.'

He nodded. 'So?' he said. His lean face was eager, and he
was tense with impatience.

'So?

'I know we don't need your permission, but I'd like to think
I – we – have your approval?'

It moved me greatly that there was a question in his words.

'Jonathan, you fool, of *course* you do!' I cried. 'I have long looked upon you as a brother, closer than a brother' – I hoped Nathaniel wasn't in earshot – 'and to have you become in truth my kinsman gives me nothing but joy.'

He nodded again, and I guessed he didn't speak in case his voice gave him away.

'Until she becomes your wife, Rosewyke is Celia's home,' I said. 'If you will allow it, if it's what you both want, I will arrange the finest party there has ever been to celebrate your union.'

Now he smiled; a wide, happy smile that I'd never seen before. 'Thank you, Gabe,' he said.

It took some time to do the round of all the people who had come to my aid. I found pairs and sometimes groups of men alert and watchful all around the boundaries, and they had concealed themselves so well that I'd had no idea they were there until one of them made himself known. Without exception they were armed, and someone – my brother, apparently – had told them what they should do. But when finally I turned back towards the house, I realized I hadn't seen Jasper. I consulted Samuel, who told me Jasper had taken a group of four men out to the spot where the path up from the river emerged.

'He's eager, that Doctor Hart,' Samuel opined. 'Wanted to post himself at the gates, where the track meets the road down there, but the coroner already had it covered.'

I thanked him and hurried off.

Jasper and his group were so well hidden that I couldn't make them out. But he saw me, and as I stood on the path staring around, he emerged from the tangle of fruit bushes that bordered the orchard and the woods and came up quietly beside me. He grabbed my arm and led me back into his shelter.

'I'm pleased you didn't spot me,' he said quietly.

'I didn't. Well done. Where are the rest of them? Who are they?' I added.

'It's four men from one of the farms on the edge of the moors,' he replied, 'father, son, son-in-law and nephew. Name of Snell.'

Yes. I'd once sewn up John Snell's forearm when he'd had an

accident with a scythe, and I'd helped Judyth when the daughter-in-law had difficulties with her first child.

Judyth.

I let her image float before me for an instant, then regretfully
put her out of my mind.

'I know them,' I said. 'It's good that they're here. They're
armed?' Jasper muttered a response, but I couldn't make out the
words. 'What did you say?'

He didn't answer.

The silence extended.

'What's the matter, Jasper?' I asked quietly.

He didn't speak for some time. Then, with a deep sigh, he
said. 'I must make a confession to you.'

There was a note of despair in his voice. I wondered what
was wrong; what, in the midst of the major threat we were facing,
could be affecting him so powerfully. Was it, perhaps, that, back
at Rosewyke and throwing himself into defending my family and
me, he was feeling guilty because earlier he'd left so abruptly?

'I've already told you that I understand your reasons for leaving
Rosewyke when you did, Jasper,' I began. 'I accept that I made
a grave mistake in my choice of Maudsley Cheverell, and although
we are taught not to speak ill of the dead, I know that his presence among you all here was an unbearable burden.'

I thought he might reply, *Yes, that's it, that's what it is.*

But he didn't.

Instead he said, so softly that I could barely make out the
words, 'They are coming tonight. As soon as the moon's up and
they have the light, they'll be here.'

I said, 'How can you be so sure?'

But even before he replied, I had a cold feeling that I already
knew the answer. 'I think you'd better tell me,' I said.

'When you asked me to take your place at Rosewyke and tend
your patients during your absence,' he began, 'you may have
wondered why I accepted so readily.'

I tried to remember. So much had happened since that day
that it wasn't easy. 'It was because you were exhausted and
burned out after dealing with the plague in London,' I said. 'You'd
hinted at that last Symposium meeting that you wouldn't be
averse to a change, and a spell of life in the country.'

It was virtually impossible to recall the meeting with any clarity. It was among that great collection of events and memories that belonged to *before*. Before this night, and the advent of a ruthlessly cruel enemy force determined to ride away with treasures I was equally determined they should not have.

He barely seemed to be listening. 'Yes, yes,' he said impatiently. 'I was in debt, Gabe. Deep in debt. Those times while the plague raged were hard in every sense, but among the worst of it was that my income dried up. I never seemed to stop working, but so many died – whole families sometimes – and the dead don't care about unpaid bills. I borrowed money,' he plunged on, 'too much money, and I discovered how one debt leads to another, and then I also found out what happens when those clever and smooth-tongued men who are so willing to offer their help hear you choke out the words that you cannot pay them what you owe.'

'So you needed to get away quickly,' I said. He had momentarily stopped for breath. 'You reckoned that Devon was a good place to run to, and no doubt you calculated that what you'd be paid would deal with the debt, and—'

'I could have gone on doing an honest day's work at Rosewyke until I'm an old man and *never* repaid it,' Jasper said baldly. 'It wasn't enough – *nothing* I could do would have been enough,' he added bitterly. He closed his eyes briefly, then opened them, and as the last light faded and the stars came out, the look he gave me spoke of profound shame and guilt, and, beneath those, dread.

'Tell me,' I said.

'When I fled from Rosewyke there was nowhere else to go but back to London,' he said. 'So that was where I went, and I tried to resume my life in Southwark.' He was speaking very quickly now, as if he couldn't wait to be finished. 'They came to call almost as soon as I arrived, and they seemed to know exactly where I'd been and what I'd been doing.' He gave a short, hard laugh. 'I thought I'd been so discreet. I only told one or two people, but I should have known better. Anyway, I'd been back no more than a few days when some men came to see me late one night. They weren't the usual thugs – they had already paid a call earlier that evening, and the biggest and most brutal of them had been on the point of breaking the fingers on my right hand one by one, until one of his colleagues with rather more intelligence pointed out that it wasn't a great idea, given my profession, to take away my dexterity.' He gave a brief, hard laugh. 'I didn't recognize any of these other men. Their spokesman said they knew all about my troubles, they sympathized, and they had a suggestion to make that would enable me to put my financial problems behind me once and for all. *You can pay what you owe, and tell those brutes that were here earlier with their threats of violence to go to hell*, they told me, although I've no idea how they knew.'

He paused, and I guessed from his fast, frightened breathing that the memory was far too clear.

'Oh, Gabe, it was a dream come true,' he exclaimed. 'The sum they were proposing to give me would pay back all I owed.' He paused, recovering. 'Believe me, it was truly a vast sum by then because I'd been amassing so much interest, although I never really understood *how.*' He shook his head. 'I should have made sure I *did* understand, shouldn't I? I'm not stupid, I ought to have listened, done sums on a piece of paper, realized what it all meant. But all I can say to explain how I came to accept is that I was *desperate* and I thought my debtors were going to *kill* me.'

'Who were they, these men who bought you?' I asked.

He winced at the word. 'I don't know. I didn't know *then*,' he corrected himself, 'but now, of course, it's clear they were working for your man, this warlord in Japan. They were Londoners, the ones who called on me, and wealthy merchants, by the look of them. Would your man have trade contacts in London, do you think?'

'Almost undoubtedly,' I replied. I wished he wouldn't keep calling Aroto Tagauchi *my* man. It was a fair assumption that he'd have extended his grasp to London, however; there was money to be made there, and the port was burgeoning. Once he knew I'd set off from Japan aboard the *Luipaard*, he'd have sent word by the swiftest means to his contacts in the city, relying on their local knowledge to inform them how best to proceed.

And, somehow, they'd found Jasper Hart.

'You betrayed me,' I said. 'You were desperate – you just said so – and you were so deep in debt that when you saw a way out, you forgot honour, and loyalty, and decency, and you took it.'

Jasper stood with his head bowed and did not answer.

The echoes of my angry words still hung in the air.

'What did you undertake to do to earn this money?' I asked softly.

He shook his head as if he wanted to deny his own actions, his gaze fixed on the ground. 'They told me you were homeward bound,' he said, so quietly that I strained to hear. 'They said you'd stolen things from an important warlord out in the East, that you had no right to them, that the lord was determined to reclaim them and was offering a very handsome reward to anyone who helped him. They knew I was your friend, they knew I'd lived at Rosewyke all those months, that I could tell them where the house was and describe your household and its daily round. I even told them about your *horse*, God help me, and that stable yard in the port that you always used,' he muttered miserably.

'How did they know we were friends?' I asked neutrally.

'We have never made a secret of it,' he replied. 'We trained together in London, along with many others, and you and I were part of a close group who kept in touch with each other. It formed the origins of our Symposium, that you were just speaking of,' he added eagerly.

I looked at him. I felt torn in two. He was my friend, my old friend, and I was aching for his abject face. I also wanted to murder him for his betrayal.

'And you were told where to lead me as we set off together from the hidden creek in Southwark,' I said softly. 'Told which roads to take, so that, knowing all the time exactly where we would be, they could bide their time until the right moment and then, one dark night, jump us, overcome us, kill me and take my child and the treasure her mother gave me to keep safe for her.'

He tried to speak but the words would not come.

'Bloody flaming Lucifer, Jasper,' I said in a furious whisper, 'just how long did you reckon *you* would have survived after they'd slain me?'

He closed his eyes. 'They promised to pay me,' he whispered. 'They gave me half before we left London, and I would give it to you, Gabe, truly I would, but it's gone, I've already handed it over to my creditors. They said they'd pay me the rest afterwards. I believed them.'

'Then you're even more of a fool than I thought you were,' I said coldly.

'I know that now,' he said. His voice was infinitely sad.

'Gabe?' he whispered after a short and very painful silence.

'What?'

'Gabe, we're still alive,' he said. 'Your daughter is asleep within the house, guarded by people whose loyalty you do not question. Your treasure is safe in its crate, and undoubtedly hidden in a dark corner in your study.'

'So?'

'They didn't jump us one dark night.'

'No, obviously. But no thanks to you.' I couldn't look at him.

'But it was,' he persisted. 'Because I took you another way.'

And I realized what he meant. Now I met his eyes. 'Go on.'

'I'd been with my contact that last afternoon, just before we set out from the secret creek. I'd told him exactly which roads and tracks we'd take. But then . . . then . . .' He swallowed. He had gone very pale. 'Then as we were leaving, we went down to that clearing in the woods, you and I, and we found your horse, and I saw the body of that groom from Redriff Old Hall. Gregory Tresham's man. He'd done *nothing*, poor fellow, just obeyed orders, and he may well have had a wife and family, a *life*, and they *took* that life, sliced off his head with such finesse that it was as if they were showing off, saying, *look how skilful we are! See how we can slice through a man's neck so efficiently that his head remains in place!* And then your friend, your poor friend Hieronymus, his skull crushed like a shell, and you had to leave him where he was and take not a moment to tend him or to mourn.' He paused, panting slightly. 'I am so, so sorry, Gabe.'

'Did your stomach turn at the thought of how they would elect to kill me?' I asked harshly. 'Of what my child's life would be like if they took her and returned her to her great-grandfather, to be locked up securely and suffocatingly in the jewelled prison her mother perished to escape from?'

'All of that, and yet not one element in particular,' he said humbly. 'I realized what I'd done. I was so deeply ashamed that all I could think about was how to make amends. First, to take you west by the very best, most secret and well-hidden route I could come up with, and then to sleep as little as I could when we stopped to rest, in order to watch over you.'

I did not reply.

'There's more,' he said presently. 'I have seen them since, in the company of others. There are a dozen of them, and among their number are my London contact and at least two of Aroto Tagauchi's men who followed you from Japan. They have recruited others. Local men who cannot find work, men who in their despair have turned to drink, abandoned and argumentative sailors in Plymouth who can find no ship willing to take them on. All of them, each and every one, doubtless accepted Tagauchi's money even more swiftly than I did, if that's possible.'

'And you know all this because you are still in these men's employ.'

'*No!*' The single syllable emerged as an anguished, suppressed shout. 'I am *not*. They *think* I am, and I am regularly reminded of the second half of my payment awaiting me once you . . . after it's all over. But, Gabe, I'm *misleading* them!' His smile beamed out as if he expected me to cheer. 'I'm no longer giving them *accurate* information about you and your movements,' he went on hurriedly, fearful I hadn't understood. 'In short, since they sought me out down here, I've given them nothing but obfuscations, evasions and downright lies!'

'What sort of lies?' I asked. 'Plausible ones that would pass the intelligent scrutiny of men employed as agents of Aroto Tagauchi?'

'Of course!' he cried. Then, his face full of eagerness, 'I hinted that you were dismayed not to have the welcome home that you had expected. I said your family were shunning you for coming home with a child and no wife, and you were planning to move away. I said you shut yourself up at Rosewyke each night with nobody for company but your dog, and were feeling very sorry for yourself!'

Other than presenting my enemies with a picture of me alone, friendless and self-pitying, I could not see what he had achieved. I made no comment.

'Gabe, they won't be expecting any opposition,' Jasper said. 'When they come, they'll creep towards the house, find it dark and shuttered, no lights showing, just as I said it would be, and they'll think all they have to do is walk in and retrieve what they want.'

I stared at him. If he was hoping that this ingenious plan of his to feed the pursuers the wrong information was going to make me shout with relief and embrace him in a gesture of forgiveness for his betrayal, he was wrong.

'I hope you're right, Jasper,' I said. I raised a hand in farewell and left him.

I hoped very much that our defences comprised more than Jasper's foolish optimism. I had a powerful sense of imminent danger, for tonight there would be a full moon.

What better time for an attacking force to creep up on Rosewyke?

I set off back to the house.

As I emerged from under the trees, I looked up at it. I remembered Nathaniel saying the shutters should be closed and secured, and just now Jasper had referred to the same thing. Whoever had undertaken the task had done their job well, and no light emerged from the edges of the windows. It looked like a blind, desolate place.

Although it would confirm the description that Jasper had given to the enemy, I didn't like it; it no longer looked like my home.

I hurried round to the front of the house and, once again, there wasn't a glimmer. It was hard to believe they were all there: my friends, my parents, my sister, my child. Judyth.

Darkness was almost total now. The moon had not yet risen, although there was a faint white glow in the east over the moors that suggested it would appear before long. The distant stars were faint bright dots impossibly far away. I felt desolation fall around me, and the danger that faced me – faced us all – suddenly seemed too much to bear.

I sensed someone standing beside me. I had heard no approach, been unaware of any movement. Whoever it was, he – or she – was just *there*. As if some mighty and mysterious force from far outside the world had picked them up and gently placed them down beside me.

I felt a quiet chord thrum through the air that just for a heart-beat felt like pure magic.

And a soft voice said, 'Evening, Doctor.'

I spun round and saw the unmistakable form of Black Carlotta standing motionless at my side.

'What are you doing here?' I asked.

She thought about the question, then said, 'I've been watching, me and some others that prefer to stay hidden. Seems to me many folk who appreciate a man such as yourself don't take kindly to this power that's disturbing the air. Don't like a danger such as this one seeking out and threatening someone they've come to trust.'

I waited, but it appeared she'd finished.

'Many people are here, yes,' I agreed tentatively. 'Word has spread that I'm back, and that I have . . . er, that I'm in danger. But how do you . . .' I paused, not sure how to phrase the question.

She chuckled. 'How do I know? How did me and my kind come to hear about the forces amassing against you, when we've been driven into hiding, we keep ourselves to ourselves and rarely speak a word to outsiders?'

'I didn't mean—'

'For one thing,' she went on, ignoring the interruption, 'you and I talked, when you were still lurking in that hut I use up on the moors. You told me a deal of things, Doctor, and I picked up much more that you *didn't* tell me.' She was staring up at the house, right at the shuttered window of my study. 'You didn't mention what else you brought back besides that pretty child. You didn't need to, mind, for even as we stood together beside the hut, I knew what was within. You might think, Doctor, that some wrapping, some padding and a wooden box hides something like that from someone like me, but you'd be wrong. And it was almost dormant then, hiding its true nature, maybe.' She shook her head. 'Can't be sure.'

She looked up at the house again, and I looked too. I could make out its black silhouette against the dark sky. Nothing more.

And then I could.

It was eerie: it wasn't there, and then it was. It was gold, and to my eyes without definition: a cloud, a patch of mist that formed, dissipated, formed again. If I blinked I saw it more clearly for an instant. If I looked sideways, very briefly it took on a familiar shape.

I wondered what Black Carlotta was putting into my mind . . .

She chuckled again. 'It's not me, Doctor. I'm not doing it.' She added something else that sounded like *no power from me could do that*.

Alarmed, I turned to look at her.

She said softly, 'I don't know what creature it is. Nothing I know.'

'It's a tiger.'

She nodded. 'Gold. And it sparkles.'

I didn't ask her how she knew. I didn't really want to be told. After a while she said, 'It's old. Very old.'

'Yes.'

'And it has a long and unbreakable tie with blood.'

I hesitated, thinking. 'With a specific family, yes. With a very ancient bloodline.'

She dismissed the distinction with an impatient wave of her hand. 'It is through blood that the link is made.'

I wished that I understood. Wished that I saw what she could see.

'I did not steal it,' I said. 'I had heard tell of it, and I knew that it belonged to a certain family on a southern island of Japan.'

'It *belongs* to nobody,' she corrected.

'Then let's say instead that it was in the keeping of that family, and had been for centuries,' I amended. 'There was an old man, and he had just one child, a daughter, and she in turn also had just one daughter. Neither woman followed the path that the old man laid down for them, and that each new generation had always followed. The younger woman's rebellion was the more forceful and—'

'And she is the mother of your child. Yes,' Carlotta said.

'Was. She died,' I said neutrally.

She looked across at me, and although the light was too poor for her to have made out any expression, I sensed she understood a lot more than I had said.

'Did this younger woman have other children?' Carlotta asked.
'No.'

'The creature in your upper room is in its rightful place, then.'

'Because my child is the sole descendant of the old man's line.'

She must have thought I was seeking confirmation, and said, 'Yes. Or so I perceive it to be.'

I smiled. 'I wasn't asking,' I said. 'I already know.'

And I told her how Natsu had given her life to make sure my child was handed to me and so was her inheritance.

'Blood,' she muttered. 'Always blood.'

I saw Natsu's body on the quay. There had been a great deal of blood.

'It came to you in blood.' Carlotta's voice sounded distant, and she spoke on a monotone, as if she was chanting. 'Then there was more blood, up there in your room where you keep it.'

'No, that isn't right, there was no violence when—'

Then I remembered. I'd put out my hand to test the sharpness of the claw on the Chrysanthemum Tiger's forepaw and it had laid open two of my fingers.

I knew by her soft sigh of satisfaction that she knew.

'Was that what you meant?' I whispered.

She shrugged. 'Blood is blood.'

I barely heard. I was remembering what had happened next. How Amy had reached out and grasped the very same claw and yet remained unharmed. How the Tiger had suddenly glowed with power and shimmered with the force of the noonday sun.

'It has acknowledged you,' Carlotta said matter-of-factly. 'It knew your child already, which is why she was not hurt. It needed to taste your blood, and when it had, it knew you too.'

'Will it – can it protect us?' I asked. I heard myself speak the words and my rational self shouted out in protest. Such things cannot be, my sensible scientific mind cried. It is nothing more than a golden statue with ivory claws that are studded with diamonds and rubies. Any power attributed to it exists exclusively in the minds of the men who make themselves believe it is there.

And yet, I thought, And yet.

Black Carlotta had turned to go. Was already a couple of paces away.

'You can stay here!' I called softly after her. 'There is danger abroad, and safety within our walls.'

She laughed. 'Doctor, the danger you speak of is because of what's within your walls,' she said bluntly. 'Thank you for the offer, but I'll be on my way.' She hesitated, as if wondering whether to go on. Then she said, 'But I am in danger, me and all those like me. Remember? What I said to you last time we spoke, about the Scots king and his fear?'

'I remember.'

'Then you'll know why. Goodbye, Doctor.'

'Wait!' I said. 'Have you somewhere to go, all of you? Somewhere safe?'

She smiled. 'Of course. We knew this was coming. We'll be fine.'

She walked away.

But then she stopped, head cocked as if listening. Then she turned to look back at me.

'My, but you must stand high in the favour of some power or other,' she remarked.

I had no idea what she meant. 'Really?' I said dryly.

She was smiling again. 'Oh, yes. You're already protected by something which, since you cannot see, hear, smell or feel it, you refuse to believe in. Although I'm surprised you can't hear it humming, since it's all but deafening now.'

'It's . . . *what*?'

'But there's another force too,' she said, ignoring me, 'and that is also on your side.' She laughed aloud. 'You'll be able to detect this one all right.'

And then, with quite amazing speed, she seemed to float across the open space and a moment later she had disappeared beneath the trees.

EIGHTEEN

The night came on.

Out in the yard, some of the men grabbed the chance to sleep while others patrolled the boundaries. Theo was standing outside the barn, frowning. 'All's quiet,' he said as I approached him. 'The patrol's just reported and gone out again.'

'Good. Thank you.'

He stared at me. 'What are we expecting, Gabe?' he murmured. 'Wish I knew, so that I could tell them what to expect. So I'd know what to expect myself,' he added. He looked down. 'No doubt you've been in this situation before?'

'Waiting for an anticipated attack? Yes, I have.' I did not want to elaborate.

'Do you think it'll be tonight?'

I shrugged. 'I sense it will,' I said honestly.

I decided not to add that a local wise woman had said it would be, and I was very inclined to believe her.

All was quiet inside the house. The door to the morning parlour was firmly closed, allowing those within to sleep while they could. Celia had settled down close to Jarman Hodge, keeping watch. Judyth was with her. Theo's wife Elaine was up in the small room next to mine, with all three of their children. My parents were in Celia's room, or so I hoped. My mother had taken over the care of her new granddaughter. I'd been delighted when she announced that she would make Amy her responsibility, although I wished that this sudden closeness hadn't been instigated by a time of such peril.

Sallie was in the kitchen. The fire would be kept burning, there would be a big cauldron of water constantly on the heat. I left her counting her supplies in the pantry. I'd suggested gently that she try to get some rest, but, although she said she would, I could tell from the tension in her thin frame that it was unlikely. Going out through the door, I turned and, on impulse, said, 'Sallie, I have no idea how we'd manage without you.'

And she made a shooing motion and said, 'Get away with you!'

They came as the moon was halfway up to the zenith.

They were slick, efficient, extremely well-drilled and eerily, frighteningly silent. Theo's men, local farmers and friends had been stationed on the boundaries; there was a large band of tough-looking types at the gate on to the road who had come at Josiah Thorn's invitation; Jasper and his quartet were at the top of the path down to the river; in the house, eyes were staring out into the darkness from behind the shutters.

Aroto Tagauchi's fighting warriors slithered black-clad and dark-masked right past every one of them.

There must have been twenty-five or thirty of them. More than half moved with the neat, efficient movements of trained fighters: those would be the main core of six that was comprised of Tagauchi men from London and off the ships that had pursued us all the way from Japan, with the addition of at least ten or a dozen more of their number, presumably posted here in Devon.

They announced their arrival at the main door, with a spear-headed attack of maybe twenty men. Finding the door locked and barred, as no doubt they had anticipated, instantly two files broke off to right and left, heading for the windows to the library and the morning parlour.

The group attacking the parlour window found the heavy shutters impossible to break. It was a small window, and it had been easy to reinforce the shutters with sturdy wooden braces. The library window was larger and more difficult to fortify. The attackers were taken by surprise when the shutters suddenly parted, bright light shone out, blinding them out there in the darkness, and even as they reacted, the windows were flung open and armed men burst out to repel them. Musket fire blasted out at them, blades caught the light as they were swept down on the attackers, and in very quick time an order was shouted – one sharp, shrill syllable in an alien tongue – and on the instant, as one the attackers formed up into a tight knot and disappeared into the darkness.

I wiped my sword. I was standing on the grass outside the library, and Theo was beside me. None of our number had been injured, but two of the attackers lay beneath the window. One was dead. He had taken the lethal lead ball from the musket fired by one of Theo's men right in the face, and not a lot of his head was left. The other man lay inert, bleeding heavily and dangerously from a deep cut to the side of his neck.

This second man, clad entirely in black and tightly hooded, was clearly one of those who had pursued us; I even thought I recognized him.

'Will you tend him?' Theo asked quietly.

'No.'

He nodded.

We went back inside and I set off on a hurried check of the people inside the house. No one had been hurt, although some of the children were crying, and after a quick few words with Celia and Judyth – including the welcome assurance that Jarman Hodge was sitting up and Theo's daughter was feeding him porridge – I went out into the yard. Men were still coming in from the boundaries, shame-faced at having let the attackers through without a single challenge. 'Didn't see, hear or even *smell* the buggers!' the blacksmith from Tavistock said resentfully.

There were no serious injuries, although one man had wrenched an ankle falling over in the darkness and another had a nasty cut on his cheek from being hit by a wood chip, blasted out of the frame of the library window by a musket ball. I sent them inside for attention.

Then I remembered Jasper. He was not in the yard, and nor were any of the Snell men. 'Anyone heard if there's been action on the path up from the river?' I asked. Nobody knew.

I headed for the gate and the men on guard opened it as I ran up. Theo thundered after me, grabbing my arm. I shook him off and said angrily, 'I should have sent more men down there! There were thirty at most attacking up here, it's almost certain they know about the riverside track, so there may be a dozen or more coming up that way!'

Theo was trying to hold me back. 'If Jasper and the others have failed and let the attackers get through, we'll know about it soon enough!' he protested. 'At least wait for more armed men, Gabe – what do you think you can do alone?'

I threw him off.

I raced across the grass and through the orchard and the band of woodland, my feet finding the narrow path as if I'd walked it every day for the last two and a half years. Which was unexpectedly lucky, not that it struck me at the time, given that I hadn't often gone that way when I lived at Rosewyke . . .

Jasper and his companions hadn't failed.

John Snell and his son had minor wounds, the son-in-law and the nephew were unharmed. The two of them were busy making a pile of five bodies, and John Snell was shouting out instructions.

'They weren't expecting us,' he said when he saw me approach. He was sitting in deep darkness under a hedge which shaded him from the moonlight. There was a bundle across his lap; someone had kept him warm with a coat. 'Three of them were locals,' he went on, 'with a couple of foreign-looking fellows in the lead. The two in the lead came creeping up without a sound, but the men following behind weren't so fit or so dainty-footed, and we heard one man trip on a step and another wheezing as he clambered up the steep stretch. That was enough of a warning, and we were ready for them.' He gave a savage smile.

'All dead?'

He nodded. Jerking his head towards his son, sitting nearby and nursing a huge bump on his forehead, he said, 'Once William there took the leader down, the others were easy prey.' There was a savagery in his voice that I hadn't expected from a Devon farmer. 'That Doctor Hart did well too. He took care of the other foreigner.' His voice had changed. He dropped his head.

I looked round. 'Where is Jasper?'

And John Snell put a gentle hand on the bundle in his lap.

Jasper lay across him, head cradled on a folded coat. I crouched down beside him. His face was deathly white but his eyes were full of excitement.

'I got him, Gabe!' he said. He paused, panting. 'The leader was one of the men from London. It was he who was going to pay me afterwards.' He paused again, this time for longer. 'He looked so surprised to see me when he came out from the top of the path!' He started to laugh. It turned into a gurgle, and his mouth filled with blood.

'Jasper, don't tell me now,' I said, my hands already inside his clothing, searching his body for the wound, trying to think what I could use to stem the bleeding.

He took hold of my hands and stilled them. His touch was icy cold. 'Don't, Gabe,' he said. 'It will not be long, and I would rather you talked to me.'

'Very well, then.' I withdrew my hands. I would have ignored his plea and gone on trying to save him, but I'd already located the wound. He was right: it wouldn't be long. A blade had stabbed right into his upper chest, and then whoever had held the weapon had twisted it sideways and down. Some major vessel around his heart had been severed, and he had no more than moments to live.

He was trying to say something. I caught the words *help*, and *fire*. He waved a hand towards the sea. I thought he was smiling.

'Jasper? What is it?'

He smiled again, shook his head.

'Is there anything I can do for you?' I asked him.

I had to bend low to hear his reply. His breath was fading. 'One thing,' he whispered.

'Tell me.'

'Forgive,' he breathed, so softly I barely heard.

But I had picked up the single word, and so had John Snell. 'Is he asking for absolution?' he whispered. 'Should we get Jonathan Carew out to him?'

'No,' I replied. 'There's no time.'

Besides, I didn't believe it was a priest's absolution that Jasper wanted.

I bent down so that my face was beside his ear. 'I understand,' I said. 'You were desperate for money and you grabbed the chance when it came. But you saw your own mistake and you did all you could to put it right. I forgive you without reservation.'

I saw him relax. He mouthed, 'Thank you.'

'Say a prayer, maybe, Doctor?' John Snell prompted.

But as I knelt beside my dying friend, I found I could not speak. I waved a hand at John, and he took up the cue.

His son-in-law and his nephew stopped what they were doing,

the son bowed his head and closed his eyes, I looked down into Jasper's bloodless face and his wide eyes. We all listened as John Snell's sonorous voice said the Lord's Prayer and the *Nunc dimittis*, and as the ancient words floated out down the steep bank to be lost in the rushing noise of the Tavy, Jasper Hart expelled his last breath and died.

The Snell men undertook to watch over the body. I ran back to the house.

I looked up, just as I'd done earlier. Now the light around the house was clear silvery-white, for the scene was bathed in moonlight. But then, as I watched, a brighter light shot up into the sky, cutting a shining path whose brilliant gold eclipsed the cold paleness of the moon.

I didn't understand what I was seeing, and my logical mind refused to believe what I thought it was.

Then it was as if Black Carlotta was beside me again, just where she had stood before. *It's changed*, I heard her say inside my head. *Just like I told you. Those night-clad men thought it would be loyal to the old ways, and believed they had its might behind them. They were wrong. It has turned. It's yours, yours and the child's. It has a far greater allegiance now.*

I stood as if bewitched.

Then the brilliant dazzling gold began to fade, very slowly at first but then quickly, folding back into itself and falling back towards the house.

They came again.

There were two more assaults. The first was aimed once again at the library, and it had the same result. 'You'd have thought they might have learned,' one of Theo's men remarked as I hastily stitched up a deep slice across his forearm. He was still full of the high elation that comes after a successful fight, and only swore at me four times as I tended him.

It was clear straight away that more care had gone into the third attack. The leader had assembled the remainder of his troops, and someone watching upstairs reported that there were thirty-six of them. Assuming the count was accurate, it meant either we had underestimated their original strength, or reinforcements had turned up. The men were preparing to advance in tight formation, two by two, straight towards the main door, and marching as they were, they offered a smaller target for the musket fire from the house.

Already the library windows were wide open and, taking my place among the massed defenders, I looked out. Some quick-thinking person had removed the shutters from the small window of the morning parlour, on the far side of the main door, and there was movement from within. They would fire on the column from that wing, I thought, and the two-pronged attack must surely fell many of the attackers, provided our forces were good enough shots and had enough ammunition . . .

Then one of Theo's men – it was Tomas, the one with the broken nose – came pounding up the track from the gates. Spotting the column marching on the house, he veered hastily to his left, ran for several paces on the edge of the trees and then hared across the grass to the library window. 'Theo,' he gasped out, bent double, hands on his knees. 'Where's the chief?' He looked round wildly.

'Here.' Theo pushed his way through the assembled men and leaned over him. Tomas muttered something, but he was so out of breath that the words were barely audible. Theo frowned and shot out a question, Tomas nodded furiously and Theo straightened up, shot me a triumphant glance and punched a fist in the air. He spoke briefly to the men gathering round him, then came over to me.

Unlikely though it seemed, there was a sparkle in his eyes. He said, 'Who would you like to be approaching up the road from Plymouth with a well-armed contingent of fighters?'

'Theo, it's no time for a jest,' I replied angrily.

'It's no jest. Go on, tell me.'

'Francis Drake,' I said angrily.

'Close.' Now he was starting to smile. 'Remember a ship called the *Falco*?'

'Of course.' How could I not? Some of my most memorable years at sea had been on board that ship, and I was of her company when I had the accident that ended my naval career.

'The *Falco*'s in port,' Theo said. 'For some reason her captain remembers you fondly. Apparently he's a man ever spoiling for a quarrel, and when I sought him out he told me it's far too long since his company did any shore-based hand-to-hand fighting. There's fifteen of them on their way, and he's leading them.'

Captain Zeke. Ezekiel Cole. I felt like cheering.

They had commandeered a flat cart drawn by two plough horses, which were quickly led away once the cart was in place. On the back of the cart were two naval guns, of the smaller broadside type that are fired at point-blank range to tear through an enemy's decking. I'd never heard of them being transported on a farm cart across country to be used in the fields and the woods of a private house, but Captain Zeke was ever an innovator. As well as the sailors expertly loading and firing the ship's guns, there were many others with muskets and muzzleloaders, and every man of them moving in the same well-drilled routine.

Even as the cart jerked to a standstill, the attackers were responding. The brief, harsh words of an order screamed out and instantly the column changed direction, moving in a tight curve to their left and heading swiftly for the cover of the woods between the house and the river. A second order, and four men spun round to open fire.

Nothing could have prepared them for the speed of Captain Zeke's gunners. It surprised even me, and I knew him. Already the two heavy guns were blasting out the first shots, one after the other, the noise deafening, and men positioned on either side were firing their muskets and muzzleloaders in the well-practised sequence that meant there was barely a pause.

Instantly the attackers were a fatally depleted force, with most of their leaders dead or dying.

The men at the front of the column were already among the outlying trees, those behind trying to push in behind them. A steady stream of fire was raining down on them from the *Falco*'s improvised gun carriage, and then there was a shattering explosion as shot from the two guns fired simultaneously blasted out on a fast, flat trajectory and landed with utter precision right where the attackers were massing beneath the trees.

Some were right in the line of fire and killed outright. Many more suffered terrible wounds as great spears of wood, splintered off the tree trunks by the shot, drove deep into their bodies.

As the deafening sound faded, we could just hear the soft patter of earth, fragments of branches, the ragged remains of garments and pieces of men raining back down to the ground. Under the devastated trees that were the outliers of the woods, nothing else moved at first, but then there were groans and sounds of distress, and the branches shivered as those men who could crawled away.

And into the silence Captain Zeke said, 'Well, I think we can call that a success.'

I remembered later that Jasper had been trying to say something as he died. *Fire*, he'd said, and *help*. He had raised a hand towards the sea. Had he known? Had he been aware that those men who normally fought at sea were bringing their firepower to our aid? I didn't know. And it was too late to ask him.

All of Aroto Tagauchi's core force were dead. More than a dozen of the local recruits were also dead. Some of the others, dismayed by the ferocity of the unexpected defence, had slunk away before the naval reinforcements turned up. The rest had hurried after them once Captain Zeke's barrage began.

Theo and his agents had taken the bodies away for burial. Theo told me later they had recognized almost all the local men. 'Looking on the bright side,' he said to me, 'this business has done the town a favour, since to a man they were thugs, thieves and brawlers, and not one of them's going to be much of a loss.' He smiled grimly. 'We'll no doubt be finding that, for a while at any rate, the forces of the law in the town will have a little less to do.'

NINETEEN

Afterwards I thought I'd been the only person to see the great golden figure of the Tiger that night and there was nobody to verify or deny whether it had really been there. Black Carlotta had witnessed it, but she had gone. Wherever she was, I wished her well. But I knew I wouldn't be seeing her again.

Then, a fortnight or so later, something strange happened.

I was with Theo when Jarman Hodge came in. He had recovered from his injury with no more than a rather dramatic scar to show for it, and he was back to his usual taciturn self. Slipping quietly into Theo's inner office, he nodded to me and, closing the door, said, 'Spot of trouble down in the port.'

'Trouble?' Theo stared up at him.

'Done and dusted now, chief, and not a single corpse for you and Doctor T to go and inspect. But . . .' He frowned, as if not sure how to go on.

Theo sighed, noisily enough for Jarman to take it as a prompt. Jarman smiled briefly, then said, 'There's been a foreign ship sighted, standing offshore. Word is it looked like a smaller version of that ship you set off on, Doctor.' He paused. 'More than one person reported a boat slipping out of the estuary very early this morning. Ship's gone now.'

The largest of the three ships that had pursued us all the way from Japan – the one we'd called the mother ship – had been like a smaller *Luipaard*.

'What was this trouble?' Theo demanded.

'Strangers down by the quay last night were asking questions. The tavern patrons didn't care for the look of them, apparently, and when questions were asked about that business up at Rosewyke, the strangers got booted out. Seems they persevered, though, and eventually found one of the locals – goes by the name of Slyke – who'd joined the attackers. Skulking in his own parlour, since he doesn't show his face outside his own hovel nowadays,' he added laconically.

If indeed these strangers had rowed ashore from the mother ship, then it was highly likely they'd have come wanting to find out the end of the long tale that had begun back in Japan. No, long before that: back in the earliest days when men first started to appreciate beautiful objects, to covet them and ascribe to them the most unlikely magical powers . . .

I stopped that line of thought before it could take hold.

'The locals down on the quay don't like to admit any of their number sold themselves to fight for Gabe's enemies,' Theo was saying. 'They'd not have taken kindly to one of them entertaining strangers coming asking awkward questions.'

'They didn't,' Jarman said shortly. 'The visitors were seen leaving Slyke's hovel, and in no time a crowd had gathered. Some of them chased off the strangers, the rest dragged Slyke outside, and punched him about a bit till he bleated out that he'd only revealed what everyone was saying, about how the battle ended when the big guns turned up and all the attackers either died or fled.'

'Slyke included,' Theo observed. 'I can't imagine he was much use as a fighter, and he probably led the charge when they all ran away.' He glanced at Jarman. 'All quiet now?'

'All quiet.' But instead of opening the door to leave, Jarman stood where he was.

'What?' Theo asked.

'Apparently that wasn't all Slyke said,' Jarman replied, lowering his voice. 'He was incoherent with drink, mind, so it may have been misreported, but more than one witness said he was raving about some vision he'd seen, some golden shape forming and reforming right above your house, Doctor. Said it was at the height of the attack, shortly before the heavy artillery arrived.' He shrugged. 'Probably a load of bollocks, but I reckoned you ought to know.'

He nodded to Theo and then to me, opened the door and walked away.

Presently a glass of brandy was pushed into my hand. 'You look like you need that,' Theo remarked.

I hadn't even heard him get up.

The brandy brought me back to the present, and I talked easily enough with Theo until I thought I could make my escape without arousing his suspicion. He seemed to think my momentary lapse was because I was remembering the events of that night, and I didn't correct him.

And as I rode away, I reflected that it was exactly what I had been doing: remembering. But the memory had been very specific, and solely of that one unbelievable moment when I'd looked up at the Chrysanthemum Tiger soaring above Rosewyke and *known*, even before Black Carlotta had confirmed it, that something momentous had happened. *It's yours, yours and the child's*, she'd said into my mind. *It has a far greater allegiance now.*

Did they know, those men who had come by night from Aroto Tagauchi's ship to discover the end of the story? Did they listen to a drunken ruin of a man mumbling about golden figures in the sky and understand what had happened? I hoped so; I prayed it was so. Because if it was, they would report back to the powerful and ruthless man who had sent them to bring back his treasures and he would know he had lost.

Most of my family and friends had slipped back into the regular and comfortable routine of their lives. My brother had donned his cloak of taciturnity once more and stomped off back to his farm, and when I thanked him for his help, merely muttered something to the effect of *I don't expect to do it again*. My parents were safely back home at Fernycombe. If, when he thought he was unobserved, my father sometimes threw out his chest with pride that a man of his considerable years still had it in him to wield a sword and go to defend his son's hearth and home, who could blame him? My mother was as happy as I'd ever seen her. She was still entranced with her new granddaughter, and the enchantment was mutual: Amy adored her. Others – especially me – moaned that my daughter had a strong will and was absolutely *infuriating* when you made her do something she didn't want to. My mother, hearing the moaning, would say with detectable smugness, 'Really? You *do* surprise me, she's as good as gold with me.'

She was.

I did the rounds of the many people who had turned out in the face of peril and unknown danger to defend the doctor who had only just returned from long absence. Most of them brushed it off, and I detected embarrassment in some of the more reclusive of the farmers. Quite a few asked if I was home for good. To each one I answered that I was.

The summons from Walter Haverleigh came very shortly after the events on the quay that Jarman Hodge had reported. I made the journey by sea, with a friend of mine who had retired from the navy to be a fisherman. He was not a talkative man, which was a pity because I could have done with some light chatter to take my mind off my memories of my friend Hieronymus Petrarcus.

Walter stood outside his porch to receive me, just as he had done on that first visit two and a half years ago. Cheverstone Manor had two large new barns now, I noticed as he hurried me inside to the warmth of the fire, and the sturdy iron gates that had opened to admit me were kept padlocked and guarded.

His staff had prepared a fine spread, and we ate and drank while we exchanged pleasantries. But he was never a man to waste much time on anything but hard business; quickly we moved to the reason for my visit. Leading the way down to his private sanctum, Walter unlocked at least two doors and finally showed me into a windowless cell deep under the house.

He closed and secured the door. 'We feared the worst, you know, when we found the two bodies,' he said quietly. 'That groom was only a young man, and to die so cruelly . . .' He shook his head, momentarily dismayed into silence.

'And Hieronymus,' I added softly. 'His skull was smashed.'

Walter nodded. 'Yes. I cannot forget the brutality of it.'

We stood together for a few moments, not speaking. Then in a different voice he said, 'We thought you would like a few mementoes of your voyage, and awaiting you in one of the barns is a chest containing amongst other treasures some porcelain, silks, some pieces of jade and a very fine Samurai sword.'

I already have mementoes, I could have said. More precious than anything you could give me.

But he meant well, so I kept quiet.

He was crouching before a heavy iron chest in the corner of the room, once more fiddling with padlocks. I turned away, not wanting him to think I was watching. Presently there were several loud clicks as the locks opened.

After a brief pause, he said softly, 'This is yours.'

I spun round. He was holding out not a bag but a leather sack, and by its weight he was finding it a struggle. He gave it a shake and it clinked.

I took it from him. It was even heavier than I'd thought. Putting it on the stone floor, I eased open the drawstrings.

It was full of gold coins.

He didn't say anything, just stood waiting until I looked up. Then he smiled. 'I think, Doctor,' he remarked, 'that it would be wise to provide you with a couple of bodyguards to ensure your safety while you transport your earnings home.'

We returned to the comforts of the fire and, pouring brandy, he proposed a toast to a successful mission.

I raised my glass, but did not drink.

'You hesitate?' He was eyeing me, a faint smile on his lean face.

I did not know how much he had learned of the final act; of the pursuit that followed me right to my own front door and ended in the deaths of many enemies and one good friend. He knew I had made off with Aroto Tagauchi's last remaining descendant – *my child*, I shouted in silent protest – and also with the old man's greatest treasure. He was still looking at me, and now he raised an eyebrow. He may well know, I thought. But we shall not speak of it.

I swirled the brandy in the heavy glass, and its powerful fumes filled the air. 'Successful in that we have made a great deal of money,' I murmured.

'Is that not the definition of a successful mission?' he asked lightly.

'Many died,' I replied. He acknowledged that with an incli-nation of the head. Angry suddenly, I said, 'Will you go on trading with Aroto Tagauchi now that you have discovered this alarmingly violent and ruthless side to him?'

He grinned. 'Not a question of discovery, Doctor. I always knew it was there. It is the nature of trade, for a man to do whatever it takes to protect his investments.'

Still I did not drink. There was a fairly uncomfortable silence.

Then Walter sighed. 'However, I can confirm that there will be no further dealings with Tagauchi,' he said, and there was definitely a note of regret in his tone. 'The old man was already unwell – his heart, they said – and this business with which you seem to have involved yourself brought on a fatal seizure.'

'Fatal?'

'Yes. Aroto Tagauchi died while the *Luipaard* was on her way home.'

I was stunned. The first thing that occurred to me was to wonder if the Tiger would still have transferred its allegiance if the old man was still alive. I thought I heard a voice in my head say, *yes*.

Walter was still speaking, and I caught a familiar name.

'. . . lost his only daughter,' he was saying, 'and, for all he never saw her because she was kept in her golden prison within her grandfather's castle, they say he mourns her.'

He was speaking of Romeu Silvestre.

Who could have no idea that he had a grandchild.

For a moment I felt pity for him, and a stab of guilt because it was I who had taken away his only living descendant. The sum of these emotions was not enough to make me act upon it: I would have to learn to live with it.

I raised my glass, clinked it against Walter's and drank.

For the next few days I was fully occupied with transporting my chest of treasures and my sack of gold back home to Rosewyke. Walter was as good as his word and sent two heavily armed guards with me and, while they looked as out of place on my friend's fishing boat as a prince on a dung heap, their steady, silent presence was very reassuring.

Back home, my household exclaimed at the contents of my chest, generously happy for me to have such gorgeous items in my possession. I hadn't yet told them I was planning to share them; that pleasure was still to come.

I found a very safe place for the gold.

The reminder of Chiyo's death and the thought of the father who mourned her stayed with me. In some way that I did not understand, it was linked in my mind with the shrine on the hillside; its beauty and peace haunted me, and I kept thinking of the moment of understanding I had experienced there.

One evening I sought out Jonathan. I found him in his church, in the little St Luke's Chapel, and he was alone. The panels high up in the wall glowed in the candlelight.

There was a glow about him, too, as there was about my sister. Their happiness was luminous.

'May I talk to you?' I asked him.

'Of course!' he began, smiling. Then, looking at me and understanding, he said quietly, 'Shall we go over to the house? The fire is lit.'

We sat either side of his hearth and I wondered how on earth to start. Then I thought I'd simply tell him.

'There was an old apothecary, and when we'd talked for some time about the mysteries of life, he told me to go to a shrine on a nearby hillside,' I began. 'It was a Shinto shrine, and . . .'

'And something happened,' he said when I did not go on.

I had the odd feeling that he knew what I was going to say even before I spoke. I said it anyway.

I described the shrine. The beauty of the natural setting, the imposing entrance, the stacked offerings of rice and sake, the powerfully affecting appeal of simple objects honestly and carefully made. The old man who attended the shrine, and his gift of the *omamori*; it was still in its silk bag on a leather thong around my neck, and, easing it out, I handed it to Jonathan.

He drew it out and examined the *kanji*. 'The calligraphy is beautiful,' he said. 'An amulet? For protection?'

'Yes.' I took it back. 'Jonathan, I had a revelation.' The words emerged quickly; if I hesitated, I wasn't sure I'd be able to get them out. 'I became aware quite suddenly and with no doubt at all that there was a power, a great creative force. It was not the God of my childhood and youth – your God – but also it *was*, but it was so much more as well.' I tried to find the words. 'It was what had made all the best of the world; what had brought into existence all that we treasure most. Beauty so great that we can only gape in wonder. Courage, fortitude, the cherishing of those we care for and who care for us. Love. Whatever had created it was right beside me, on the track leading to the shrine, and its strength and its majesty were all the greater and more affecting because everything was so natural, so simple. I thought the realization was simple, too, and for those few moments it was.'

Jonathan said very softly, 'And then it went away.'

I bent my head and waited for him to castigate me. To tell me I was a sinner and guilty of apostasy. To look at me with profound hurt in his expression because I'd just denied the beliefs he held so dear.

I went on waiting and he didn't speak.

Eventually I nerved myself to look up at him.

'I have felt the same,' he said quietly. 'Like you I have gazed into the wonders of this world, and, deep in thought, sensed the same revelation that you describe.' He stopped, and I noticed his lips were moving, as if he was talking to himself. 'Unlike you, Gabe – or so I believe – I have studied other religions, and in some depth. What I cannot understand is how every one of us is so convinced of the truth inherent in our own faith that we must utterly dismiss every other.'

'All gods are one, and behind them is the truth,' I murmured. He looked at me enquiringly. 'Someone said that to me once. Not someone I see any more,' I added quickly.

'What a pity,' he replied. 'He sounds like a wise man.'

It was a woman, I wanted to say. And she is indeed wise, although because of the superstitious, infantile fears of our King, she has had to take her wisdom far out of reach.

In my mind I was on the hillside by the shrine, and a specific memory came back to me. 'You were in my thoughts that day,' I said.

'Was I? Perhaps because you anticipated this conversation?'

'I did, but it wasn't that, not to begin with. You told me once about some ancient writer who tried to make sense of the mysteries that seem so far beyond us by saying we only saw them as shadows on the wall of the cave, and we could not hope to penetrate further until we understood what caused the shadows.'

'Fancy you remembering that,' he said. 'It was a Greek philosopher called Plato.' I thought he'd finished, but after a moment he said, 'I think we must accept that mystery is at the heart of life. I am not sure we shall ever see what makes the shadows; not that it should prevent us from trying.'

'And that's what you do?'

He smiled. 'Yes. Of course.'

For some time I found I had nothing to say. I had undergone

a crisis, back there by the shrine on the island, or so I'd thought. I had found my true spiritual nature and discovered I was not an English Protestant. Even worse – or so it had seemed – I had glimpsed something far beyond the man-made religious systems with which I'd grown up. What I had experienced, far too briefly, was nothing to do with church doctrine, angels on a pinhead, virgin birth and a man rising from the dead; those – or so it seemed to me – were merely symbolic, to be seen as man's attempts to explain to himself something far outside and way beyond the everyday world he inhabited. They were like the Greek myths that Grandmother Oldreive had read to us, to my brother, my sister and me. They were illustrations.

I leaned back into the chair. I closed my eyes. I felt worn out, as if I'd been involved in some arduous physical effort. I was aware of Jonathan moving about, and I heard noises coming from the scullery. I think I slept briefly . . .

'I've brought some bread and some slices of ham.' His voice woke me, and I opened my eyes to see him putting a platter on the small table beside me. 'Eat up, Gabe.' He smiled down at me. 'You need to strengthen yourself for the ride home. Thinking deeply, I find, tends to take it out of you.'

I tucked into the food. 'Just as well, then,' I said flippantly between mouthfuls, 'that I don't do it very often.'

Meeting his eyes, I reckoned he too thought it was time to lighten the mood.

Jonathan saw Gabe on his way, then went over to the church. He knelt for some time, deep in thought. He was about to return to the Priest's House when the church door opened quietly.

Slowly he stood up.

She was standing just inside the door, as if she was waiting for him to invite her closer. She was pale and unsmiling, and her eyes were wide. With a shock of apprehension he perceived that she was full of dread. Fear rushed through him. Was someone hurt? Was *she* hurt? Had something made her change her mind? His heart gave a painful thump. Perhaps she . . .

But then the apprehension left him and he smiled in relief.

He knew why she had come.

Celia said, 'Jonathan, there is something I must tell you.'

He walked to meet her as she approached, taking her outstretched hands. 'Are you quite sure?' he said gently.

For an instant her stern expression faltered and he saw the anguish. 'Yes. I wish I . . .' She stopped. She raised her chin. 'But I must. There cannot be lies between us.'

'Lies?'

'No, I don't mean that – unconfessed sins.'

He led her through to the vestry, closing the door. The remains of a fire in the small grate still threw out some warmth. He pulled up a bench and they sat down. She was, he noticed, hunched tightly in on herself, as if she mustn't let herself touch him.

'Jonathan, I have to tell you that I killed someone,'[3] she said, her voice low and toneless, as if such words could not be uttered in the way she usually spoke.

'Dearest one, I—' he began.

She took no notice. 'You have heard that my young husband Jeromy was murdered. He was, and he died at my hands. He had tried to kill me and he was going to keep trying, I knew it, and I had prepared to defend myself, stealing a weapon from my father's barn.' She drew a shaky breath and he sensed she was remembering the full horror.

'Celia, my love, there's no need—'

Once again she didn't let him stop her. 'I stabbed it into his belly and up into his heart,' she whispered. He could see that she was trembling. 'Once he was dead, I put his hands on the weapon's shaft and left him there.'

When the silence had stretched almost to unbearable, he said, 'My beloved, I have three things to say. The first is that, as your brother said to Theo's brave daughter Isabella only a short while ago, to kill someone who is going to kill you is not against the law, and even the church accepts you have a right to take a life in self-defence. The second is that I also have something I must share, which is that I have killed too.'[4]

Her eyes widened in shock. 'You? But you can't have done, you're a priest!'

So he told her. He described an old man in a filthy cell, accused

3 See *A Rustle of Silk.*
4 See *The Angel in the Glass.*

of a crime against the state and facing more torture, and agony that would continue until he died. He described taking it upon himself to ease the pathetic old soul into death, as gently and painlessly as he could, and how he knelt in vigil after it was done while the old man's soul departed.

He waited to see how she would respond.

After quite a long time, she turned to him, put her arms round him and kissed him.

'What was the third?' she asked presently.

'Hmm?'

'You said you had three things to say. You've only said two of them.'

'Oh. Yes.' But he was doubtful now, and wished he'd kept all reference to this last to himself.

'Go on,' she insisted.

He held her face between his hands. He loved her for her bravery, her forthrightness, her intelligence. And her beauty. He could still hardly believe she was going to be his wife.

But she was waiting.

He leaned close and whispered, 'I already knew about Jeromy.'

She sprang away from him. 'You – *what?* But you can't have done, nobody knew except Gabe! *Who told you?*'

'No one,' he replied.

'Then *how* did you find out?'

'I know you,' he said quietly. 'I know you're a fighter, and that you're not deterred by even the most fearsome challenge. I know Gabe, too.' He paused, finding the right words. 'Neither of you said much about what happened to your husband, and I think perhaps I read the truth of it in the very silence.'

Slowly she nodded. 'Have you always known?'

'Always suspected. Knew as I became closer to you.'

'Yet you still grew to love me?'

He leaned forward and kissed her again. 'Of course,' he whispered.

TWENTY

Celia and Jonathan were married at the beginning of December, in the parish church close to Fernycombe where my parents had always attended and where my siblings and I had been received into the faith. The priest was a good friend to my family, and he appeared delighted to perform the ceremony. I had nothing against the church, but it didn't have a place in my heart like St Luke's did. But then, a priest can't officiate at his own marriage. The day before, Celia and Jonathan had asked me to go down to St Luke's late in the evening, and I took it as a great honour that they wanted me to be there for their own private moment of commitment in the powerful atmosphere of the ancient building, magical in the candlelight and with the colours in the glass panels high in the wall making patterns on the stone floor.

Celia made a beautiful bride. As I watched her, I thought back to the day of her first wedding. She had been much younger then, naive, self-centred; determined to exercise her right to choose her own husband, even though practically everyone thought she was making a mistake.

Nobody thought she was making a mistake now.

Jonathan and Celia settled into married life in the Priest's House at Tavy St Luke. I was a frequent guest, and Celia's talent for homemaking was very swiftly apparent. I wanted to help, and I had insisted on buying them a splendid bed, a deep feather mattress and smooth, costly bedlinen as a wedding present. They thanked me graciously and both managed to hide their embarrassment.

I had a sackful of gold hidden under my house; my share of the profits from the *Luipaard*'s voyage was vast. But I knew better than to offer money to the new Reverend and Mrs Carew. Instead I made what I thought was a well-reasoned case, expressing the point that the church accommodation for a married priest needed to be larger (and a lot more comfortable) than for a bachelor, and I put up the necessary funds disguised as a donation to the church. Then I sat back and watched with considerable satisfaction while the small house was extended and modernized.

Celia told us all firmly that she had no need of a housekeeper. My parents, Sallie and I told her equally firmly that it was unseemly for a woman in her position to do for herself. Sallie had a widowed sister-in-law who came highly recommended (by Sallie, but that was more than good enough for Celia), and the woman came over to meet Celia and Jonathan (although he managed to maintain a diplomatic distance, saying it was entirely up to his wife; I guessed he really loved saying *my wife*, judging by the frequency with which he did so). She and my sister took to each other straight away and she joined the household. Her name is Katherine but she prefers to be called Cat.

We were all secretly relieved when she arrived to share the work because my sister was pregnant.

As for me, I was back where I started from. But this time there was a difference, because I was there by choice. I no longer yearned to be somewhere else.

I developed a close friendship with Josiah Thorn. I had the strong impression that working again during my absence, albeit only part of the time, had rejuvenated him. I dare say it was gratifying to discover not only that there had been no diminution in his healing skills, but also that people turned to him willingly and seemed to need him. He told me he would not be averse to continuing on the same basis, if it would be acceptable, and I agreed without even having to think about it. We met several evenings a week to talk over our patients and, when the day was sunny and my work not too pressing, I often joined him for an afternoon's fishing.

Together we tended Jasper Hart's grave in Jonathan's churchyard.

'I liked Jasper,' Josiah said to me on a bright winter's morning when we were planting daffodil bulbs on the grave. 'He was a fine doctor. If I had a criticism,' he went on thoughtfully, 'it's that he was a little too much the slave of his fears and imaginings.'

'He worked tirelessly throughout London's last major outbreak of plague,' I said.

'Ah. Well, that would explain it, then.'

The inscription on Jasper's headstone was simple. It read:

> Here lies Jasper Hart, who died in November 1607.
> A fine Doctor who for a time
> tended the sick and injured of this Parish.

Amy thrived in her new home from the start. She had inherited a look of the Oldreives, and it wasn't just about the eyes. My mother wasn't the only one to remark that it was like seeing Grandmother Oldreive reborn. Amy's hair was coppery now, smooth and glossy. She was the product of a mother who had been half Portuguese and half Japanese and an English father; her features belonged to everywhere and nowhere. She was very pretty, and I don't think that was solely a father's pride expressing itself.

She had a rich, vivid imagination. Often she entertained herself chattering away in her own inimitable way to invisible friends, giving orders, handing out praise and reprimands, accompanied by appropriate facial expressions. This had concerned me at first, but Sallie, observing my reaction, said not to worry, many children made up invisible companions for themselves. 'Especially,' she added meaningfully, 'when they don't have any playmates.'

I took the hint, and, with Celia's and Judyth's help, set about introducing my child into the circle of the sons and daughters of friends and neighbours who were around the same age.

Sallie never witnessed Amy up in my study with the Chrysanthemum Tiger, and I told neither my housekeeper nor anybody else about what I'd seen. It happened several times – always at the enchanted hour of twilight – and the repetition meant I couldn't tell myself it had been a fluke, or I'd imagined it, or, tired after a long day, had slipped into a brief sleep and dreamt it.

To put it simply, under Amy's chatter and the touch of her little fingers as she stroked the golden fur along the length of his back, the Tiger moved. Nothing dramatic such as leaping down off the shelf and snarling. Not even that extraordinary metamorphosis I'd once seen when the claws changed from ivory chrysanthemum petals to steel-sharp daggers; I'd have doubted the veracity of that, if it wasn't for the scars across my fingers.

No. The movement induced by Amy's clumsy, childish hands

was far more subtle. As the Tiger felt her touch, his long back at first bent down in a curve so deep that his belly almost touched the rock he stood on, then arched right up in the opposite direction. Delighted, Amy, like any child absorbed in a game, would have gone on for hours. But the Tiger had his own way of announcing when he'd had enough; he returned to solid, unchanging gold. It was surely only in my head that I heard him give a low, admonitory growl.

Sometimes I feared for her future.

Our King, God rot his ignorant, superstitious, misogynistic mind, had a pernicious history when it came to dealing with what he believed was witchcraft. Often when some disturbing new report of his latest move reached us in the far south-west, I would feel a flood of relief that Black Carlotta and her companions had gone. If proof were needed that they were out of danger, it was that nobody in the vicinity was arrested, tried and hanged for that most ill-defined and illusory crime; surely more open to abuse in the form of the settling of old scores than any other. As we heard rumours of the wretched King's latest scheme, often I feared for Judyth's safety. The King appeared to be aiming at an all-out crackdown on 'witches', although in this context the word apparently meant any female, young or old, who was different. Who lived alone. Who was skilled in the old ways of hedgerow healing and who willingly helped anyone who asked.

I had seen Judyth many times in the course of the day's work. We had remained brisk and businesslike, chaffing each other sometimes, slipping back into the professional relationship we had built up before I went away. I had held her in my arms once, but it had been as we danced at the celebrations following Celia's and Jonathan's wedding, and both of us had danced with almost everyone else as well.

We were waiting, but as the days and weeks went past, I could not work out what for.

So, late one afternoon when the sun was setting and the frost creeping across the grass, I went to call on her.

I didn't need to raise the angel door knocker to announce my presence. She already had the door open as I walked up to it.

She stood back and I went inside. As always, her cottage was warm and welcoming; clean, tidy, sweet-smelling, and the colours of her various small treasures that were arrayed around her parlour shone like jewels in the firelight.

She did not invite me to sit down. She did not offer food or drink. She stood before me, and a faintly raised eyebrow was her sole communication.

I had not planned what I should say. I had tried out a few approaches, but they sounded juvenile and naive to my critical ears. We were in a strange middle ground, Judyth and I: far beyond being new acquaintances attracted to each other, but a long way short of any casual assumption of intimacy.

I opened my mouth and started to speak. The words came without any thought.

'Some time ago,' I began, 'down there in the passage by your front door, with the enemy outside, I thought you were hugging me and I took you in my arms. You resisted because we were facing great peril.' She had actually said, *Gabe, I want to hold you more than anything, although not now*, but I didn't say so, since it was very likely the words had stemmed from the heat of the moment and a reminder might well have discomfited her. 'But the danger has passed,' I ploughed on, 'so I've come to see if we might do it again.'

She watched me for a long moment. Then she stepped into my arms.

I think it's fair to say that we did not look back from that moment on.

My old horse Hal remained in the stable with Judyth's gelding that night. Judyth and I became lovers at last, and, perhaps because we were already friends and knew each other so well, for both of us there was an ease and a familiarity that led to a high degree of delight.

Some time in the small hours, warm under the covers, while the frost made crackling white stars on the window panes, she lay with her head on my shoulder, her arm across my chest, my hand on her belly. Neither of us had any clothes on. We were silent for some time. As if we couldn't bear to part from each other even into the unawareness of slumber, we hadn't yet slept. Then she gave a sigh.

'What is it?' I murmured.

She didn't answer for a moment. Then she said softly, 'That day you came to see me after you came home.'

'Yes?'

'You were preoccupied with worries, and you were in a hurry to leave.'

'Not to leave you,' I protested. Never that.

'No, I know.' She paused, and I felt her draw a breath. 'As you left – do you remember? – I said, *When it is over, I shall be here.*'

Of course I remembered.

'And here you are,' I said when I could manage the words.

'Here I am,' she agreed.

Some time later, full of joy, I knew even as I fell into sleep at last that life with Judyth was unlikely to follow the usual pattern. She was a dedicated woman who lived for her work, she had been independent throughout her adult life, she loved her little house, and I didn't propose to ask her to give it all up to be a doctor's wife and run his house for him. I wasn't even sure if she would agree to marry me. Perhaps she would, if we were blessed with children; with sons and daughters to join Amy in the next generation.

But none of that concerned me; not then, and not since.

Judyth reminded me that night that she'd told me she would be there. I believed her. She *was* there, that enchanted first night together. I knew, as well as I knew my own heartbeat, that she would always be there.

It was more than enough.